Praise for Shelly Laurenston's
Here Kitty, Kitty

Rating: 4 Stars "Laurenston wins again with this delightful addition to her shape-shifter family. Ang is a strong heroine who uses her brain as well as her heart to get what she wants."

~ *Faith Smith, Romantic Times Book Reviews*

FAR Recommended Read "The hilarity and the laughter that comes with a Shelly Laurenston book gets better and better with each story that I read from her. She is a master magician with her words and knows how to draw you into the story and have you laughing your self silly in the first page that you read."

~ *Missy, Fallen Angel Reviews*

Look for these titles by
Shelly Laurenston

Now Available

Pack Challenge
Go Fetch

Here Kitty, Kitty

Shelly Laurenston

A SAMHAIN PUBLISHING, LTD. publication.

Samhain Publishing, Ltd.
577 Mulberry Street, Suite 102
Macon, GA 31201
www.samhainpublishing.com

Here Kitty, Kitty
Copyright © 2009 by Shelly Laurenston
Print ISBN: 978-1-59998-787-3
Digital ISBN: 1-59998-521-7

Editing by Angela James
Cover by Scott Carpenter

First Samhain Publishing, Ltd. electronic publication: July 2007
First Samhain Publishing, Ltd. print publication: May 2009

Dedication

To Princess Cammy. Without your guidance through the frightening world of high fashion, this book could not have been made. And, yes! Those shoes DO look fabulous on you!

Prologue

He didn't actually see the wall until he walked into it.

"Dang, Nik. You okay?" His brothers could at least have the decency to hold off laughing at him until they made sure he hadn't caused any real damage.

He rubbed his forehead. "Yeah. I'm fine."

Better than fine. With a woman like that in his sights. He took control of himself. He had to. He suddenly had the overwhelming desire to shift and run her down like a red deer.

He walked toward her. She reeked of dog, but it wasn't her. No, to his huge disappointment, he realized she was human. He thought for sure she had to be cat, with the way she moved and all. Leopard or cheetah. Something other than just another boring human female.

She leaned back in her chair, a martini in her hand, crossed her legs—and both his brothers groaned.

"Oh, man. Who the hell is that?"

His brother Bannik chuckled. "Mine, little brother."

Nik ignored them both, instead letting them argue so he could focus his attention on the conversation between the woman and her itty-bitty friend.

"Fine," she sighed. "You wanna live life alone and bitter, be my guest."

"Trust me. Fucking the Viking isn't going to change the living alone and bitter thing one bit."

"Whatever." A boarding announcement rolled through the terminal and the woman cocked her head to listen. "Come on, sassy girl. Let's get your ass on a plane."

She finished her drink and carefully placed the glass down on the table. Nik took two long steps toward her. She pushed back her chair and stood up, slamming right into his chest. Her hair slid across his hand and he immediately imagined that hair trailing across his body as she slipped her head between his thighs.

Nik shook his head, what in hell—he usually had more control of himself than this. But her scent...goddammit. Her scent slid around his throat, caressing his cheek. It was as erotic as a lover's touch that effectively put him in a chokehold.

He swallowed and stared down at the top of her head, forcing himself to speak, "Sorry, darlin'."

She finally looked up at him. He heard her sharp intake of breath and the increase in her heart rate. He could feel the change in her body temperature. Heat radiated off her in waves.

Funny thing was, the same thing happened to him. When he'd caught her scent, he didn't think she'd be this beautiful. What a gorgeous face. Damn, but no one had a right to be that pretty. And the loveliest brown eyes he'd ever seen on a female. Dark, dark brown. Like the richest imported dark chocolate. Long, dark brown hair made those eyes even more devastating. Her light brown skin damn-near glowed and she possessed the cutest little nose.

She let out a shaky breath.

"You all right, sugar?"

"Uh..."

He waited for her to say more, but she appeared to be a bit slow witted. Kind of like his Uncle Billy whose baby sister had hit him in the head with a brick.

Her friend, who Nik had barely noticed she was so tiny, slung a bag over her shoulder. "Sorry about that. We need to get to my plane."

"No problem." Nik smiled down into that beautiful face. "Y'all can slam into me any time." At least *she* could. He could care less about the midget. Although, as usual, his brothers took an immediate interest in anything with a pussy. They stared at the tiny woman like she was a Happy Meal.

"Hey, Ang. We need to go." Her tiny friend grabbed her arm and tugged. Then she yanked.

The woman blinked, glancing around. "Uh...oh yeah. Yeah. We better get moving." She gave him a soft smile. "Sorry."

"Not at all." He wanted to say something else but, really, what the hell was he supposed to do with a human?

Fuck her until the end of time?

No. He'd sworn off the full-humans. Like the dogs, they got mighty attached to a man. His kind happily lived alone. He didn't need or want some female spending every night wrapped around him like an anaconda in a bed that could easily accommodate them both sleeping apart.

So, instead of bending her over the table, ripping her panties off, and fucking the hell out of her—Nik walked away.

"Well that was entertaining." His youngest brother Aleksei winked at him and grinned.

"Shut up."

"I thought for sure you'd do her right there, big brother."

"I told ya both to shut the hell up." Nik's phone rang. He grabbed it off his belt and flicked it open. "This is Nik."

"Mr. Vorislav, it's Annie. Your father has asked that you return home."

Nik stopped walking, afraid of losing the faulty connection in the terminal. "What? Why?"

"He needs you involved in a last minute deal. He didn't give me any details."

"What about the Kingsley Park deal?"

"He asks that you let your brothers handle that negotiation."

Nik stared at his kin. Apart he had no doubt they could broker a deal with the old wolf they'd come to see. But together? Together the two of them could be the biggest idiots on the planet. Leaving them alone to handle this could be a huge disaster.

"Mr. Vorislav, I need your answer."

As usual, his father didn't leave him much choice. "Tell him I'll be home in a few hours."

"Yes, sir."

Annie disconnected and Nik turned to his brothers. "I gotta go back."

"What's up?" Bannik asked.

"Some last minute deal of Daddy's. He wants you two to handle this."

His brothers shrugged nonchalantly. *Not* the response he wanted.

"We've only got a temporary pass on this territory, so don't screw it up."

Aleksei sneered. "What the hell does that mean?"

"It means keep your goddamn dicks in your pants and focus on the deal. Now go."

His brothers moved around him and headed off toward the exit. "Y'all." His brothers looked at him. "Stay outta trouble."

They grinned at him. Then at each other.

Nik watched them walk away with a very bad feeling in the pit of his stomach.

Sighing, he headed back to where they'd left the jet. As he moved through the terminal—hoping to see that hot female one more time—he saw "them" coming down the hallway.

But even if he hadn't seen them, he would have smelled them. He'd recognize their scent anywhere. He'd known quite a few over the years.

There were about fifteen of them, but they gave him a wide berth as they passed. Except the head female. She tried to stare him down. He knew her. Knew that pretty face. Dianne Leucrotta. Matriarch of the Leucrotta Clan.

She nodded at him and continued on down the hall.

Nik shook his head. Those hyenas were on a mission. He could see it in their beady little eyes. Thankfully, the hyenas were smart enough not to mess with his kind. Because all he really wanted to do was head home and think about a serious pair of long brown legs, instead of killing someone—even hyenas—on such a gorgeous Texas day.

Although, he wondered, *who the hell was dumb enough to piss them off?*

Chapter One

Six days later...

"I see now why they're on The List."

"Uh-oh. Is the rodeo clown still lurking?"

Angelina Santiago tightened the strap on her Chanel shoes, while trying not to fall on her ass. Not easy. Hopping became involved.

"I think he still can't believe I turned down a cowboy."

"I think I have to agree with him on this."

"Honestly, Sara. What is your thing for cowboys?"

"Dude, they're hot."

"And poor you. Stuck with tiny, weak Zach." Angie stood up, smoothing out her silk skirt, once again elegant and composed—at least that was the illusion she gave. An illusion she worked hard to maintain.

"I didn't say Zach was a letdown or anything. If I could just get him into a cowboy hat, I'd be one happy bitch."

"You're already happy. Much more and you'll be walking around in a state of constant orgasm, which would get on my last goddamn nerve."

"Everything gets on your last goddamn nerve."

"This is true." Crouching down, Angie grabbed her bag from behind the counter. She briefly debated whether to grab the solid wood bat lying next to her Louis Vuitton purse. She'd owned the "Bitch's Hammer" ever since she took it from the guy trying to use it on her. She smiled at the memory.

Never underestimate a teenage girl wearing Candies.

Angie decided to forgo her trusty weapon of choice since she had her sweet little Glock .9mm shoved in her bag. A birthday gift three months ago from Sara and Miki.

She stood up and nodded at her two saleswomen. They would make sure to close up her shop later and handle everything while she was away. Normally, she'd stay until closing, but she had packing to do. A rather dramatic and time-intensive event for her.

She re-adjusted the headphones attached to her cell phone. "Did you hear again from Mik?"

"Not since they stopped to get gas. I don't know what's going on, but that was a 'dangerously calm' Miki I spoke to. Not a good thing."

Angie winced. "My God, that can't be good."

"No shit."

No. Not a good thing at all. Although Sara was no better. When she got quiet—the universe needed to notice.

"And Conall? Recovery a-okay?"

"He's fine. Although I'm pretty sure he's the one who pissed her off."

"Probably. But not really surprising. This *is* Miki we're talking about. Think she told him she loves him yet?" Angie headed toward the exit, her ridiculously expensive bag swinging casually from her hand.

"Are you kidding? He's going to have to work for that."

Angie stopped and looked at the two men who'd been in her store every day for the past week. She remembered them from the airport when she dropped off Miki. They were damn gorgeous, but she really liked the other one. Shame he didn't seem to be with them.

One of the men stared at the scarves, pretending that they hadn't been staring at her.

She smiled while trying to keep a straight face. "That teal scarf would look fabulous on you."

The one holding the scarf in his huge hand looked at it and back at her. Frowning.

She laughed and strolled away. *What boneheads.*

Angie pushed the glass doors open and walked out. "My plane arrives tomorrow at four ten. Flight eight-sixty."

"Don't worry. I've got all the info. We'll meet you at the airport." Sara sighed. "And look, until you get here, I want you to be careful. They targeted Miki specifically, but I don't know if they're coming after you or not."

"Please don't start. Again. Besides, I'm in Pack territory and Marrec will be taking me to the airport. I'll be fine." She sauntered toward her Mercedes.

"Angelina, don't ignore—"

"Bye, Sara. Call me when Miki gets there." She ended the connection. Her friend could be quite the mother wolf when her friends were threatened.

Angie remotely unlocked her door and stopped, the hackles on her neck snapping to full attention. She spun on her expensive heels and came face-to-face with a woman.

Well...at least she thought it was a woman. A woman she'd seen once or twice the past week at the diner, just outside town. Angie didn't like the woman staring at her then. And she sure as fuck didn't like it now.

Whatever. All Angie needed to know was this woman wasn't Pack, too small and boringly dressed to be Pride, and definitely not completely human.

Sometimes Angie wished she could be more like Miki with her fast-moving mind. Mik could analyze anything in seconds and come up with a satisfying solution. Or like Sara. With her calm, controlled demeanor—as long as no tequila was involved. Angie wasn't like either of her two best friends, and specialists had actually analyzed her fight or flight response. Because she never did what everyone else did. Ever.

Angie slammed her handbag, heavy with her Glock, against the head of the woman across from her. Squealing in surprise, the female stumbled. Nope, they never saw Angie coming. Always their mistake. And to prove that point, Angie hit her again. The buckle on the side of her bag cut a gash across the woman's face. Blood splashed across Angie's arm and ruined her bag.

The female hit the ground, and Angie slammed her foot against the woman's windpipe, pushing down.

Gasping, the female fought to get Angie's foot off, but Angie gritted her teeth and pushed harder.

Something, a movement from the corner of her eye or a sound, distracted her from the prey under her feet. She spared a glance to the left of her. The two men, the ones from her shop, were moving toward her.

At first, she wondered if they were coming to rescue her or the woman whose windpipe she happily crushed under her Chanels.

She heard another sound and turned to see animals, not lions but not quite dogs either, bursting full-throttle from the woods behind her store's parking lot.

Angie reached into her bag for her Glock while turning to warn off the men. But limbs shifted, fur grew, fangs appeared. Then they were launching themselves at her.

And her last thought before all went black—*There are tigers?*

CR80808CR

Nikolai Vorislav, rolling onto his back, let the morning sun warm his belly as he quietly waited in a soft patch of tall grass. Waited until his breakfast walked up to one of the many lakes he had on his property. And, as always, breakfast did come walking up. Slowly, Nik rolled back over onto his belly, watching to see if it saw him. It hadn't. Instead it drank from the lake, completely oblivious to his presence.

He waited a moment more. Then he silently charged. The deer made a run for it, but Nik had his paws on its hindquarters and under him before it got more than ten feet away. Nik gripped its neck and bit down until it stopped thrashing. With a happy sigh, he settled down to a nice hot meal.

When done, Nik went for a swim in his lake, letting the water go through his coat, washing all the blood away. He looked up at the sun. It was getting late. He needed to get on a conference call although he'd rather stay outside for the rest of the day playing. But his father would have his head.

As it was, Nik barely tolerated the old bastard these days. He loved his father, but he didn't understand him. And he really didn't want to. Still, he needed to leave his father be. The old man had begun to slowly transfer the business over to him and Nik's momma would have his hide if he started any crap now.

So, resigning himself to a Sunday trapped on a trans-Atlantic call, he headed back to his house.

He padded quietly through his backyard, glancing at his pool. He fought his desire to dive in headfirst and stay there for the next four hours. Instead, he trotted over to the patio, stopping before he moved into his house. He sniffed the air and groaned. His brothers were around somewhere. Why? He'd left them in Texas with explicit instructions not to come back until they had a signed property deal from that old wolf Marrec so they could build some stupid amusement park his father had his heart set on. Nik should have known better. Trying to get a wolf to sell its territory was not easy, if not damn-near impossible. But this deal was Alek's baby. He'd brought the property to their daddy's attention. How he knew about wolf property, Nik could only guess.

Nik didn't want to walk through the back doors into his kitchen. He knew he'd probably find them there, eating his food and finishing off his sweet tea. No. Not a good idea to deal with those two without his morning coffee. It would be in everyone's best interest if he made them wait a bit. So Nik went around to the side of the house, took a step back, and leaped up to the second-floor balcony. Clearing the railing with ease, he silently landed on the marble floor. With a couple of nudges from his muzzle, he opened the glass door and stepped into the hallway.

He needed a shower and coffee before his call. Man, did he need coffee.

So focused, in fact, on getting his coffee, it took Nik a good thirty seconds to catch the strange scent in his house. He slowed down, but kept walking, trying to locate its owner. Maybe his sisters had brought over one of their friends. Whoever she was, he just had to meet her. Anybody smelling that damn good was a must-meet, if not a must-have-in-your-bed. And the scent was so familiar, it must have been someone

19

he'd met. So intense he started purring. Wow, he hadn't done that in awhile. It felt good.

He walked past one of the unused guest rooms and stopped in his tracks, his tail twitching expectantly. He took several steps back and turned his head.

It was her. The tasty piece of ass from the airport.

His eyes roamed over her body. She sat up in the bed, the sheet tucked under her arms, and she had definitely been in a recent fight. Though she didn't look too much the worse for wear. A few bruises. A few scratches. A good-sized knot on the side of her forehead. Yet nothing life threatening. Still...why the hell was she in his house?

She stared at him, her breathing coming out in shallow pants, and Nik suddenly realized he was still tiger.

No wonder she looks scared to death.

Nik shifted, making sure not to move too quickly and frighten her even more.

Leaning against the door jamb, Nik crossed his arms in front of his chest. "Well. Hello, sugar."

"Oh, shit..." she let out softly.

He grinned. So pretty. No. Pretty didn't do it for her. Beautiful. Gorgeous. Astounding. Even those words were weak.

"I...I..." She shook her head, then the panic kicked in.

She slid off the bed and stumbled to her feet. She still had the sheet around her body, but she tripped over it and started to drop to the floor.

Nik moved quickly, going across the room and grabbing her around the waist before she could hit the floor. She moaned in pain and he held her gently, slowly slipping to his knees, her naked back pushing against his naked front. She was so weak, she couldn't stand on her own.

"Breathe, sugar. Just breathe."

He had to fight hard to keep his self-control. Not easy with her naked flesh pressed against his. And before he took hold of her, he spotted the sexiest damn tattoo in the middle of her back. He didn't have a chance to get a good look at it, but knowing she had one set his teeth on edge.

"I'm going to be sick."

Uh-oh. Well, that killed the libido right quick.

"Come on, darlin'. Let's get you in the bathroom." Each bedroom in his house had its own bathroom and he had never been more grateful. He stood up, bringing the woman with him, and swiftly took her inside. He held her with one arm while he lifted the toilet seat cover and the toilet seat. Kneeling down again, he brought her with him, making sure her head hovered over the toilet.

"It's going to be okay, sugar. Just relax."

Moaning, she gripped the sides of the toilet and leaned forward. He was about to reach around and pull her hair off her face, when her head swung back, slamming into his nose. His brothers had broken his nose years ago, but this bitch literally knocked it out of joint. He heard the bone pop.

"Goddammit!"

Releasing her, he fell back to the floor.

He looked up in time to see her smoothly get to her feet, the sheet sliding off that sweet, *sweet* body, leaving her naked and oh so beautiful. With a coldness he'd never seen on a human not born cat, she turned and yanked the top of the toilet tank off.

"Wait—" was the last thing he said before she brought the hard, heavy porcelain down on his head.

Angie winced. She never wanted to hurt something that pretty, but it's not like he gave her much choice.

Damn! When did tigers get involved in this little drama? She wrapped the sheet around her body and ran out of the bathroom into the adjoining bedroom.

She saw no sign of any of her stuff, but that wasn't very surprising. She wouldn't exactly expect them to leave her .9 out and loaded.

She ran out into the hallway, heading in the opposite direction from the one the tiger had been taking. She'd only gotten a couple of feet, though, when she skidded to a stop. Two other tigers sat quietly at the end of the hallway near a set of stairs. They looked at her, and she was positive she saw surprise on their cat faces. She knew that if they could register surprise they were at least partly human. Hell. She'd rather deal with real tigers. No ulterior motive except dinner.

"Shit!" She turned and ran down the other way. The hallway stretched long and sported two exits. Boy, this wasn't just a house. This was a mansion. *A very nice mansion.* Shame she didn't have time to enjoy it. She skidded toward another stop at the top of the stairs. Two women, chatting quietly, sat on the bottom step. They looked up at her, eyes glinting in the dim light of the stairwell, and frowned. Nope. They weren't completely human either.

"Fuck!"

She tore back the other way, but saw the tigers loping toward her. She went into the first room she found, slamming the door shut behind her. No lock. Shit.

Angie desperately glanced around the room.

There must be a weapon around here somewhere.

"Oh, my God, Nik! What did that evil bitch do to you?"

Nik forced his eyes open to see his sister and cousin kneeling over him. "Help me up."

They each grasped a hand and hauled him to his feet. He couldn't let them go right away. Still too shaky.

"Maybe we should call the doc?" his cousin Reena asked as she used a wet washcloth to wipe blood off his face and out of his eyes.

"No. I'll be fine." He pulled away from them, slowly walking back into the bedroom. He looked over at the two tigers standing in the doorway.

"Shift. Now."

The two tigers looked at each other. For a minute, Nik thought they might make a run for it. But they knew better. Knew he'd track them down and kick the living tar out of both of them.

They shifted to human and looked at their brother sheepishly.

He stared at them. "Why is there—" He stopped, putting his hands on both sides of his nose, and snapped it back into place. Nik closed his eyes against the pain. When he opened them again, both his brothers were trying to ease out of the room.

"Don't make me come get you."

They stopped and turned around.

"Where is she," he barked. If he'd been more human, the crazy woman would have killed him. Luckily, his people were very hard of head.

"Your bedroom."

"Great." That's all he needed. Some insane woman ripping up his bedroom. He pushed past his brothers and stalked down the hallway.

He'd just gotten in front of his door when his sister, Kisa, spoke, "Isn't Granddaddy's shotgun in your room?"

Nik looked at his bedroom door, then hit the ground as wood exploded around him. A hole the size of a basketball punched through it.

Who the hell is this crazy heifer?

Angie ejected the shotgun shell and aimed the gun again. Her feet braced firmly apart, her eyes on the hole she'd just created. She needed to get to a car. Or a phone. Preferably both.

This was bad. Really, *really* bad. She didn't even know they had tiger shifters. What did tigers do? Christ, weren't they man-eaters or something? And what about all the Pack-Pride bullshit? Were all cats involved in that or the lions only?

Goddammit! Where the hell is Miki when I need her ass?

Angie realized how quiet it had suddenly become. Real quiet. She strained to hear anything as she took several small steps forward.

She stopped abruptly, closing her eyes. She didn't know how long he'd been behind her, but she knew he stood there now. She could feel him.

She steadied the gun in her hand and spun around to clobber him with it. But he was fast and strong. He grabbed her around the waist, yanking her up against his naked body with one hand while the other snatched the gun from her.

They stared at each other as he threw the gun out the open balcony window he'd come through. She could feel his hard chest against her tits. Her legs straddled one of his enormous, rock solid thighs.

Holy shit, he's fuckin' gorgeous.

He glared at her. "You are so payin' for that door."

Then he dropped her on her ass.

Chapter Two

"You rude, motherfucker!"

"You try to kill me in my own home and I'm rude?"

"*You kidnapped me!*"

"Woman, I did no such thing." As he spoke, he looked up and saw his brothers staring at him through his poor abused door. He saw the truth in their eyes. Christ, they *had* kidnapped her. *Those idiots!*

"Well, how do you explain me getting here, hillbilly?"

He looked back at the beautiful woman sitting on his floor. Man but she was pretty. Shame she was such a highfalutin' bitch.

"There seems to be some kind of misunderstanding—"

"Really, Jethro? Ya think?"

He closed his eyes and counted to ten. He needed to remain calm. Although this woman seriously tested the tiger in him. When he opened his eyes again to answer her, calmly, she was diving for the open window.

With a roar that shook the house, he went after her. He had her by the waist before she even reached the balcony. That's all he needed. Some crazy heifer with a broken leg because she jumped out his second-story window.

"*Motherfuckingbastardsonofabitchwhorecocksuckerprick!*"

Nik dragged the kicking, screaming woman out of his bedroom and to the room that had belonged to his old Aunt Abby. A crazy tigress, she'd believed everyone plotted constantly in hopes of stealing her valued "possessions". So when she moved in for the last year of her life, she'd insisted on a walk-in closet with a lovely lock on it. For the first time since the old woman died, Nik locked that closet. Right after he tossed her crazy butt inside.

She kicked and screamed louder, but Nik ignored it as he adjusted the padlock. He had to find out what the hell his brothers had been up to and he still hadn't had his cup of coffee.

Nik was not a happy man.

Angie banged on the door one more time, but she knew he'd left the room. She *felt* him leave, even though he did it silently.

"Goddamn redneck!" She hadn't been this angry in a long time. Not since the judge ordered her to go to anger management. One little incident with a baseball bat and a guy's knees and suddenly she's marked as a raging lunatic. Typical.

She felt around in the dark and eventually found a light. Flicking it on, she yelped in surprise and jumped back as far as she could manage.

She stared at the stuffed wolf silently staring back at her. Angie didn't want to know if it was once like Sara since, upon death, the shifters didn't change back.

She bit back a sob of absolute rage. She wanted to go home.

Now!

A pair of jeans quickly pulled on, Nik walked into his kitchen. A cup of fresh, hot coffee found its way into his hand and his butt forced into one of the kitchen chairs.

"Drink it, Nik," Reena ordered as she poured herself a cup. "Before you say or do anything that we'll all regret, drink your damn coffee."

With a low growl, he took a sip. French roasted. His cousin and sister knew him well. He had what he considered "foo foo" coffee in his cabinets. But he kept that for company—when he had company. He liked coffee strong enough to remove old paint.

"Feel better?" Kisa asked as she handed Aleksei, her twin, a piece of cantaloupe. Aleksei took it and took another step toward the exit. As did Bannik. *Idiots.*

"Don't even think about leavin'." Nik took another sip of his coffee. His head hurt. Man, that woman had a lethal way with a toilet.

"Why is that woman in my house?"

Bannik and Aleksei glanced at each other. Apart, they were two of the brightest men Nik knew. Predators with hearts of gold. But together...Lord, they could be stupid.

"It's the girl from the airport," Alek offered. Like that was an explanation.

Reena sat down catty-corner from Nik. "What girl at the airport?"

Ban grinned. "Big brother here practically tackled that poor girl at the airport 'cause he thought she was cute."

"I didn't tackle her." Nik looked at his cousin, who was really more of a sister to him. Her mother, for reasons no one could quite put their finger on, had shunned Reena when she was barely seven. The tigress stopped caring for her, feeding her, or anything else. Reena wandered over to their territory and his mother took her in, raising her as one of her own. "It was an accident."

Reena raised an eyebrow. "I'm sure. You are known for being quite clumsy."

"Shut up."

"Anyway, we got to this town Daddy wants so bad and there she was. Struttin' around all those wolves like she owned the place. A full-human."

"Still doesn't explain how she got in my goddamn house."

"I'm gettin' to that." Ban scratched the scar across his stomach. The price he'd paid for his daughter. Tiger females were brutal lovers, but Ban loved his daughter and Nik feared for any man who would one day come into her adult life. "See, she has this little store with really nice stuff in it. Me and Alek would go and check it out, ya know, every day or so. Anyway, last time we were there, she left early and when we walked out, we smelled hyena. Which seemed strange, 'cause it's wolf territory."

Nik's head fell back with a sigh. "I am so bored by this."

Ban didn't use less words, but he did talk faster. "Anyway, we go to the parking lot to see if she was okay, and she's got this hyena female down on the ground and is crushing the holy hell outta her windpipe. Which we would have let her go on doin', but this Clan of hyenas came out of the trees and she was kinda outnumbered at that point. So me and Alek stepped in. She got banged up a bit, but that was kinda our fault 'cause we kinda hit her when we leaped over her to get to the hyenas."

"That still doesn't explain why she's *here*," Nik roared in frustration.

"We couldn't just leave her there. Clearly them wolves were

not takin' very good care of her."

"That's really gallant, but both of you have quite substantially large, albeit tacky, homes, so I'm not sure why her skinny ass is in mine."

"Well, me and Alek knew you liked her too. So on the way back, we rolled dice for her, and you won."

"It seemed only fair to include you when we were playing since you saw her first."

Nik stared at his brothers. He prayed that there were cameras all over his kitchen and someone was going to jump out at him and scream, "You've been punk'd!" But that didn't happen.

"You two do realize you've brought her over state lines?"

"How else do you think we got from Texas to here?"

Nik lifted his coffee mug, about to chuck it across the room at his brothers, but Reena's cool hand on his arm stopped him. "What he means, you two Neanderthals, is that it's now a federal offense. Life in prison mean anything to you?"

"We rescued her. I didn't see any wolves out there trying to help. Ask me, she should be damn grateful."

"She is not grateful. She's crazy. Look what she did to me." Nik pointed to his still oozing forehead. "And in case you're wonderin', yeah, this hurts!"

"If you don't want her, I'll take her."

Alek shook his head. "No. We should roll for her again."

"You're right. That'd be the fair thing to do."

"You're not takin' her anywhere!" Nik snapped. "The only place she's goin' is back to her people."

"Um…" Kisa, always painfully shy, cleared her throat. "Actually, the town she lives in, those aren't her people."

"Because she's human."

Kisa shook her head. "Actually, she is considered part of a Pack. Just not that Pack." She cleared her throat again. "After I cleaned her up last night—"

"You cleaned her up?" The words were out of Nik's mouth before he could stop himself and his brothers were all over it.

"Don't worry, big brother," Ban offered.

"We didn't see her naked," Alek finished.

He glared at both of them. "I don't care if you did." Yes he did.

Nik looked back at Kisa. "Go on, darlin'."

"Well, I did a little research on her. You know, to find out what we were dealin' with. And she's part of Alek's little girlfriend's Pack now."

"She ain't my girlfriend," Alek sighed out.

"What girlfriend?"

"Nessa Sheridan."

Nik finally grinned, "Sweetie pie Nessa?"

Alek glared at his kin. "Don't call her that."

"Is that how you found out about that property Daddy wanted? From your little girlfriend?"

"She ain't my girlfriend."

It had been years since Nessa Sheridan brought that pretty little ass of hers to visit. One of the few wolves they ever allowed on their territory. College friends for four years and for some unknown reason his usually suave brother couldn't quite get what he wanted from her. But, in usual Vorislav fashion, the man kept trying. His phone bills must be brutal, though. The woman had lived in Europe for quite awhile now.

Of course this still created a very big problem. "If we're

talkin' the Sheridans...we're talkin' the Magnus Pack." He'd never met the other Pack members but he remembered Nessa's brother and father well enough. And he knew the rest of that Pack's reputation. Wolves. Bikers. Nut cases. Since he last had to deal with that "little gang", they'd wiped out the Withell Pride and had taken on a new Alpha Female. Some psychopath who had the entire Cat Nation double-checking the locks on their doors at night. She'd only been Alpha for six months, but apparently she was damn scary.

"The..." Reena's sharp gold eyes lasered over to her cousins. *"The Magnus Pack!"*

"Why," Nik asked Kisa carefully, "is an unmarked human part of any Pack?"

"She's best friends with their Alpha Female."

"The crazy one?"

Alek and Ban ducked as Nik's coffee mug went flying. He didn't throw it, Reena did. *"You idiots! Do you have any idea what you've done?"* Apparently Reena had heard about the Magnus Pack's Alpha Female as well.

"Don't yell at us," Ban shot back.

"You're right! I should just kick your butt!"

"Stop," Nik barked.

"Um..." Kisa raised her hand like she was back in fifth grade. "Anyone else think she's gotten kind of quiet up there?"

They all looked up at the ceiling. And Nik was almost surprised not to see blood seeping through the walls.

The lock removed, the door swung open and Angie squinted at the bright sunlight pouring through the windows. She leaned against the wall, her arms crossed in front of her. Once her eyes adjusted to the light, her breath almost caught in her throat.

Damn, but the man was beautiful.

So tall. Six-five, maybe. Black thick hair with hints of red and several streaks of white. Not grey. White. And what she'd missed when she crashed into him at the airport were the big round swirls of white hair behind each ear. That looked unbelievably weird to her, and yet she had the almost overwhelming desire to run her fingers through it and find out if it felt any different than the rest of his hair. She also noticed he kept it short in the back, but he let the front get a little long, so it fell into his eyes. His nose, long and slightly flat at the tip, reminded her a bit of a cat's muzzle. And his gold eyes with green flecks reflected the sunlight coming into the room. The lids of his eyes slightly slanted, so she guessed he had some Asian in him.

He'd finally put some clothes on, too. Loose-fitting jeans and an old blue T-shirt with Navy written on it. He didn't wear any shoes on his big cat feet. Good. If necessary, she could break his foot.

The pair eyed each other for a full minute before Angie couldn't stand the silence anymore. "Well, hillbilly, ya lettin' me out? Or are you going to stand there staring at me all day?"

He scowled and stepped back from the door. "Fine. Get your skinny ass out here."

Angie's attempt at being elegant flew out of the room, because his words caused her to trip right into him. She didn't know whose skinny ass he was talking about, but it couldn't be hers. She hadn't been skinny a day in her life and thankfully never wanted to be. Angie had many issues, but problems with self-image had never been one of them.

He grasped her by her arms to stop her fall and she felt the heat from his hands go right through her skin. His gruff tone from a mere second ago changed, as he asked, "You okay, sugar?"

She yanked her arms away from him. She detested being touched. Always had. And she found his touch particularly annoying. His voice, though, with its damn Southern accent sent her pulse racing through her entire body like an out-of-control wildfire. "I'm fine. And don't call me sugar." She walked into the middle of the bedroom. "Now what, country?"

He shrugged, an annoying smile tugging at his lips. Then he walked over to the side of the bed, grabbed the cordless phone off the bedside table, and tossed it to her. She caught it with one hand, but she didn't know what he expected her to do with it. Did he want her to call and make a ransom demand? Or just shove it up his tight ass? More likely that before she made Sara pay the bastard one damn cent for her freedom.

"What the fuck do I do with this?"

"Well, sugar, it's called a phone. They're these amazing new inventions—"

"I know what it is, you mother—" She gritted her teeth, cutting off her curse. If she let the full weight of her fury go, she'd stand there and curse him for the next seventy-two minutes.

She clocked it once.

"I'm not going to ask them for ransom."

"Ransom." He laughed. "Who'd pay ransom for you?"

"Why you slimy little—"

"I'm giving you the phone so you can call your friends and tell them to pick your skinny ass up. Today." At her frown of confusion, he added, "Trust me. I didn't kidnap you. My idiot brothers did. Thought they were doin' a good thing. Personally, I would have left your ass there. Let the dogs take care of ya."

She didn't ask for hillbillies to kidnap her, but she sure as hell didn't need to hear she wasn't worthy to be kidnapped either.

She quickly punched in a number on the keypad and put the phone to her ear. The phone rang while she moved past the hillbilly and easily pushed herself up onto the empty dresser. Her feet didn't touch the floor and she was glad to see her pedicure had held up quite nicely under the recent abuse.

By the fourth ring, "Yeah?"

Man, she'd never hear the end of this shit from Sara and Mik. Letting herself get carried off by hillbillies. "Hey, Sara. It's me."

Okay, she thought to herself, *let the abuse begin.* But all she heard was a little sniffle.

"Angie?" Sara's voice sounded so small. *What the hell?*

"Yeah?"

Then Sara Morrighan burst into tears.

Her friends didn't cry...*ever.* She cried once but anyone would cry if a jealous cheerleader tossed them down a flight of stairs. "Sara, what the hell is wrong?"

"I...we..." Sara couldn't speak she was crying so hard.

After a moment, another voice came on. "Who is this?"

"Zach, it's me. What the fuck?"

"Jesus, Angie. Shit." He spoke away from the phone. "Sara, it's Angie. Honey, she's fine. Sara," he growled, "stop crying."

Angie shook her head. That Zach. He sure knew how to be Mr. Compassion. Turned out just what her best friend needed, too. "Marrec called us early this morning," he stated into the phone. "They found your purse, blood, and some torn up hyenas."

Angie closed her eyes. No wonder Sara was crying. She thought Angie was dead.

"No one called you and told you I was okay?"

The hillbilly winced and she realized he also thought her friends had been informed.

"Nope."

"I'm fine, Zach. Really."

"Where are you? What happened?"

"I have no idea what happened. And as far as where I am..." She glanced over at her captor to find he'd stretched himself out on the bed. One arm hung over the side, swinging back and forth, his fingers brushing the carpet as he blatantly stared at her legs.

"Hey. Hillbilly. Where the hell am I, anyway?"

He looked up at her through long black lashes. "North Carolina."

Angie stared at the man. "I'm sorry. Could you repeat that?"

"North Carolina. That's where you are. At the moment."

"Zach. I'm...I'm in North Carolina."

"North Carolina? How the hell did you get into North Carolina?"

"I don't know. But I'm ready to come home now."

Zach muttered a soft curse, then, "Okay. Okay, we're coming right now."

The way he said that...something was going on. Something that wasn't about her. She knew it.

"What's going on, Zach?" She reached down and rubbed her calf. *Damn Carolina bugs.*

"Nothin'. We'll be there in a few hours."

"Zach," she warned, "of the three of us, I am *not* the nice one. So I'd like it if you answered me."

Zach sighed and Angie could hear him moving.

What the hell was going on? And what the hell did the hillbilly think he was doing? Instead of a bug, it was his big fingers brushing against the skin of her ankle, causing her entire body to clench.

Again with the touching.

She moved her leg away and covered the receiver. "Cut that out."

Zach returned. She had the feeling he switched rooms. "Okay, Angie. This is the deal. The hyenas made a grab for Miki. A full-on assault right at her school."

"Yeah, I know. Conall got hurt, but when I talked to Sara last night she said he was doing okay." She reached down and slapped away the hand caressing her calf.

"Yeah. Yeah. He's fine. It's just...well, we're pulling in the Pack right now to protect Miki."

"Protect Miki? What the hell for?" One of the last people she could think of who needed protection was Miki. And one of the last people she could imagine *wanting* to protect her was Zach.

"Not permanently or anything. Just for the next...uh...nine months or so."

Angie froze, her eyes growing wide. She barely even noticed the big hand wrapping around her ankle.

"Zach, are you...are you saying that Miki..."

"Yeah. Her and Conall, uh..." Zach chuckled. "Got kinda close."

She squealed. Of the three, Angie was definitely the most girly. And when your best friend got pregnant, you squealed, causing the hillbilly to snatch his hand away. "Holy fuckin' shit, Zach! You're fuckin' shittin' me!" She may be the most girly, but bikers still raised her.

"Nope. Our little Conall's going to be a dad."

Man, did she have work to do. Sara would be completely useless in this situation. She hated kids. And Miki, being Miki, would be so busy analyzing she would neglect important things like items for the baby. A crib, some diapers, a desktop computer that could patch into hypersensitive government databases undetected—it would be a Kendrick after all. So, Miki would need her to help.

Hell, Angelina Santiago was going to be an aunt!

But that also meant she needed to see the bigger picture right now. She looked over at the hillbilly cat who'd stormed into her life. He rolled onto his back and stretched both arms over his head, legs stretching out long. The man had to have the biggest thighs she'd ever seen on a human being.

Yeah, this has disaster written all over it.

She shouldn't trust him. Not really. But her instincts were never wrong. The only power she inherited from her grandmother. When she met Sara and Marrec she automatically knew they were different, but good people. And before Sara's grandmother ever spoke, Angie smelled the woman's evil and insanity all over her. Those same instincts told her clearly this big idiot could be trusted. At least with her life he could.

"Zach, I want you to do something for me."

"Anything. Name it."

"Wait 'til the Pack's there. Protect Miki."

"Ang, I can't leave you there. If for no other reason, your friend will have my head."

"And if something happens to Miki?"

Zach had no answer for that. And with good reason. "Please, Zach. Do what I'm asking. I'll be fine."

"I don't even know who you're with."

"Hey, hillbilly."

He looked up at her, his head back against the bed. "Stop calling me that."

She wouldn't, but he didn't need to know that. "What's your name?"

"Nikolai Vorislav, but I wouldn't tell him that."

She ignored him. "Nikolai Vorislav."

A cold, brutal silence hit her from the other end of the phone. *Uh-oh.* "Zach?"

"Put him on."

Nik stared at her feet. She had the prettiest toes he'd ever seen on a woman. And her skin. Christ knew how she kept it so soft. When he marched upstairs to let her out of the closet, his anger marched right beside him. But one look at her, leaning back in the closet like the queen of goddamn Sheba, and his dick almost pounded past his zipper. Lord, the things he could do to that body.

As it was, she still only had on the sheet. She wore no underwear and he was dying to get another look at that tattoo on her back. Especially if that meant he could see her completely naked. He already knew she looked good completely naked.

Human, you idiot. She's human. Too needy. Too...boring. *Remember?* Of course, how boring could this woman be when she used toilet parts as weapons?

No, he needed her gone before he ended up doing something he'd regret for a real long time.

She stared at him for a few seconds before shaking her head and muttering under her breath, "Those goddamn bitches better be worth this bullshit." She covered the receiver of the phone. "I need to stay."

Nik's eyes snapped up to her pretty face. "Where?"

"Here."

Nik shook his head and turned over on his stomach. "I don't think so, sugar. You hit me with a toilet."

She raised one eyebrow and he felt little comfort from that expression. "And your brothers snatched me across state lines—several of them. Your choice, hillbilly. I stay here for a couple of days and you keep me safe or your brothers go where they so clearly belong and learn not to bend over. And since they let my friends twist for the last few hours, you know I have no problem with that."

Nik let out a growl. A low, threat-growl. They normally lasted no more than a few seconds. His stretched out for about fifteen. The woman pissed him off that much. Yet she didn't react. She didn't move. Didn't cower. Didn't do anything except stare at him. She was like a freakin' house cat. Except he did see the tiny goose bumps that ran down her arms and across the exposed part of her upper chest.

"Is that a yes?"

He blinked, his nostrils flaring. If he didn't know better he'd swear his growl just turned her on.

Okay. Now this woman is starting to scare me.

"Do I have any choice?"

"No," she responded coldly. "Now you talk to him, assure him that you'll keep me safe, and you be goddamn nice and charming."

"Or what?"

"Or I start setting things on fire."

And he knew she meant it. He at least knew she'd try.

He held his hand out and she tossed the phone to him. He

brought it to his ear. "Hello?"

"Vorislav?"

"Yeah."

"Zach Sheridan."

Nik smiled. "Hey, Sheridan. How's your sister?"

"Great. How're your balls?"

Ah, yes. What a college graduation that was. Degenerating into an ugly fight between two families. They didn't even shift, just began beating the shit out of each other. And Nik clearly remembered Zach Sheridan trying to put his balls through the roof of his mouth. Actually, that was the last thing Nik remembered about that fight.

The only ones who didn't fight? Alek and Nessa. After all that, the two were still friends, although long-distance ones.

"So, why exactly did your brothers pull her out of Wolf territory?"

"I don't know. You'll have to ask them. But I'm sure it had something to do with impressing your sister."

Nik reared back when that dog growl leaped at him through the phone. "Keep your brother away from my sister."

Oh, this could prove to be mighty fun. "I don't know. My brother thinks she's awfully cute."

"I wonder how cute she'll think he is when they start finding pieces of him all along the Eastern Seaboard."

"Do you have a point, little puppy? Or you gonna keep nippin' at my heels?"

"Hey," Angelina whispered. "Is that you being nice?"

"Sssh, darlin'. Big boys talkin'."

From the expression on her face, Nik thought for sure she would launch herself off that dresser and beat the living tar out of him.

Man, what an uptight little thing.

"Look, hillbilly-pussy, how do I know my friend will be safe with you?"

"My brothers saved her, didn't they? And they didn't see any wolves out there helpin' her. But if you're so worried, ask your sister."

"What does that mean?"

"She's been here. On our territory. Stayed in my momma's house. Eaten our food. Hunted our deer. It's been quite a few years since then, but not much has changed."

"Don't bullshit me, Vorislav. There's no way my sister was ever on your territory."

Normally Nik would kick the hell out of anyone who accused him of lying. Because he prided himself on his Southern honesty. But now he smiled. He couldn't help himself. "She never told you, did she?" The silence he got back answered his question. Poor Nessa. He knew she'd be getting a call soon from one angry big brother. "Your little human will be just fine. Don't worry about a thing."

Good Lord, he wanted her to stay. He *really* wanted her to stay.

"You better protect her, Vorislav. The hyenas have gone postal and we don't know why."

"Don't worry, little doggie. I won't let anything happen to her." He reached over and grabbed hold of her ankle. Just like he thought she might, she yanked her foot away from him. But in the process, slammed her head against the heavy gilt frame of the mirror behind her. Nik winced as she gripped the back of her head. "I'll even protect her from herself."

"Yeah. Well, good luck with that one."

He tossed the phone back to Angie, hitting her in the forehead since her hands were still massaging the back of her head.

"Ow!"

"Sorry."

She caught the phone before it slid off her lap and hit the floor. She glared at him as she put it to her ear. "Zach? We cool? Okay. And don't take any shit from Sara and Miki. If they got a problem, they can call me. But do yourself a favor...don't eat anything Miki fixes for you." She ended the call.

"Well, now. Looks like I have myself a guest."

"Yes. You do."

"So, what's the first thing? Hungry?"

"That's mighty Southern of you, but I'd prefer clothes first."

"But they're so unnecessary." The woman hit him with a toilet and he ends up flirting with her. This simply couldn't be normal behavior, even for shifters. He blamed his father and the man's defective tiger genes.

She slipped that amazingly hot body off his dresser and moved toward him slowly.

"Dude." She crouched next to him. "Maybe we should get some things straight."

"Dude? Did you just call me dude?"

"I'm only staying here temporarily because I have to. Not so you can have a party with the Texas girl."

He propped himself up on one elbow.

This was a woman who could easily make him crawl. Happily. "But we have such great parties here, sugar. The body shots alone can be quite entertaining."

"Clothes. Food. Now." She stood up. *Mmmmhhmm. Tall.* "Or

43

I really will set shit on fire—and I'll make sure to start with you."

He willed his dick to behave as he stared up at her. Maybe he'd break his "no full-humans" rule this one time. Just for her.

"So shift that ass into gear, hillbilly," she walked out the door, the damn sheet she wore blocking his view of her delectable tattoo. "I don't have all fuckin' day."

No. He shook his head. He would not be abandoning his rules for this one. He knew crazy when he saw it. The majority of his family was crazy. And he wasn't about to add another one to the pile.

As hot as the woman was—and good Lord she was hot—he would only worry about making sure she survived the next couple of days. With that mouth, it wouldn't be easy. Then, when the wolves arrived, he'd toss her skinny ass out of his house.

Her head popped back through the door. "I'm sorry. Was I not clear when I said move your fuckin' ass?"

Nik growled and followed after her.

Oh, yeah. When this was all over, he was going to beat the living tar out of his brothers.

Chapter Three

"I don't see the problem, sugar."

Angie crossed her arms in front of her chest. "First off. Stop calling me sugar. Second, I would never allow that...*thing* to touch my body."

He looked at the dress he held in his hands. "What's wrong with it? It's a nice, simple sundress."

Did he really believe for a second she'd wear the dress of a dead woman? "It would be fine. If I were ninety...and boring." *And dead.*

"Look, until we get you something else—"

With a growl, Angie advanced on him. Startled, he backed up until he hit the wall. She reached around his waist, digging into his back pockets.

Smiling, "What the hell are you doing?"

"Doing what I always do. Taking care of it myself." She located his wallet, pulling it out and stepping away from him. "I swear. The shit I have to do just to get through the day." She quickly found his credit card and took it out. He had one of those all-black credit cards. A redneck the man may be, but a painfully rich one. You couldn't even order this card...you had to be invited. *Nice.*

She tossed his wallet back at him, making sure to hit him in the face and moved toward the door.

"Where are you going?"

"Apparently, I'm going to be walking my Brazilian-Mexican ass into whatever dinky town you have around here."

"Dressed like that?"

She could hear the laughter in his voice and she had the overwhelming desire to punch him in the face. "Even this sheet is better than that fuckin' dress."

Angie got as far as the stairs before his arm slid around her waist. She shuddered at the contact. No, she never liked being touched, but this felt different and she had no idea why. She just knew it was freaking her the fuck out.

Snatching herself away from him, her feet slid on the sheet. She would have tumbled head over ass down the marble stairs, but he caught her, turning her so she slammed flush against him.

"Oh, no you don't. Be clumsy in your own house."

She frowned. Okay. First he said something about her non-skinny ass. Now he was saying something about her being clumsy. She was *never* clumsy. She was the elegant one. What the hell was it about this man that had her falling all over herself?

"Something happens to you, those dogs of yours will drive me insane with their howling. I hate that sound." Carrying her against his side, he walked down the hall.

"Where the hell are we going?"

"My bedroom."

She tried to pull out of his grip, but he held her easily. "I don't think so."

"Don't flatter yourself." He walked into his bedroom and

dropped her to the floor. She stumbled back and almost had to grab him to keep herself from hitting the floor—again.

"Okay, sugar, now let's get you something at least tolerable to wear. Can't have you embarrassing me in front of the neighbors."

"Where are the clothes I was wearing when those idiots brought me here?"

"Ripped and blood covered. Can't have you walking around in that, now can I?"

Angie expected him to pull out some other woman's clothes. Some piece of ass he had in his house before. But apparently, the old lady's wardrobe was all he had because he pulled out a big white T-shirt. He glanced at her and then, with an adorable, wicked smile, tossed it so it landed on her head.

Angie snatched the shirt off, only for a pair of shorts to hit her full in the face.

She snatched those off as well. "What are you doing?" Angie shoved the hair out of her eyes.

"Trying to get you to loosen up. You are one uptight filly."

"Sorry, kidnapping does that to a girl."

"No, I'm pretty certain you were born with that stick up your ass."

"Why you motherfuck—"

"You throw those things on, sugar. There's a drawstring, so that should tide you over until we get you some clothes. And sorry, no shoes for now. But this is the South. Shoes are always optional."

He walked past her. "I'll meet you downstairs, sweet cheeks."

His hand slapped her rump, but by the time she spun around, her fist pulled back and ready, he was already gone.

ဆ၈၅ဆ

"What about these?"

Nik took a deep breath. He did that every time she shoved her size ten hooves into his lap. Especially when she'd adorned those hooves with eight-hundred-dollar Prada shoes.

Shoes that he would be paying for. Who knew a slap on the ass would cost him so much?

"They look fine." His jaw began to hurt. All that talking through his teeth. But he couldn't help himself. The woman had moved through his town like a demon. A demon with *his* credit card.

"Just fine? Is that all?"

She'd purchased new clothes. Lots of new clothes. At the moment, she wore an adorable mini-dress that cost him enough to feed a family of four full-humans for a week. Every time she lifted up her legs to show off a new pair of shoes, he caught glimpses of her white lace panties. He hated himself for his weakness. The more she showed him those panties, the more he wanted to tear them off.

It couldn't be normal to dislike someone and want them all at the same time.

She lifted one long leg, holding her foot up right near his face. "Well, which do you like better? These or the black strappy ones?" She'd already bought three "black strappy ones". How the hell was he supposed to tell the difference?

"I don't care."

"Hhhmm." She lowered her leg. "Then I better get both. And the Ferragamos."

He bit the inside of his mouth so he wouldn't start cursing at her.

She slid her feet out of his lap, grazing his crotch, and easily got to her feet.

"I'll take these, too." She motioned to Janette, the owner of the store. Janette glanced at him and he nodded. Unable to hide her grin and unwilling to stop laughing, Janette followed the evil viper across the shop.

Angelina Santiago. He finally got around to asking the evil viper's name. Now it would be the name he would forever associate with deep, passionate annoyance. The woman had spent nearly twenty grand of his money in little under three hours. Actually, the Ferragamos put him way over the twenty grand mark.

And what amazed him was how she simply didn't care. She spent his money like they'd been married for twenty years and she'd found out he was cheating with his secretary.

How full-humans put up with this he would never know.

"I'll be right back." She strutted past him toward the exit. And it was a *strut*. The kind of walk bands like ZZ Top wrote songs about. She didn't move like a supermodel. She moved like a stripper.

"I'm supposed to be protecting you."

"Well, good job!" She gave him the thumbs up and strutted her fine ass out the door.

Janette sat down next to him.

"How's your day, Nik?"

He looked at her. She smiled, her fangs peeking out a bit. *Damn leopards.*

"Fine. Not as good as yours though."

"Very true, Nik." She patted his thigh. "Very, *very* true."

CR8O8O

"A permit?" Angie gave a little pout. "Really?"

"Sorry, darlin'. You can buy a huntin' rifle now, though."

She debated the salesman's suggestion, but her shoulder still hurt from using that damn shotgun from earlier in the day. She really preferred handguns. Besides, she would still need ID and all her stuff was in Texas.

Angie shook her head. "No thanks." She glanced around the sports and firearms store, deciding to go back to the standard weapons she once used before she became old enough to start buying guns.

Quickly grabbing what she needed, she had the lovely man charge it to Nik's account. It seemed everyone in town knew the hillbillies. And every woman definitely seemed to know Nikolai Vorislav. Not surprising, though. Even she had to admit he was damn fine. *Especially* when she found ways to annoy the living shit out of him.

She took her bag of purchases and walked out the door, heading to the store she'd left Nik in. Halfway there, a sweet black leather skirt caught her eye in one of the shops.

Angie walked in and immediately a salesgirl was at her beck and call. She really liked this town. They knew how to treat people. Of course, almost everyone she'd met so far was a little less than human. But after finding out about most of the people in her own town, she really wasn't too concerned.

Taking the skirt from the clerk, Angie put her bag down in one of the chairs. She held it up against her body as she stared at herself in the mirror. *Cute.* And an Armani original.

"Does Nik Vorislav have an account here?"

"His family does, yes."

"Great. Charge this to that—and anything else I find to amuse me."

"Yes, ma'am."

She giggled and wondered the best way to make sure Vorislav saw the price tag. She loved the look he got on his face when she did that.

"Enjoying Vorislav's money, are we?"

Angie glanced over her shoulder, quickly realizing they had her surrounded. Six of them. All gold and gorgeous.

She turned slowly, her eyes straying to the bag she'd brought into the store with her. Nope. She'd never make it before they ripped her apart. And, yet...she got the feeling they didn't want to hurt her.

"As a matter of fact, yes I am."

One of the females laughed. "Good."

Another one, holding a phone, looked Angie up and down. "Are you Angelina Santiago?"

No point in lying now. But Angie couldn't help but return the once over before answering, "Yeah."

She handed Angie the phone. "Here."

Completely confused, Angie took it. "Hello?"

"Is this Angelina Santiago?"

"Yeah."

"Well, hi there! This is Victoria Löwe."

"Who?"

"Long story short—I'm a lioness looking for a truce."

"With who?"

"With the Magnus Pack."

"What does that have to do with me?"

"Well, I've tried to communicate with Sara Morrighan, but she refuses to talk to me or any of us."

The other females stepped away to look at the clothes while Angie used the phone. "You think that could be because you killed her mother?" One of them picked up a hideous dress and Angie frowned. The woman caught her expression. She held it up and Angie shook her head. "No way," she mouthed at her.

She didn't know these people and they were the mortal enemies of her best friend, but dammit, bad fashion was bad fashion. And she couldn't let someone go through life thinking that dress was okay.

"I didn't do anything, Ms. Santiago. In fact, I wasn't even born yet. But all that aside, the Withell Pride is dead and gone. I'd like us to move past this. The entire Cat Nation would like that as well."

Cat Nation? There's a Cat Nation?

Angie took the horrid dress from the woman's hands and put it back on the rack. She grabbed a sexy little gold number and held it up against the woman's body. "So what do you want from me?"

"Talk to her. Get her to speak to me."

The dress would look great on the woman, so Angie gave her a strong nod of approval. "I don't get into Sara's business and she doesn't get into mine. It's helped us have a very long, healthy relationship."

A tug on her arm turned Angie around to face a cute outfit on the wrong female. She grimaced. "No. No." She took the outfit and tossed it on top of the racks.

"No, no, what?"

"Not you." Angie dragged the female over to another rack

across the floor. She found an elegant suit with the woman's name—whatever name that may be—written on it. The female blinked in surprise, then smiled.

"Look. I can talk to Sara, but talk don't mean shit to her. If you want a truce with Sara Morrighan, you better be prepared to show her how far you'll go."

"And how far is that?"

"I have no idea." Hell, with Sara, it could be Mars.

"Look. All I want is to talk. And wouldn't you like that too?"

"Personally, I could care less." Another tug, she turned and gave an immediate nod of approval. At least one of them had some taste.

"What about your friend? The one about to breed? You'd like her to be safe, wouldn't you?"

Angie froze. "Are you threatening me?" If she had to, she'd kill every cat in the Continental United States if it kept Miki and her future niece or nephew safe.

"No. But we want our kids safe, too. See what I'm saying? This could be a benefit for all of us."

Angie pried a dress several sizes too small out of another female's hands. "Don't be ashamed. There's nothing wrong with the 'X' in front of that 'L'." She gave the woman something more her size.

"I'll try and talk to her. But I'm not promising anything."

"Fair enough."

Angie waved away a bad pair of sandals as she closed the phone, handing the device back to one of the females.

"Should I be concerned that you people found me here?"

The one holding the phone shook her head. "No. We weren't looking for you. We just happened to see you walking around town. Everyone knows Victoria is trying to get a truce going. We thought we might be able to help."

"And how did you know who I was?"

"Are you kidding?" She laughed. "Everybody in town knows the Vorislav boys took you. Those tigers. They're crazy."

"Besides," another added, "you don't smell like you're from around here."

Angie let that freaky and disturbing statement pass as Nik stormed into the store. "Where the hell did you go?"

The lionesses all smiled. "Hey, Nik," they all said as one.

Nik's face dissolved into a delicious grin. "Well, hey, ladies. How y'all doin'?"

Angie rolled her eyes in disgust. *Christ, is there any woman in this town the man hasn't stuck his cock into?*

Angie grabbed her bag from the sports store and the clerk handed her a bag holding her new skirt. She walked up to Nik, but he seemed much more interested in the lion females.

But she knew exactly how to get a man's attention. *Any* man's attention.

"Look at what I got, hillbilly." She took off the watch she'd purchased when he'd gone to the bathroom nearly an hour before. She held it up in front of his face. "A Tag Heuer. The lovely gentlemen at the jewelry store said he'd be happy to put it on your account." Angie backed up, dangling the shiny new watch. "Isn't it pretty and shiny, little kitty? And expensive?"

Laughing at the expression on his face, she walked out of the store and knew, without looking, Nik would be right behind her.

He thought for sure she'd make him take her to one of the many expensive restaurants in town, to really solidify the afternoon of overindulgence, but instead she grabbed a cheeseburger, fries, and a cola from the local diner. She took her food and headed into the park. He followed, with a separate bag just for her ketchup. Seemed she couldn't tolerate her fries without loads of ketchup.

Now, as they sat across from each other at a picnic table, Nik couldn't help but wonder if she were always like this or if she'd simply gone off her meds.

She silently ate her burger and fries, staring out at the park. For a human, she really was mighty feline. She liked watching other people, her shrewd eyes taking in everything. And she loved to flirt. Not with him, but with everyone else. On their way to the diner, they'd passed a small group of Pride breeding males. In typical lion fashion, the males checked her out like prime rib at a steak house. She didn't return their appraisal with any shy glances or beguiling smiles. Instead, she watched them walk past her, turning and walking backward on those four-inch heels like she was born with them on her feet. And then, she nailed them with a killer grin that stopped them all in their big lion tracks. He knew that smile. He'd used it himself. It was the smile that said, "I'll fuck you and no one will ever be good enough for you again."

Unfortunately, she didn't smile at him like that. She mostly glared, smirked, or mocked. And she seemed to be a real big fan of pissing him off.

"So there's a Cat Nation?"

"Of course there is. The dogs breed like rabbits. They kind of outnumber us. But being the biggest cats, tigers don't worry too much."

She grinned around her burger. "And a humble breed, I see."

"What can I say? Not a lot of breeds are like us. Last I weighed in, I was damn-near seven hundred pounds."

"Too many carbs?"

"Funny."

"I am...and I look fabulous in my new shoes."

Again with those damn shoes. "Do you goad everybody this much?"

"Me? Goad? Of course not. I bring joy and life to all. I'm sweet, charming, have a great sense of style—and if you wanna keep that hand, you'll get it away from my fries."

Busted. "Come on. Little gal like you can't pack all this away by yourself."

She stared at him for several long moments. Then, with a shrug, she slapped his hand away when he came in for a second pass at her fries.

"Aren't you a little worried about staying here under my protection? You don't know me from Adam."

She chewed on her food thoughtfully before answering. "No. I'm not worried."

"That seems a little strange to me. I think I'd be worried."

She took a sip of her soda. "I slammed you with my head, hit you with a toilet, and shot a hole through your door. You, however, threw me in a closet." She shrugged. "So, no. I'm not worried."

He unwrapped his fourth burger. "I guess ya got a point."

"I figure if you were gonna kill me, you would have done it by now."

"I could always sell ya to the lions."

"Well, if they look anything like that group we passed outside the diner—sell, sell, sell away!"

He debated about whether to hit her with the burger in his hand, but his hunger overrode his impulse.

She watched him eat for a moment, then asked, "So you're not married, are you?"

Nik choked on his burger. He hit his chest several times to dislodge the beef while she watched him quietly.

"Why do you ask?" he wheezed out.

"Just a question."

"My kind don't get married. We don't settle down. We live alone. Happily."

"So you're not like the wolves?"

He shuddered. "No. We are *not* like the wolves."

"Interesting."

"Really?"

"No. Not really. I'm just looking for shit to say."

Angie's phone rang. He'd gotten her a new phone but with her old number so she could keep in touch with her friends.

She pulled the gold-plated phone out of her Dolce & Gabbana handbag. Nik guessed it would be those dog friends of hers. He expected tears, soothing words about how she was doing fine.

What he didn't expect...

"Don't you dare yell at me, Sara Kylie Morrighan!"

"We're coming for you. Tonight!"

"Like hell you are!" Angie stood up. "I swear to God, you push me on this and I'll make that scar on your face look like a fuckin' scratch!"

"Here!" Sara yelled away from the phone. "I can't talk to her!"

Angie began pacing around the table. "*She* can't talk to *me*? She's being an irrational psychopath and she can't talk to me?"

Nik worked on another burger—*how many was that now? Forty?*—and watched her, but didn't say anything. She suddenly wanted to punch him in that handsome face, but that was because she felt a little tense. She stopped taking out her anger on others a long time ago. Or at least she worked really, really hard not to.

"Hello?"

"And when the hell were you going to tell me you were pregnant?"

"I just found out! I didn't even have tests yet!"

"What do you mean you haven't had any tests? Then how the hell do you know?"

"Because they can smell it on me! Like that's not fuckin' freakin' me out! *And why are you yelling at me?*"

"*I don't know!*" With a sigh, Angelina sat back down at the table, right beside Nik.

"Miki, you need to get control of Sara. Now."

"I don't think she's wrong. I think we should come get your ass this damn second."

"Miki Kendrick, I swear to God—"

"Angie, we don't know these people you're staying with."

"They're tigers."

"Siberian," he offered.

She glared at him over her shoulder, but barked into the phone, "Siberian, apparently."

"Oh, really. Well, according to page six hundred and ninety-five of the *Encyclopedia of Mammals*, male tigers are one of the most vicious and deadly predators known to man. The males kill cubs just so they can get the female back into heat so they can get her pregnant with their own."

Angie used her free hand to rub her forehead. "That's fascinating, Kendrick. But I really don't think I have anything to worry about here. You do. So why don't you focus on yourself for awhile? You are the one about to breed."

"I wish everybody would stop fucking saying that."

"Oh, I'm sorry. How about you're the one about to experience the wonders of childbirth?"

"You are such a bitch."

"And you are such a psychopath."

"Fine!"

"Fine!"

Angie slammed her phone closed, then slammed it down on the picnic table. She picked it up and slammed it down two more times.

"Do you and your friends fight like that all the time?"

"That wasn't really a fight. That was a disagreement. Fights usually involve finger pointing and the occasional headlock."

"And parts of the toilet?"

She smiled, her anger evaporating in seconds at his humor. "Naw, *sugar*," she mimicked back in her best hick accent. "That was a full-on assault. Texas style."

Not even realizing her actions, Angie reached over and gently touched the cut she'd given him right above his eye. Already it damn-near healed completely. *Must be nice to have that awesome shifter metabolism.*

"I didn't hurt you too bad, did I?"

He didn't answer. Instead he closed his eyes, her fingers stroking along his brow, and leaned his face against her hand.

At that point, she really should have taken her hand away. Normally she would have. Normally she wouldn't have touched him in the first place. But after being kidnapped by hillbillies, "normal" seemed the least of her worries right now.

Nik tilted his head down, rubbing it against her hand. His eyes still closed, she could just watch him. He had the longest black lashes she'd ever seen on a man. And his hair wasn't black but a deep, rich brown that felt incredible against her hand. Not really knowing why, Angie dragged her fingers through his hair...and Nik purred back in response. A low one, from deep down in his gut.

Startled, she snatched her hand back. Two weeks ago she'd been arguing with the rodeo clown about how she didn't like to be touched in public. She finally admitted she didn't like *him* touching her. Now here she sat, running her hands through her kidnapper's hair in front of God and everybody.

Have I lost my fuckin' mind?

Nik's eyes snapped open to find her staring at him like *he'd* done something to *her.* When, in fact, she was the one twisting him around her very well-manicured finger. Many women had touched him before this one and many would after he got her skinny ass out of his house, but no one had ever made him lose himself like that before. And this one had done it with a simple touch.

She scrambled to her feet. "We...uh...better get back. The clothes...ya know."

True, her twenty grand worth of clothes were in the back of his pick-up, but he really needed a moment to, er, compose himself.

"Are you coming?"

Well, that's a loaded question.

He tossed the keys to her. "I'll be right there. Gotta clean up all this stuff."

She nodded and practically sprinted back to the car. He, however, willed his poor dick to behave.

Why did this suddenly feel ten times more dangerous than when he thought an entire Clan of hyenas was out to kill her?

Chapter Four

"Did you buy her a pony, too?"

"Don't start, Reena."

"I mean, exactly what is wrong with you? Has all rational thought left you to blow that kind of money on some woman that you don't even know?"

Nik wouldn't look at his cousin. Instead he buried his head into the couch cushions.

"Well? Answer me!"

"I think she's cute," he mumbled sadly into the expensive leather.

"Oh, good Lord!" Reena launched herself onto Nik's back, batting his head around with her hands. Funny, it never hurt this much when they were tigers. "Have I taught you nothing?"

"Stop doing that. Now."

She grabbed hold of his T-shirt and pulled. "Send her ass back."

With a sigh, Nik sat up, knocking his cousin off his back. When she hit the floor, he barely glanced at her. "I can't. I'm supposed to protect her."

"Just 'cause they're afraid to transport her. Send her in the jet."

Nik found himself suddenly interested in his bookshelves. Maybe he should get new ones.

"Nikolai Vorislav, them dogs don't know about the goddamn jet, do they?"

"It's none of their business."

"They left her here because they had no other way of safely gettin' her back to wherever the hell those dogs roam. But if we can take her ourselves—"

"She's stayin'. And I'm not discussing this anymore."

"The woman hit you with a toilet."

"She was scared. I almost think she regrets it now."

"*You* think she regrets it. *I* think the bitch is crazy."

Nik sighed again. "Yeah. But damn if she don't look good in a sheet."

"I'm leavin'." Reena stood, clearly disgusted by her cousin. "The boys will be home from their daddies' soon and you're starting to piss me off."

Reena took several steps away from him and spun around. "And just so we're clear, you're turning into your daddy."

Fangs burst from Nik's mouth. "I am *not* turning into my daddy."

Reena folded her arms in front of her chest. "Did you care that Alek and Ban didn't see her naked?"

Nik glared at his cousin, but didn't answer.

Reena chuckled. "Too late."

CSÐEJBÐ

Angie sat on the floor of the bedroom that was now her

temporary home. Shopping bags surrounded her and she went through each one, pulling out and meticulously folding each item. It gave her hands something to do while she silently beat herself up.

What the hell had possessed her to rub the man's forehead?

She wasn't like Miki and Sara. Though they hid it well, both craved affection and love. Angie craved occasional sex and not to get the shit annoyed out of her. Otherwise, she happily co-existed with herself. She didn't even have a pet. The only full-time companions she needed were her two best friends, but even they went home at night.

Angie carefully folded a gold tank top and laid it on the pile. She shook her head.

Why the hell am I unpacking? Getting comfortable?

Sara wouldn't get comfortable. Sara would have gotten drunk and beaten the brothers within an inch of their lives. Miki would have...well, Miki would have dug an underground tunnel, extricated herself a safe distance, and then blown the house up.

Neither of them would be unpacking clothes after a little shopping spree with their kidnapper.

Wow. She really was a girl. Could she be any more girly? Any more dull? Any more dangerously weak and stupid and female?

"Hey, darlin'." That came from the balcony of her room. Without missing a beat, Angie grabbed one of the baseballs she'd purchased from the sports store, crouched, turned, and pitched it.

The ball slammed right between the eyes of one of the hillbilly brothers. "*Shit!*"

Startled and hurting, he went to grab his head, forgetting he was on the other side of the balcony. The *outside* of the balcony. He fell back, disappearing from sight.

"Uh-oh." Maybe she should have waited before attacking. She wasn't too sure how well the family would take to her killing one of their own. Especially after trying to kill the other brother earlier.

Grabbing another baseball—just in case—she quickly walked to the balcony, and leaned over the railing.

Three of Nik's siblings were down there and she guessed the two hysterically laughing were the ones who had *not* been on her balcony.

"What are we looking at?"

Angie gasped, his voice right in her ear. Big arms braced on either side of her.

The motherfucker is in my space!

Angie turned and swung with her free hand at the same time. Her hand contacted with a concrete slab...or a hillbilly chest. Either way, she felt like she'd broken her knuckles.

"Motherfuckinggoddamnsonofabitch!"

"Aw, sugar. Did you hurt your hand?"

Angie didn't know what annoyed her more. The fact her punch didn't even faze him or that he hadn't moved back away from her. Yeah. She was sure of it.

Both annoyed the shit out of her.

"Lemme see." He took her hand, but she snatched it back before he got a good enough grip on it.

"Keep your hillbilly paws off me."

He held his hands up. "Okay. Okay. No need to get all hysterical."

"*I am not—*" Angie took a deep breath and did the counting technique her anger-management counselor taught her. *Ten. Nine. Eight...*

"And what exactly are you gonna do with that?" His eyes glanced at the baseball in her hand and back at her.

She looked up into his smiling face. No. He didn't smile at her. He smirked.

Condescending prick.

She looked at the baseball in her hand and, for a brief moment, Nik thought she might try and shove it up his ass. Man, this woman was quite the hellcat.

Instead of rectally damaging him, she muttered, "Three, two, one," under her breath, and calmly looked at him. "Pick something."

Nik looked down into that pretty face. "I'm sorry?"

"I said pick something. Anything around here, and I'll nail it. Dead on. I used to date a minor-league baseball player."

"Really?"

"Yup. He loved teaching me stuff." Nik just bet. "It was the only time I didn't tell him to get his fuckin' hands off me."

Nik rubbed his nose to stop from laughing. He leaned against the balcony. "Anything, huh?"

Ban stared up at them, rubbing his forehead. When he realized Nik watched him, he began making kissing faces and pointing at the pair of them. When Angie turned around, he stopped.

Sarcastically, "How about nailing my bonehead brother in the head again?" Since he assumed it had already happened once based on the knot already growing there.

She shrugged. "Okay."

"Wait, I was kid—" But it was too late. She sent the ball blazing down from the balcony and popping Ban right in the head...again.

Man, that baseball player taught her well.

Ban let out a stream of curses he probably hadn't used since he left the Marines and again gripped his forehead.

Nik ran his hands through his hair. No, he'd never hear the end of this one.

While Ban rubbed his head with one hand, he grabbed the ball from the ground at his feet with the other. Nik knew exactly what he had in mind. "Don't even think about it."

"That nutcase hit me in the head! *Twice!*"

She put her feet between the bars and leaned far over. "Who the hell are you calling nutcase, slow boy from down the lane?"

"She sure did hit ya." Nik laughed. He probably shouldn't be so proud of that fact, but he couldn't help himself. "Why the hell were you up here anyway?"

Ban dropped the ball and took several steps away, closer to Nik's side of the balcony. "I wanted to see if she wanted to come with us to the dinner tomorrow."

Angie suddenly perked up, pushing Nik aside to look down at Ban. "A dinner? Like a party?"

"Yes. But I changed my goddamn mind!"

"Well that's plain mean."

"Forget it. I ain't takin' you anywhere. The slow boy from down the lane has spoken."

Nik placed his hands on the railing, "accidentally" rubbing against Angie's bare arm. "Good. 'Cause she's comin' with me."

She turned on him. "I am not."

He didn't want to analyze why she seemed more than comfortable going with Ban, who she popped in the head with a baseball, and not him. He was definitely better looking than Ban.

"Sssh. Don't interrupt, sugar. Big boys talkin'."

"We are not bringing her now," Ban snapped.

"Sure we are. Daddy'll love her."

"Momma won't. She hurt me. I'm gonna have a knot on my head." Yeah. And once he made up some bullshit story, every tigress there would be falling all over their Christian Dior dresses to take care of the big idiot. They loved Ban. He was a proven breeder.

Nik brought his head right next to her so he could whisper in her ear. "He's got a point, sugar. You done gone and hurt her baby boy. Ban's her favorite."

She didn't answer him. She was too busy leaning away from him. He didn't understand it. He'd bathed that morning.

He wondered how far she'd go, so he leaned over a little more. Immediately, her body leaned farther away from him. He wasn't even sure she knew she did it. He stood up straight, and so did she.

He leaned over again. So did she. So he kept going, now desperate to see how far she'd go.

She hit the floor.

"Dammit!"

He stretched out his hand to help her up, but she slapped him away. She got to her feet and looked damn cute doing it, too.

"You all right, sugar?"

"Yes." She brushed non-existent dirt off her dress. "And stop calling me sugar."

"Naw."

"Naw?"

He shrugged. "Naw." He smiled at her. "Besides, ain't you sweet as sugar?"

She snorted. "Naw."

Aleksei suddenly appeared on the other side of the railing. "Ya gotta come with us."

Startled, Angie jumped back. "Are there stairs or something next to this fuckin' balcony?"

"Naw," both brothers answered.

She leaned over the railing, giving Nik an amazing look at those legs. *Damn, girl.* "Then how..."

"It's our hind legs. Tigers can jump really far," Aleksei offered.

"Really?" She bit her lip. "You must have amazing thighs."

What the hell did the woman think she was doing? Flirting with *both* his brothers. And completely ignoring *him!*

Aleksei stared at her, completely lost. "They're not bad."

"Interesting."

Alek leaned in closer and all Nik wanted to do was toss the man's ass off his balcony. *Why is he on my territory anyway?*

"Ignore Ban," Alek insisted. "Just come with us."

"I'd love to. I do love a good party." She glanced at Nik. "And I think I have just the dress."

Nik barely bit back a snarl. "Only one?"

She shrugged innocently.

"Great." Aleksei grinned. "Well, I better take care of Ban's big fat head. I still hear him whimpering."

"I ain't whimperin'," Ban yelled from the patio.

Aleksei winked at Angie. "Yes he is."

She gave a wave of her hand. "Do what you must, hillbilly. But I want my baseballs back."

She headed back into her room. Aleksei leaned in close to his brother. "Man," he whispered. "That woman is hot. And I think she likes me."

"I think she likes anyone dumb enough to be controlled by her."

"You mean like you, Mr. Twenty Grand Man?"

Nik glared at his brother, slapped his hand over the man's face, and shoved him off the balcony.

"That wasn't funny," Alek yelled once he landed.

Nik leaned over the railing. "Yes it was."

Angie placed her newly purchased clothes in the chest of drawers as Nik walked back into the room. He closed the balcony doors and she almost screamed at him to open them back up. She finally had to face it, the man made her nervous. And closing her off in a room with him wasn't really helping.

He picked up the bat she had laying on her bed. "And what do you expect to do with this?"

Kill you in your sleep?

"Pretty little thing like you. What? You gonna beat up the big, bad hyenas with it?"

She carefully smoothed out a chemise she'd placed in the drawer, and turned to face the hillbilly, closing the drawer with her backside. She folded her arms in front of her chest and silently regarded the man for several moments.

"Is there a problem, hillbilly?"

"If you keep calling me hillbilly there will be."

She stepped away from the dresser. "Oh, I'm sorry. Do you prefer redneck or Jethro or—?"

"You could use my name."

"I sure could. But I choose not to."

Anger flashed across his face, but it quickly disappeared. Replaced by a slow, easy smile that almost had her melting at his feet. "I wonder what it would take to get you to say my name."

Uh-oh. "Don't go gettin' any funky ideas, hillbilly." Especially since she had so many of her own.

He dropped the bat back on the bed. "Like what exactly?" When she didn't answer, he walked toward her. "I asked you a question, sugar."

"I'm not playing this game with you."

He stopped right in front of her, gently taking a lock of her hair and twining it around his big index finger.

"I don't play games. I'm a real sore loser."

He stared at the hair he had wrapped around his forefinger, his thumb smoothing it against his skin. It took Angie a second to realize he'd stepped even closer to her. She wanted to take a step back, but if she did he'd end up yanking her hair. And she didn't want to look like she was trying to run away from him.

When, exactly, did she lose control of this situation anyway?

Freakin' cats!

"Damn, girl. You sure are pretty."

Well, at least he didn't try and bore her with "beautiful". Men said that crap to her all the time, but they wouldn't know beauty if it came up and kicked them in the nuts. Miki, who they all but ignored, was beautiful because if the girl set her mind to it, she could destroy *the universe.* Sara went beyond beautiful with her strength. The woman had lived in pain and with that fucking bitch Lynette for years and not only survived but kept her soul. *They* were beautiful.

Angie had a really great sense of style, amazing friends, and absolutely no delusions about herself. Or anyone else for that matter.

"That's very kind of you."

"Not really." He continued to wrap her hair around his finger until his hand rested close to her cheek.

He had her trapped with the tall dresser at her back and her hair wrapped around his hand. She had to lean her head back to get a good look at him. The hillbilly towered over her. The man was big. Huge. Conall-sized. Just a little leaner.

She cleared her throat, trying her best to maintain a bit of pseudo-calm. Of course, she didn't feel calm. She didn't feel scared either. She didn't know what she felt except extreme panic and a growing wetness between her legs very few men had been able to get out of her without their hands or mouth on certain parts of her anatomy. And that sound. What the fuck was that sound?

Thump. Thump. Thump.

Ever since he took hold of her hair, she kept hearing that damn sound.

Good God. That was her! That thumping noise emanating from between her legs. Was her clit supposed to sound that loud pounding against her panties? And could the hillbilly hear it? This could get seriously embarrassing.

"Look, hillbilly," she looked for a way around him, but he wouldn't move and he seemed in no hurry to release her hair, "if I'm gonna stay here, maybe we should get a few things straight."

He leaned in suddenly, his grip tightening on her hair. And, man, but did that feel good. He put his nose right against her neck. *Is the man smelling me?* "What exactly would those few things be, sugar?"

"First off, stop smelling me."

"Sorry. It's just..." He took another sniff. "You smell good enough to..."

"Don't you dare say it."

"...lick."

Then he did. Right across her jugular. His tongue, warm and dry, pulling the skin of her neck as it rasped across it.

She almost dropped. Right there. Right at his giant, hillbilly feet. But at the same time, her fight or flight response kicked in and she did the only thing she could think of. She brought her knee up, aiming for his nuts.

But the fucker moved like lightning. He grabbed her knee before it ever touched him. His hand slid around and up, bringing her leg up and out. He leaned his body against hers, his lean hips between her thighs, and he wrapped her leg tightly around his hip.

He did it so fast, she didn't even realize what the hell had happened until his body pinned her against the dresser, the heavy wood banging against the wall behind it.

Thump. Thump. Thump.

Nik knew he had to stop. He knew he needed to back away and let her get on with her packing or unpacking or whatever the hell she'd been doing when he walked in. Then he would go outside as tiger and kill the first unlucky thing that came across his path. Hopefully one of his brothers.

But he couldn't. He couldn't walk away from her. He never

met a woman capable of making him this *feral* before. He considered himself out of control at the moment, at least by Vorislav standards. She really did smell good, though. She tasted even better.

Damn his brothers to hell and back! Why the hell did they bring this vicious, foul-mouthed piece of ass into his home? Yesterday his life had been going so well. Quiet. Simple. With the occasional elk thrown in for good measure.

Now, more than twenty grand in the hole and a healthy knot on his forehead, he had some stranger pinned up against his furniture while he ground his painfully hard erection into her amazingly hot crotch. And, man, but did *that* feel good.

Her hands, still covered in scratches and scrapes from the day before, grabbed hold of his T-shirt. But instead of pulling him in for the kiss he desperately wanted to give her, she shoved him away.

"Get the fuck offa me!"

Nik released her and her hair immediately. He didn't want to, but never in his life had he ever forced a woman to do anything she didn't want to—and making his baby sister eat dirt didn't count—so he wasn't about to start now.

Like an alley cat trapped under his couch, she hissed at him, "Don't ever put your fuckin' hands on me. I don't like to be touched."

"Really? 'Cause it *smells* like you didn't mind much."

Goddamn, motherfuckin' shapeshifters! As far as Angie was concerned—they cheated! Being able to smell fear, panic, pain, and now lust ripped away her ability to lie her Latina ass off.

And, to her growing rage, he was right. She didn't mind much. For the first time ever, she didn't mind being cornered.

By a lunatic hillbilly, no less. A lunatic hillbilly who made her feel like she hadn't had sex in a thousand years...and that this might be her one and only chance.

No, sex with the hillbilly wouldn't be the problem. Her lack of control would be the problem. She could see it in his eyes. Angie would never be able to control him. Never be able to tell him what to do and just have him do it. His brothers were easy. A few complimentary words, a few glances from beneath her lashes, and she could lead them anywhere. But not this one.

This was not some big kitty she could lead around by his cock. This one was a big, mean, woman-eating tiger. And she'd do well to keep her legs closed and her body off-limits.

Controlling men and sex were the only things she ever had going for her, she wasn't about to give that up to this asshole.

No matter how badly she wanted him to push her onto all fours and fuck her from behind.

"You need to go now." She pushed herself away from the dresser. His eyes narrowed at her sudden and brutally cold detachment. Scooping some folded clothes off the floor, she pulled open the dresser drawer and carefully placed them inside with the others.

"So it's like that, is it?"

She glanced at him over her shoulder. "Like what?"

He shook his head. "You know, sugar, if you wanna pretend what just happened didn't. And that what we both felt, we didn't. Well, that's on you."

The bedroom door opened as he headed out. "But we'll both know you'll be lyin' your pretty little ass off."

Then he was gone, the door closing quietly behind him.

Angie glanced down at her hands. They were shaking. Badly. Not from fear, though. She didn't fear the man. Not even close.

And for the first time ever, Angie regretted she really hated being touched.

Chapter Five

Nik leaned against the kitchen counter, his arms crossed in front of him. He watched the food on his stovetop bubble and cook. He could feel his face frowning. He'd let some woman make him frown. She also made him hard. Unbelievably, painfully, mind-alteringly hard. But the frowning definitely pissed him off more.

He didn't let women get to him. Why should he? There were others. More than enough to keep a man damn happy without attaching himself to just one.

Known for their brutality and solitary ways, most tiger females and males spent little time together except for the occasional vicious mating.

But the Vorislavs weren't raised like other tigers. Not with the father the good Lord cursed them with. The rest of his kin didn't even call his daddy eccentric. They called him weird. The less friendly ones called him a freak. A freak among freaks. And he was Nik's sperm donor.

Nik knew he should never come home from hunting and find his siblings sitting in his kitchen. Eating his food. Drinking his beer and coffee. And if they were, he shouldn't let them live. But he did. The old man had insisted on it since they were cubs. He'd wanted a family from the very beginning and did everything necessary to ensure that. He prided himself on two things: surviving the Vietnam War and making sure all his children were with the same female.

Nik understood the first. But the last boggled his mind. There were few, if any, tigers who only bred with one female in their lifetime. Most of the tiger families consisted of half sisters and brothers. But not his. It wasn't that his mother didn't want other males either. But if any got too close, his father made sure they never got too close to much of anything ever again.

Really, if you favored your balls, you kept away from "Vorislav's female"—his poor mother's nickname among the tiger community.

Nik didn't hate his father. He simply didn't understand him. He definitely had no desire to be like him. True, he hadn't yet had the need to have any cubs of his own like Ban, but his sexual appetite was as healthy as any of his breed. So, to avoid the nightmare of dealing with a tiger female in heat, he spent his free time getting his itch scratched by other cats. Lion females were great because they only bred with their own kind. So, if they needed or wanted simple sexual gratification, they came to him. Same thing with leopards and jackals.

But Nik avoided humans like the plague. They could be as bad as wolves. Some were happy enough to bump from one bed to another. Yet too many others wanted to commit their lives to one person. Forever! Why the hell would anyone do that? Why the hell did his father?

No. He needed to stay away from Angelina Santiago. Far, far away.

Of course, not easy with her living in his house—even temporarily. And pushing through his kitchen door with that half-crazed look on her face, storming up to him, and grasping his T-shirt between those soft, cool hands.

Yeah, a problem waiting to beat him over the head...again.

"Where is it?" she demanded.

"Where's what?" He wanted to pull her hands off his shirt, but if he touched her again...

"The TV. Where is it?"

"I don't have one."

"*What do you mean you don't have one?*" Panic wafted off her in waves. "*What grown man doesn't have a TV?*"

"One who likes to read instead."

"Read?" He loved her face. Especially when she looked so beautifully perplexed.

"Yeah. I read. And I have a whole bunch of books you can borrow."

Her face twisted in disgust. "What? I look like Miki to you?"

She released him and stormed back out.

He stared at the door she went through. "Who the hell is Miki?"

Growling in annoyance, Angie moved through Nik's house. They were alone. His family members long gone. Just her, the hillbilly, and books. Books!

She shook her head and wandered into what she could only assume was the library and his office. One wall had a floor-to-ceiling bookshelf. Books filled it and he even had books on top of books. The other wall had a floor-to-ceiling case as well, this one filled with CDs and actual vinyl albums. She went straight for the music. He set up his music chronologically starting with stuff from the fifties. She frowned. Clearly a big Elvis fan.

"No TV. And Elvis. Could this get any scarier?" As she moved past the different decades, she finally hit the eighties and nineties, and smiled in relief. He had a nice selection of alternative music and a butt load of some great tech. He seemed to be quite the Lords of Acid fan. Considering their music usually had to do with fucking while being bound, she wondered briefly if he was a bit of a "kinkoid". Into tying up girls and fucking them senseless.

Thump. Thump. Thump.

Goddammit! She really needed to get control of that. Having such a noisy clit really was unacceptable.

She grabbed one of the earlier Lords of Acid CDs and popped it into what had to be the most amazing sound system she'd ever seen. She turned on one of her favorite tracks, "Rough Sex", then went through a pile of magazines he had on his desk. He had a stack of news magazines like *Time* and *Newsweek*, but she had no interest in reading anything that depressing. Thankfully, buried down at the bottom, was a recent copy of *Vogue*. The name on the subscription label said Kisa Vorislav. Must be a sister, since Nik wouldn't dare have a wife.

With a sigh, she sat down at his desk, put her feet up on the exquisitely carved wood with the magazine on her lap, and promptly fell asleep.

Nik could hear her moving around his house. He could imagine the way the skirt of her mini-dress swirled around her thighs. And those shoes. The black "strappy ones" she debated about getting. They really did look good on her. Twenty grand well spent as far as he was concerned.

His cell phone went off and Nik let out a sigh of relief. Anything to distract him from the thought of that woman in those shoes.

"This is Nik."

"Hey, Nik, darlin'."

"Sahara. Hey, baby." A lioness. She belonged to the Lyon Pride from this afternoon. He and Sahara had gone a few rounds in the past. The woman did know how to have fun.

"My sisters said they saw you in town today. And I started thinking, I'm free tonight…"

Nik smiled, then groaned. "I can't. I'm babysitting a dog-lovin' human."

"Get your brothers to do it. From what I heard about her fabulous taste in clothes, they won't mind a bit."

Nik's good humor fled. He thought about his brothers lingering around his territory, watching Angelina walk around his house in those shoes. He didn't like that thought one goddamn bit. Then he realized he felt territorial about a woman he had no intention of breeding with. That particular realization pissed him off even more.

No way. He *was not* his father's son. He'd meet up with Sahara tonight. Meet her and fuck her into oblivion, completely blocking out Angelina Santiago and her strappy black shoes.

"Ya know, Sahara, as a matter of fact—" Tech music suddenly pulsated through his house. But not just any tech music. The Lords of Acid. Specifically "Rough Sex" by Lords of Acid.

That heifer.

Thoughts of the evil viper bent over his kitchen table, taking his dick, while screaming out his name almost had him coming in his jeans. Especially when he added in the handcuffs.

"Sahara, I can't. Really. I made a…" he sighed heavily, "…a commitment."

"You?"

Nik's frown returned. "Yes. Me."

Sahara chuckled. "Uh…okay."

Angie woke up when she felt her chair kicked.

"What?" she asked, not bothering to be polite.

"Hungry?"

She nodded, yawned, and stretched. Arms over her head, legs stretched out with toes pointed. When she finished, she looked up to see Nik staring down at her with his hands clenched into fists. "What?" she asked again.

"Nothin'," he growled.

Strange man, she thought as she followed him from the room.

Angie expected him to go to the dining room, but he kept walking right into the kitchen. She wondered how long she slept, because it had gone pitch black outside. She'd look at her new watch, but she'd left that on the dresser in her room.

She followed Nik into the kitchen and stopped in the doorway. He had the table laid out with food, wine, and lit candles.

Oh, but no. That wouldn't do one damn bit.

She popped on the overhead light. He looked up at her with a frown. At first, she thought it was annoyance, but she realized the bright light bothered his eyes.

"It's too dark," she gave as way of explanation.

"I guess it would be."

"Does it hurt your eyes?" She didn't know why she suddenly cared. Honestly, she hated candlelight dinners. To quote Miki, "You never know what the hell they're puttin' in your food, dude."

"Not really. Just not used to it. I don't really need lights at night." He placed a huge bowl of food on the table; the salad and bread were already out. "Sit, sugar."

She realized she'd been standing like an idiot for the last two minutes. She grabbed a seat and plunked herself down.

"You talk to your friends again today?" he asked conversationally.

"No. I'll call 'em tomorrow. Give 'em the night to cool the fuck off."

"How long y'all been friends?" He sat down catty-corner from her and began ladling out the food.

"Since we were eight."

"Got any brothers or sisters?"

"No."

"Not a real chatty gal, are ya?"

"Exactly how am I supposed to expand on not having siblings? Should I cry?"

He smiled and held up a bottle. "Wine?"

"Please."

"So you can say that word. I thought you were physically incapable."

She watched him pour the white wine into glasses she was damn-near positive were Riedel Vinum stemware. *Nice.*

She definitely appreciated a man with taste.

"I say it when I feel it's necessary." She glanced down at the food he'd ladled out for her. "Macaroni and cheese? Classy."

"I pull out all the stops for my unwanted guests."

"I can see that." She took a bite, closing her eyes and letting the flavor roll around her mouth. "Oh, my God," she finally bit out.

"Is that good or bad?"

"Good. Definitely good."

The hillbilly grinned. "Why thank you."

"Where did you learn to cook like this?"

"Momma. She taught all her boys to cook. She said with our attitudes, we could never expect a woman to stay very long."

Angie's head snapped up. Unlike her grandmother and her best friends, her parents' love always remained in question. So, the fact that someone's mother would say that to them bothered her.

Nik caught her look. "Don't worry. She says the same thing about Daddy." He sighed. "And Lord knows she still hasn't gotten rid of him."

Angie didn't know if he meant divorce or murder. And she wasn't about to ask.

Instead, she decided to change the subject before they got around to her family. "What do you know about Victoria Löwe?"

He shrugged. "Not much. Her Pride's territory is out your friend's way. Up near San Francisco, I think." Angie had no idea lions lived so close to the Pack. "And I know she's making lots of changes among the Prides. But the tigers don't involve ourselves in too much of that Pride crap. Always seemed to me they brought that war on themselves."

"I thought you were all part of a Cat Nation."

"I guess. I mean, honestly, none of it is really my business."

"It is now."

"Well, you can blame my brothers for that."

"You know, I don't remember seeing you with your brothers. Exactly why did I end up here? Did they not have enough room in their trailers?"

Nik glared at her as he bit into a piece of bread. "Actually, they rolled dice for ya—and I lost."

"They rolled...for...and you...*lost!*" She threw her fork down and started to get up, but Nik's hand grabbing her arm stopped her. "Get off me!"

"Sit. Now."

She didn't have much choice. He had an iron grip. She sat back down but wouldn't look at him.

"That was mean. I'm sorry." He released her arm. "My momma raised me better than that."

She finally looked at him. "So you didn't roll dice for me?"

"Oh, no. They did." He gave her that goddamn devastating smile again. "But I won."

No. She'd *never* be able to control this one.

"As a matter of fact, you did win. And don't you forget it."

"Don't worry, sugar. I won't."

CB&O80

Nik rolled onto his back, his arms behind his head, eyes locked on the ceiling, his cock hard, ready, and demanding satisfaction. Preferably from the hot piece of ass a few doors away.

He could smell her. She'd taken a hot shower and her scent now flowed through the entire floor. His mouth watered. His heart hammered against his rib cage. Christ, he wanted that little lady. He wanted her bad.

He closed his eyes, trying to sleep. But that was a mistake. As soon as he closed his eyes he saw her...with her head in his lap. Her mouth on his dick, her tongue swirling around the tip. Her cheeks hollowing out as she sucked him long and deep.

No. That wouldn't help him sleep. He opened his eyes.

He wondered what she'd do if he sauntered on down her

way and knocked on her door at one o'clock in the morning. Welcome him in or kick him in the nuts? Probably welcome him in only to kick him in the nuts once she got him in there.

A growl from underneath his balcony pulled him away from his fantasies about Santiago riding him like a cowboy on a buckin' bronco.

His brothers. They wanted to go hunting. Not a bad idea really. Besides, as much as his brothers drove him crazy, he did love 'em.

They growled again and Nik laughed. They wanted to go hunting. Now. And they basically told him to get his head out from between Angelina's thighs and get a move on.

Smart asses.

Well, anything had to be better than lying here all night pining for a woman who treated him like an annoying alley cat she couldn't get out of her backyard.

He shifted while still in bed and slid out from under the covers. Bounding across the room, he leaped over the balcony. His brothers were already running, the scent of deer filling their heads, and he followed. Loving the feel of the cool Carolina night on his fur and the power of his people flowing through his veins.

Angie sat on the balcony staring out at the yard through the bars of the railing. Wearing an oversized sweatshirt she'd gotten that day and nothing else, she had her knees tucked up under her chin.

When the two tigers suddenly appeared, she almost dashed back inside, but she forced herself to stay put. She knew they had to be shifters. They roared at the house while simultaneously batting each other around with their enormous paws. Within a few minutes, another tiger she could only guess was Nik jumped down and the three ran off into the trees.

They were beautiful to watch. Their long, powerful limbs moving with such precision. It must be interesting to watch them hunt, to see them take down their prey. As long as that prey wasn't her.

Angie finger-combed her wet hair. Except for Sara, Miki, and Marrec, there was no one else to tell she was okay. That dangerous shapeshifters hadn't killed her. Her parents didn't know she'd been missing and she wasn't really sure they'd care. Last she heard, they were on a dig somewhere in the Sudan. Two scientists who had just enough love for their work and each other. Angie had been an accident from the beginning and eventually they couldn't even pretend to care anymore. They left her with her grandmother and every once in awhile they'd stop by to remind her she had parents.

She remembered her parents coming to visit when she turned ten. They'd promised to take her away on a family vacation. Instead, they spent thirty minutes telling her why they couldn't. She listened with absolutely no emotion while her grandmother slammed pots around in the kitchen and cursed in Portuguese. But Miki and Sara were there too. They didn't say anything, but she soon learned their silence was a very, very bad thing.

Sara limped into the kitchen and returned with a glass of what looked like milk and orange juice. A revolting mix. While staring at Angie's parents, Sara handed the glass to Miki, who gulped it down in two big swallows.

Three minutes later, Miki staggered up and over to Angie's mother and projectile vomited all over the woman. Twice.

To this day, her mother wouldn't even mention the two women who had become such an integral part of Angie's life. And until the day she died, both Sara and Miki always had a place at her grandmother's table.

Angie's anger-management counselor seemed convinced her issues with physical contact were due to her parents' lack of affection. Perhaps, but knowing that didn't make it better. Or make any of it hurt less.

Although she knew she was too old to worry whether her parents cared or not, she did. Still. After all this time.

Angie laid her head on her knees and sighed. She didn't feel lonely often. But when she did, she felt it all the way to her bones.

She looked up as Nik—at least she really hoped it was Nik—burst out of the trees. He sprinted across the backyard and took a wild leap up to her balcony. He didn't clear it, but clung to it with his big claws and forearms. His giant tiger head dipped over the railing as he looked at her.

So stunned by his return and launch at her balcony, Angie didn't move or run for her life. She simply stared up at him. She'd never seen a tiger this close before. She couldn't believe how enormous he was. His gold eyes glinted at her in the darkness and his huge tongue hung from his mouth.

"Is this your way of saying goodnight?"

He dragged that big tongue across her cheek.

"Dude! Disgusting!" But she laughed in spite of herself and immediately let go of her sadness.

One paw released the banister and he hung off the side. He stared through the bars of the railing and it took her a moment to realize he was staring at her. Well, her and her no-panty-wearing ass.

"Hey! Eyes front, cat!"

He again gripped the banister with both paws and let out a weird sound through his nose. Like two big puffs of air.

Strange, but she got the feeling it didn't mean anything bad. His head came farther over the banister and he quietly waited. She had the feeling he wouldn't leave until he got what he wanted.

Praying she would get her hand back intact, Angie reached up and ran her fingers through his fur like she'd done with his hair earlier that day. She kept it up for about three minutes, just petting him, lost in the feel of his fur against her fingertips. Eventually, he made that puffing sound again, licked her wrist with his dry, rough tongue, and released the banister. He fell back to the hard ground, but landed on his feet. He turned to look at her once more before bounding off into the trees.

She had no idea what had happened, but she did know her hard nipples, wet thighs, and that damn thumping noise were freaking her the fuck out.

Chapter Six

Nik didn't come back. At least, she never heard him if he did. Around eleven in the morning, she rolled out of bed and scrounged up a bowl of cereal, made a fresh pot of coffee, enjoyed two cups and the newspaper before throwing on a pair of denim shorts and a T-shirt, and heading out to the backyard. She draped herself onto a lounge chair and dialed Sara.

No answer on her cell. So she tried Miki.

"Yeah?"

"Hey. It's me."

"Yeah."

"Oh, come on. You're not still mad at me."

"No. *I'm* not."

"But Sara is?"

"She's mad at everybody. Zach, Conall, me. The universe."

Angie grimaced. It took a lot to piss off sober Sara. But once done, the woman wasn't satisfied until someone lay bleeding and crying.

"Well do something."

"Do what? She won't even talk to me. She's pissed. I mean p-i-s—"

"Yes, Miki. I know how to spell pissed. I can actually spell it in several languages."

"I still have you beat by two."

"I'm sorry but Klingon and Elvish don't count."

"Says who? Klingon is really tough."

"Miki, hon, I really need you to focus."

"Yeah. Well, if I were you, I wouldn't get too fuckin' comfortable."

"Am I the only one who sees the big picture here? Hyenas are trying to kill you. True, there are many who have wanted to see you dead, but these are the first that have actively tried."

Miki snorted. "Look, I do understand. And I appreciate you caring and all."

"But—"

"There's no but. I mean, I did do a little research on this Vorislav guy last night and found some pics of him and his brothers on his company's web site. And imagine my surprise when I realized he's the guy from the airport. But, of course, I'm sure that has nothing to do with you staying there so comfortably."

Fucking, researching bitch!

"It has nothing to do with that. I'm waiting for the Pack to get here. Then I'll be back."

"Well, they seem to be taking their sweet time, but I'm sure you'll find some way to survive."

"Oh for the love of all that's holy. Look, I'm doing this for your—oh my."

"What? What's wrong?"

"Um...puppy."

"Don't call my baby that!"

Angie rolled her eyes. "I'm not, you garden gnome. I see an actual puppy."

An adorable black lab puppy specifically, running through the grass of Nik's backyard.

"Puppy? Why don't you call him what he is? A mid-day snack."

Her crazy friend was right. Tigers roamed this property. A cute little thing loping through the grass was really just a moving Snickers bar to these people.

Angie secured her phone to her shorts and made sure her headphones were on, then she moved across the grass toward the puppy while yelling at her best friend.

"All I'm doing is trying to protect my family. You think she'd appreciate it."

"Aw, you consider me family?"

"That is the dumbest fuckin' thing you've ever said. Of course I do!"

"Well, ya don't have to get nasty."

"Yes, I do. When you ask me stupid questions. You, Sara and Marrec are the only family I have since my grandmother died."

"The breeders still live."

"Yes, but they don't count." She caught up to the puppy as it came to the very edge of where the lawn ended and the acres of trees and tall grass began. "Come here, cutie."

She crouched low and picked the little beast up. "What are you doing around here, little one?"

"Maybe he's suicidal."

"Shut up."

"How come you're nicer to the dog?"

"The dog doesn't make it his goal in life to piss me off."

"This is true."

The puppy squirmed out of her hands. "Shit." She grabbed for him, but froze when she watched the puppy climb on top of the tiger less than five feet away from her. So well hidden in the grass, she never saw him. Her real problem? His markings were different from Nik's. His ears bent a little differently. His eyes a little more slanted. This wasn't Nik. Which meant she didn't know how safe or unsafe she may be.

"Shit," she barked again and scrambled back.

"What's wrong?"

"Uh..." The tiger moved forward, his big body raising up out of the grass. He shook himself, the puppy tumbling off. He caught the little beast between his teeth by the back of its neck. Angie flinched. She really had no desire to watch a dog become anyone's lunch. Really. But the puppy hung from the tiger's mouth without any fear.

The tiger walked forward slowly, eventually dropping the puppy at Angie's feet. She scooped him up and backed away until her ass sat back on the lounger.

The tiger watched her for several very long seconds. Then he charged into the woods.

"Are you still there?"

"What? Oh. Yeah. I'm here."

"What's going on?"

"Tiger antics."

"Don't ever turn your back on one."

"Excuse me?"

"Tigers. They attack from behind."

Angie closed her eyes on a sigh. "Good God, you've been

reading."

"It's what I do. Research."

The tiger returned, a rabbit in his mouth. Unlike the puppy, the rabbit didn't fair too well. The tiger dropped the bloody carcass in the middle of Nik's lawn, and looked at her expectantly.

Another tiger, this one's markings different from Nik's as well, wandered out of the woods. He caught sight of the other tiger. Looked at Angie. Then the dead rabbit. He turned and charged back into the woods. After a few moments. He trotted in with his own rabbit. A bigger one. He dropped it on top of the first one.

"Uh-oh."

"What uh-oh?"

The two tigers glared at each other, and charged back into the woods.

"Something's going on."

"Something bad?"

"Not for me."

They returned, each carrying a deer. One held a doe, the other a buck. They dropped their prey, roared at each other, turned and charged back into the woods yet again.

Angie giggled. "Dude, this is gettin' weird."

"How weird?"

"Well, I could be wrong but...I think I'm being wooed—tiger style."

"What does that entail?"

"So far? Rabbit and deer."

"What?"

The brothers returned, both carrying their own elk. They

dragged and dropped them on the pile. Then one slapped the other in the head with his paw. The other hit him back. Before she knew it, they turned into a mass of snarling, biting, slashing stripes.

"What the hell is that noise?"

"Cat fight."

"They're fighting over you?"

"I don't know."

"They are so fighting over you." Miki laughed. "Angelina and those mighty legs strike again."

"Oh, shut up."

"You're wearing shorts, aren't you?"

"Shut up!"

A third tiger charged out of the woods. Nik. She easily recognized his markings now.

Using his massive jaws, he grabbed one brother by the scruff of the neck, flinging him into the woods. The other went to follow, but Nik knocked him back with a well-placed paw. Then he chased that brother in the opposite direction.

"It's all clear. Big brother handled it."

"I swear, everywhere you go—"

"*Oh, shut up!*"

Nik returned. He trotted past Angelina, barely glancing in her direction, and ungracefully belly-flopped into his pool.

Angie laughed again.

"What?"

"Nothing. Just Tiger-Nik jumped into his pool. Like that goofy fat kid in eighth grade swim class."

"Well, I read that tigers love water. And they don't purr."

"This one purrs."

"Really?" Angie could hear Miki "thinking". "Interesting. Tigers are the one cat that doesn't. It must be the human in him."

Shaking her head and smiling, Angie watched the seven-hundred-pound beast splash around like a little kid.

"Look, Angie. Are you sure you're okay? Really?" Miki's concern for her bled through the phone connection and it warmed Angie's hard heart.

"I'm doing fine, Mik. The man took me shopping. I spent twenty thousand dollars of his money, and he didn't even blink an eye. Nor did he ask for sex."

"You must have terrified another one."

I wish. Angie chuckled as she watched Nik pull himself out of his pool.

She froze, that chuckle caught in the back of her throat. He'd shifted back to human. Naked human. Nik stood up, shaking the water from his hair. The bright midday sun made his skin look like the gods had bronzed it just for her. Every muscle perfectly formed and begging to be touched.

Her mind stopped functioning. Her heart felt like it would burst out of her chest and she openly stared at him. She couldn't help herself. She couldn't turn away. She was mesmerized.

Thump. Thump. Thump.

"Angie? Are you listening?"

Nope. She couldn't hear a damn thing. Nothing. Everything else, even her best friend, blocked out by this man's beauty.

Her eyes trailed down his hard body and she saw it. His cock. And like him, it was perfect.

She swallowed.

"Calling Angelina Santiago! Come in, Angie!"

Nik walked toward her, water dripping down every long, wonderful inch of him. With his long legs, it took him no time to reach her chair. He crouched next to her and gently, with one of those big hands, closed her mouth.

"Catchin' flies, sugar?"

His hand slid across her chin and down her neck. Then it kept going. For an ecstatic moment, she thought he would cup her breast. But, instead, his hand petted the puppy she still had in her grip.

Nik leaned in close, his hot breath against her ear. Softly, so only she could hear, "And, sugar, if you're gonna sit out on that balcony at night, half-naked, smellin' so sweet and sighing like you just had the best fuck of your life, then you might as well put a leash around my neck and call me yours."

He pulled away, gave her the biggest shit-eatin' grin she'd ever seen, and went back into his house.

"*Angie! Either you answer me or I'm coming out there my goddamn self!*"

"*Don't you dare!*" Whoa. She didn't mean to yell that. Or sound so hysterical. But Jesus Christ, who was this guy? She took a calming breath and licked her lips. "I mean. The important thing right now is that Pack baby."

"Stop calling her that!"

CR𝒮CRBO

Nik pulled his front door open and his sister and cousin stormed in, carrying armloads of dresses.

"Where is she?" Reena demanded.

"Angelina?"

"You got some other Yankee livin' with you at the moment?"

"Bite your tongue. Like I'd have a Yankee in my house. She's a Texan."

"Come on." Kisa motioned to the stairs. "She's probably in her room."

The two females dashed up the stairs and Nik shook his head. He didn't know what his sisters were up to, but he saw no claws, so he wasn't too worried.

He started to close his front door but Ban and Aleksei walked up.

"Hey, bro!"

Nik closed the door in their faces and headed back to his office. He still had dead elk in his backyard.

"That's not funny," Ban yelled through the thick oak.

"Yes it is," Nik cracked back.

Angie stared at herself in the full-length mirror. She wore two different shoes. Both high heels, both exceptionally hot.

She didn't even look up when the banging on the door started.

"Fuck off. You said we weren't leaving 'til seven." She debated which shoes to wear. She didn't want to think about it too much, but she wanted to look nice tonight.

"It's us."

She frowned. There was only one "us" in her life and they didn't sound anything like that.

"Fuck off until seven."

With no locks on the doors—*damn shapeshifters*—nothing stopped the two women from rushing into her room.

"I'm sorry. I don't think I said come in."

The smaller one stopped and stared down at Angie's feet. "Oh, Lord, she's even got cute shoes. We don't have cute shoes."

Turning to face them. "Who are you?"

"Don't you remember us? You met us yesterday before you left with Nik."

Angie shrugged. Very few people held her interest, especially from one day to the next.

The bigger one spoke. "I'm Nik's cousin Reena. This is his sister Kisa."

"Great. Now I've got the whole rootin', tootin' clan in here."

"You gotta help us," the smaller one begged.

"Help you? How?"

They dumped the clothes they had in their hands on the floor. Angie grabbed the first thing she saw and held it up.

"Going as a nun, are we?"

Reena nodded. "Exactly."

"Ya see?" Kisa insisted. "Ya gotta help us."

"Why me?"

"We saw those Pride whores today," the taller one said. "They looked amazing."

"It's all over town you helped 'em."

"*That's* all over town?" Angie snorted. "Not a lot goes on around here in Shifterville, does it?"

"Look, you reek of style," the smaller one offered. "We, however, don't."

Angie looked at the two women. The problem wasn't their looks. They were gorgeous shapeshifters and you could barely make out those scars on their necks. But the little one could barely look her in the eye. Shy. The other one clearly a hard ass. Probably the one saddled with the constant responsibility of keeping the youngest boys in line. That task always seemed to fall to the oldest females.

Hell, who could it hurt? And, to be honest, she kind of enjoyed helping the fashion helpless.

"All right. Why not?" The two women smiled in relief and she gave a big grin. "But we need champagne to do this."

His brothers walked into his office.

"What's that look on your face?" Ban threw himself into one of the wingback chairs. "And what the hell are you listening to?"

"Lords of Acid."

"Devil music, O-E-G would say."

"What's wrong?" Aleksei sat on the edge of Nik's desk. "And stop calling our grandmother that, Ban."

"There's over twenty thousand dollars in my account."

"That's all you have left in the world?" Alek demanded.

"Bro, why didn't you tell us? We can lend you some money."

"You idiots, I don't have twenty thousand left...there's suddenly more than twenty thousand extra there." He checked a few more things, then leaned back in his chair. "She paid me back."

Kisa rushed in. "Champagne?"

"Wine cellar."

"Chilled?"

"Fridge in the basement."

"Thanks." She tore out of the room.

Ban shrugged and turned back to Nik. "Who paid you back?"

"Who do you think? And did you get your damn dog out of

my backyard?" Ban was the only tiger he knew who insisted on picking up strays, even dogs. Not for a "munchie" either as their mother called it. But for pets. The local rescues loved Ban because he gave them money, helped during fund raisers, and came over to pet the cats and walk the dogs. His brother was so weird.

"Yes. He's back at my house. And do you mean the delectable Ms. Santiago paid you back? By the way, she can handle my puppy anytime."

"Angelina Santiago," Alek sighed. "That name rolls right off the tongue, don't it bro?"

"I'm sure lots of things roll off the tongue when it comes to her."

"Sewing kit?"

The brothers looked up to see Reena in the doorway.

"Aunt Abby's room, I think."

"Thanks." She disappeared.

With a shake of his head, Nik turned and stared at his siblings. "Let's get this straight, shall we gentlemen. You stay away from her. She's my guest. I promised those dogs I'd take care of her. So you two idiots back off."

Aleksei winked at Ban. "I thought you didn't want her."

Ban grinned back, and Nik felt his hackles rise in anger. "Which means, big brother, she's fair game."

Kisa rushed past the room, heading back where she came from. "I took cheese and crackers too!" Then she charged up the stairs.

Nik didn't know what the hell the women were up to, and he didn't want to know. Instead he focused on his brothers. "She is *not* fair game."

"Oh, come on, Nik. Ya can't keep 'em all."

"I don't keep 'em all. And I'm not keeping this one."

His face perfectly innocent, Ban asked, "So we can get her when you're done?"

He knew his brothers would never go after his leftovers, but still...even the thought of it made Nik want to rip the hides from their backs. They knew it, too. They knew they were getting to him. That they were making him dangerously angry. And they were enjoying every minute of it.

Chapter Seven

Nik took the snifter of brandy Ban handed him and crashed down on his couch. Ban joined him and Alek, and the three men dropped their big feet on Nik's fifteen thousand-dollar coffee table. Cut from a solid piece of wood, Nik bought it because he liked it. Yet he always knew that any furniture he brought into his home had to be sturdy enough to withstand the abuse of his entire family. Like most cats, they enjoyed being comfortable.

Alek glanced at his watch. "It's seven-o-five. Where are they?"

"What is your thing with time?"

"I don't like to be late, is all."

Ban glanced at Nik. "Kind of uptight, ain't he?"

"Shut up, Ban."

Nik shook his head as he sipped his brandy. He hadn't seen her all day. She'd been holed up in her room with his sisters for hours and, to his growing horror, he realized he'd begun to miss her. But that was her fault. Sitting out by *his* pool, wearing those damn shorts, and looking like she truly belonged in his home—more than any woman had a right. Without meaning to, he swallowed his brandy with one gulp.

Physical. There was nothing more to this than physical. Angie Santiago was one hot piece of ass and all he wanted was to find out if her legs would look any better resting on his shoulders.

The study door opened and Reena swept in. She twirled once in the extremely tiny mini-dress she wore, then looked at her cousins. "Well?"

"Dang, girl," Ban offered. "You clean up nice."

"What does that mean?"

Nik punched his brother in the head. "He means you look nice."

"Well say that, then. Can't believe no woman's killed you yet." She glanced back at the partially opened door. "Kisa's coming. Now say somethin' nice," she whispered fiercely.

Reena stepped back from the door as Kisa stepped in. He'd never seen his sister so elegant before in a full-length gown that swept the floor as she moved. "Aw, darlin'," Nik said with utter pride. "Look at you."

"Do I look okay?" Kisa unnecessarily smoothed the dress down in front. "I feel kinda silly."

Nik stood up. "You look amazin'. Both of you do."

The two women smiled in delight and the five of them stared at each other. For the first time in a long time, they weren't yelling, mocking, or fighting each other. Just a nice, quiet, adult moment between relaxed shapeshifters.

"Well," Angie strutted into the room, "let's go people. It's time to get this party started."

"Now, sugar, I—" Nik stopped. Stopped and stared. How could he not? She wore her long hair swept up off her shoulders, curly tendrils teasingly touching her shoulders and neck. The dress, an expensive number he remembered rolling his eyes at when informed of the price, slid over her curves like someone designed it specifically for her delicious frame. Yup. Definitely the best fifteen hundred dollars he'd ever spent.

She walked over to him. Already a good five-ten, she still had the nerve to wear four-inch heels. He liked that. Her cool fingers brushed against his jaw. Gently, she closed his mouth. "Catching flies, *sugar*?"

They stared at each other, everyone silent until Reena cleared her throat. "Um...why don't we wait out in the car for you."

Reena grabbed Ban's arm, yanking him out of the room. A firm hand in his back by Kisa propelled Aleksei out the door as well.

Angie smiled. "Get that look off your face, hillbilly."

"What look?"

"The one that says I'm suddenly Ned Beatty in *Deliverance*." She took a step back. "And the food at this thing better be good. I'm starving. The cheese and crackers wore off."

She effortlessly turned on those impossible heels and Nik almost dropped to his knees. The dress, completely backless, revealed her tattoo. A Celtic-Mayan design radiating power and protection magick that clearly showed a cat. A big one. His claws tearing across her flesh. The artist even added some red to show blood. One of the nicest pieces Nik had seen in a very long time, but on her...

Add in the way her hips moved, and he was seconds from coming in his pants like a thirteen-year-old.

"Well, come on, hillbilly. I don't have all goddamn night."

Of course, she really had to stop calling him hillbilly.

CB 80

Angie leaned against the bar. Her eyes on her lemon martini, but her ears completely tuned to the older couple next to her. In their mid-fifties, they'd been arguing since they came up to the bar.

She felt bad for the man. The woman wasn't giving him an inch. In a way, she reminded Angie of Miki. Blunt, brutal, and to the point.

"Go away," the woman hissed again.

"Why? You know we look wonderful together."

"*We do not...*" The woman took a breath. She towered over the man, her black hair streaked with grey, white and red swept up off her shoulders and held by a platinum hair clip. "Stay away from me or I'll make you regret that no one's killed you yet."

She turned to walk away and he slapped her on the ass. The tigress—and really what else could you call this particular female?—stopped, growled, then stomped off.

"She hates when I do that."

Angie didn't answer him, since she really wasn't supposed to be listening.

"I know you're listening."

Damn. She glanced at him. "Sorry."

He shook his head and moved closer to her. "Not a problem. We're quite a fascinatin' pair."

Angie realized if she took off her shoes, they'd be the same height. Compared to all the men in the room, he was damn-near tiny.

He motioned to the bartender for another scotch. "You ain't from around here."

"And what gave that away?"

"That accent of yours."

She blinked. Being the darkest one in the room, she simply assumed that would be his problem.

"Texas."

"Good. I'd hate to think anybody brought a Yankee to my party." Angie laughed and he returned her smile. "Damn, girl. That is the prettiest smile I've ever seen...next to hers, of course."

She glanced at the woman he seemed completely lost to. "She doesn't seem too interested."

"She's a stubborn woman. Won't just admit she loves me. Always has."

"I have a friend like that."

"So what's your name, darlin'?"

"Angelina."

"That's a gorgeous name. I'm Boris."

"Boris, huh? That's a very Russian name." They shook hands. "Have you even been to Russia?"

"What for? It gets really cold there. Besides, I'm an American, darlin'. Born and bred. Just like my daddy and my granddaddy before him. Everything I need is right here in the U-S-of-A."

He stood right next to her now, but not close enough to have her backing away. Good. He understood personal space. That seemed to be a problem the hillbilly hadn't quite grasped yet.

"So, this is your party?"

"Yup. It's the only way I can get money out of these rich snots."

"Money for what?"

"Poor families from where I used to live. Up in the holler, not far from here."

Dear God, I'm near a "holler".

"You haven't always had money?"

"Oh, heck no. Lived up in the holler until I turned seventeen. Then my daddy made me join the army."

Based on his age now that meant only one thing. "Vietnam?"

"Yup. Worst nightmare of my life, too. But it made me a man. When I got back, I put myself through school and got into computers real early on."

"And now you're here."

"Now I'm here."

"I like that story, Boris. That's a good story."

He took a sip of his scotch. "So what exactly is a full-human doing here anyhow?"

"Got kidnapped by hillbillies."

"Did ya now?"

"Yup. It's a long sordid tale I'm not sure I'm in the mood to discuss right now."

"You don't need me to rescue you or nothing, do ya?"

Angie smiled and shook her head. "No. I can handle them fine."

"Which ones are they?"

Angie glanced over her shoulder and nodded in Nik's direction. He stood with his two brothers, a throng of gorgeous women surrounding them. Not that she blamed the females. All three men were gorgeous, but Nik outshone them all. He must have personal contacts with all the great designers. She didn't know Armani, Gucci, and all the rest made clothes big enough to fit a man his size. And fit him they did. He didn't wear a tux like some of the other males. Instead he wore black shoes, black slacks, and a black silk Tee. He threw a black leather mid-length jacket on over that and, if she were the drooling kind...

"Them."

"Ah. I see." Boris's face suddenly went stern. "They are bein' nice to you?"

"They bring me elk and deer."

His big grin returned. He had to be the happiest man she'd ever met. "The woo-in'! They must like you."

"So it would seem."

"Not that I blame 'em. You're a charmin' girl."

"As are you."

"Yes, I *am* a charmin' girl."

Angie snorted and went back to her martini. She liked this hick. He made her laugh.

"So, you interested in any of 'em?" Boris asked lightly.

"No."

"Why not? Is it 'cause you think they're hillbillies?"

"They are hillbillies. And I don't want to talk about it."

"Why are you women so difficult?"

"We're not difficult. We just don't take shit anymore."

Boris looked at the current object of his lust. "She sure don't. That's one of the things I love about her. She'd rip your throat out as soon as look at ya."

"That's lovely, Boris. You should have that printed on a greeting card."

She felt Nik behind her even before she saw his big hands brace against the bar on either side of her body. Why the hell did he insist on doing that?

"Back off, country."

"Don't worry. I'm not touchin' ya."

"No. But you're invading my personal space."

"Of course I am. It's as big as Montana, so I really don't have room to go anywhere else."

She glared at him over her shoulder, but he was staring at Boris. The two men watched each other for several long seconds.

"What did you do," Nik finally demanded.

Angie immediately jumped to Boris's defense. "Hey, hey, hey! He didn't do anything." She turned in the circle of his arms, careful not to touch him. "He was being a perfect gentleman. So back the fuck off."

"I'm not talkin' about you." He raised an eyebrow at Boris. "I mean what did you do to Momma?"

Boris shrugged. "Nothin' I haven't done a thousand times before."

Nik glared and spit between gritted teeth, "You're disgusting."

Boris became deadly serious. "I'm also your father. So watch how you talk to me, boy."

Angie ducked under Nik's arms and stepped between the two men. She put her hand on Boris's chest. "Calm down."

"Sometimes my boy forgets his place."

"*My place?*"

Oh, man. This was getting bad. She never argued with her parents. There had never been a point. Of course, that also meant when they left again, she'd find someone to physically harm. Usually at the playground or the local diner.

But she was having a wonderful time so far and didn't want

it ruined by Nik's bullshit.

With one hand still on Boris's chest and one on Nik's, she stood between the two men. "Gentlemen. The last thing you want to do is piss me the fuck off. So why doesn't everybody settle the fuck down. And try and enjoy this goddamn evening."

Father and son looked at Angelina, then back at each other.

"Now, how can we turn down an offer like that." Boris laughed. He took her hand from off his chest and kissed the back of it. "You know, Miss Angie, I would love for you to sit with me at dinner tonight."

She grinned. "I'd love to."

Her hand still on Nik's chest, she felt that growl long before she heard it. She stepped away, not even bothering to look at him. The dinner announcement rang out over the room and everyone slowly made their way into the main ballroom where all the tables had been set up.

Angie took Boris's offered arm. "You know, Boris, it's such a pleasure to finally be around a gentleman."

"Why, thank ya kindly ma'am."

She didn't even have to look back to know Nik still stood where she left him...glaring.

"Is that the girl your brothers stole?"

Nik nodded. He couldn't believe his father had made him jealous. He knew there was no reason to be jealous. The man still loved Nik's mother. Always had, to hear him tell it.

"Yes'm."

"She's a pretty little thing." His mother, still so beautiful and reeking of class and old money, stepped in front of her son and straightened the collar of his jacket. "And probably not good enough for one of *my* sons."

"It doesn't matter one way or another if she is, Momma."

"Oh? Are you trying to tell me you're not interested?"

"I'm not interested."

She sighed as she took her son's offered arm. "I'll never understand, son, why you insist on taking after me."

"Well, mostly because you try *not* to embarrass the family."

Boris pulled out a chair for Angie. "Sit, darlin'."

"Thank you." Boris sat down next to her and the pair smiled at each other.

"You know," Angie delicately chastised, "you should have told me he was your son."

"Now where would the fun be in that?" Boris leaned into her, but she still didn't feel remotely threatened by his presence. "Now tell me true, darlin'. You ain't got no man waitin' for you back in Texas, do ya? Some cowboy with your name tattooed across his chest?"

Angie chuckled. "No. I don't."

"Good."

"I thought Nik's mom was your lady-love."

"Oh, she is, darlin'. But I ain't thinkin' about me."

Nik walked up to the table, pulling out chairs for his mother and sister. He looked up to find Angie and Boris staring at him. "What?" he asked in confusion.

Angie couldn't help it. She began giggling, Boris joining her.

The dinner was another Boris Vorislav success and one of the few events one could find an enormous group of tigers at together. Nik spent the majority of the evening chatting with his mother and aunts, ducking the advances of some of the females, and avoiding some of the more aggressive males since he'd rather not kill someone at one of his father's parties. Especially an important fundraiser like this.

He also spent a good portion of his evening making sure none of the males got too frisky with either his sister or his cousin. Their sudden transformation seemed to have gotten them a lot of male interest. He didn't worry about Reena. She could handle anything and already had two cubs from two different males. But Kisa...well, he did worry about her. Of the entire family, she remained the best hunter among them. But only when tiger. As human her shyness became painful to watch. And he'd be damned if he'd let some overbearing prick push his baby sister around. But when he wasn't worrying about that, he spent the rest of his time keeping his eyes on Angelina. To his great annoyance, the woman got along with his father like they were old friends. She also had the attention of almost every male in the room. Every time she got up to go to the bathroom or stretch her legs, every male eye focused on her.

He didn't like it. Not one bit. And it bothered him that he didn't like it.

His father finally walked away from her, leaving her alone at the huge table, and made his way over to his son.

"Boy," he barked in way of greeting.

"Daddy."

"This turned out well, don't ya think?"

Nik shrugged. "Sure. But it won't change a damn thing. They still don't think we're good enough." And Nik blamed his father's wolf-like mating tendencies more than his past poverty.

Fierce gold eyes locked with his own. "They're right. We're not. We're better. And don't you forget it."

Nik nodded. "Yes, sir." He wasn't about to start another

113

fight with the old man. He did still respect him. His father was the toughest man he'd ever known. A door gunner in the war, those men had the shortest life expectancy. Yet his daddy survived to tell the tale. Put himself through school, made his own business, and was one of the wealthiest tigers on the East Coast. At the same time Boris never forgot where he came from. And he refused to be ashamed. God forbid his children ever were.

The man's only weakness—Nik's mother, Natalia. They'd been playing their game for at least thirty-five years and never seemed to tire of it. Personally, Nik didn't like games. A person said what they felt and meant it. As soon as he thought a woman was trying to bullshit or manipulate him, he bailed.

"Now, listen up. All three of ya." His brothers moved to stand beside him at his father's order. "I want you to keep that little lady safe."

"Excuse me?" Nik growled.

"You heard me. She's a lovely little thing, and I don't want you gettin' lazy."

Nik growled again. Why his daddy insisted on pissing him the hell off, he would never know. Especially when he was trying so hard not to rip the old bastard's throat out.

"Daddy, that's not fair," Ban cut in. "Nik's takin' great care of her."

"And maybe you should mind your own business," Alek added.

"This family and everything that happens in it, *is* my business."

"What's going on?" Nik's mother stepped in front of her sons. As if they were still cubs, she continued to protect them.

Boris's eyes dragged down Natalia's body like he was

checking out a stripper and not facing off against the mother of his children. *What a horn dog!*

"Just talkin' to our boys, darlin'. Is there a problem with that? Somethin' we should straighten out in private?" He wiggled his eyebrows and she snarled in annoyance.

"I hate you."

Before his parents could really get out of control, Kisa rushed up to them, Reena behind her.

"We've got a problem. Szervác is making a move on Angie."

The entire family looked at where Angie was sitting. Next to her, Szervác had moved in close. Too close, Nik knew.

"Let's go kick his ass," Ban sneered.

"No one move." They all looked at Nik and he shrugged. "I wanna see what she does."

His mother turned on him. "Nikolai Vorislav, you cannot be serious!"

"Fifty bucks says she takes him out."

His mother glanced at Angie, then back at her son. "A hundred."

Angie turned to look at the idiot invading her space. "I need you to back away."

"Now, now, sweetheart. Don't be so difficult." He ran his index finger against the inside of her arm. "I can make it good."

Angie shuddered in anger and disgust. It amazed her how much she hated non-requested physical contact. She knew she could call for Nik, but she'd grown up taking care of herself. True, she wished she had her bat, but she'd have to make do with what she had available.

She pulled her arm away from his touch, bent it, and

slammed her elbow into the man's face, breaking his nose.

Blood gushing, he let out a roar of pain.

Angie slid out of her folding chair, grasped it with both hands, turned, and swung. The metal slammed into the back of his head, knocking him into the table, which crashed into the floor.

Angie dropped the chair. Calmly, "Next time a woman tells you to get your hands off her, get your fuckin' hands off her."

She spun on her Ferragamos, but stopped when she found the entire Vorislav family staring at her like the freak she suddenly realized she was. She didn't mean to embarrass them. Actually, she felt almost a physical pain knowing she probably ruined Boris's important evening.

Christ, can this night get any worse?

She decided to face the nightmare head on. No point in ducking and running. Besides, where the hell would she go?

She moved swiftly away from her prone admirer before he could get back to his feet. As she approached the Vorislavs, she realized they were swapping money.

"Boris, I'm really—" she began.

Boris held up one finger, cutting her off. He glared down at Kisa. "I do not owe you a hundred."

"You do, too, Daddy. I told you she'd find a way to use that chair."

"It was fifty."

"Hundred."

"You'd take money from your own daddy?"

"In a heartbeat." Kisa held her hand out. "Now give it over."

Grumbling under his breath, Boris handed his daughter a crisp hundred from the wad of money he held in his beefy grip.

Angie turned to Nik. "You were betting on me?"

Nik nodded. "Yeah. The odds were too good to pass up."

"Momma and Daddy underestimated you." Ban counted his cash. He didn't even look at her.

"But didn't I embarrass you and ruin your evening?"

They stared at her, just before they burst out laughing.

"Oh, darlin'." Nik's mother put an arm around Angie's shoulders, and Angie fought the desire to scramble away from her. The woman was being so nice, how could Angie tell her to get her cotton-pickin' paws off her? "You've got to do much more to this family than that. Besides, Szervác only did that because you're human. He'd never have the guts to try that move with one of us."

"Well, thanks for being so...nice?"

"My pleasure." She winked, and then glanced at Nik. "I think you need to take your houseguest home, son. Before things get difficult."

Szervác's family had picked him up off the ground, and were looking at the Vorislavs with a less-than-friendly glare.

"Good idea." He grabbed her hand and dragged her out of the room.

Angie waved at Nik's parents. "It was nice meeting you both!"

She let him hold on to her until they got outside and then she snatched her hand away. "You know, I can walk without your assistance."

Nik moved on her so fast she stumbled back, slamming up against a limo. Again he braced both of his arms on either side of her and leaned in close, but not quite close enough to touch.

"So it's okay for my father to touch you, but I can't. Is that it?"

"He didn't touch me. *I* touched *him.*"

Nik blinked. "What?"

"He held his arm out and I took it. Your father never touched me. Unlike you that man understands boundaries."

"I see." He moved away from her. But he wasn't angry. Far from it based on the grin spreading across his handsome face.

"What are you smiling at?"

"Get your pretty ass in the car, sugar. Before Szervác's family gets out here and starts somethin' they can't finish."

Angie didn't like this one bit, but she wouldn't argue the point. Not now. Not here. But she had the feeling this was far from over.

Chapter Eight

Angie had to admit, she'd never slept so well before in her life. Between the fresh smell of real pine trees, the wonderful bed she currently slept in, and the soothing sounds of absolutely nothing, Angie found herself catching up on any sleep she may have missed over the last few months.

She rolled out of bed sometime around eleven. Took a quick shower, and changed into a comfortable pair of denim cut-off shorts and a T-shirt. Then, barefoot, she headed to the kitchen. A fresh pot of coffee waited, and Nik had even put out a mug for her.

Damn him. Why he suddenly felt the need to be so nice she would never know. On the drive back from the party, he didn't say anything to her unless she asked him a question. But he did keep smiling. She hated that smile. True, it was gorgeous, but that wasn't the point. It was a cocky, I-own-the-world smile. And it annoyed the living shit out of her.

He heard her bare feet slapping against the marble floor as she headed back to the stairs.

"Hey. Angie. Could you come here a sec?"

He knew using her name would freak her out, but he needed to keep her a little off balance. She didn't answer him or move for a good minute. He bit the inside of his cheek to keep from laughing. And when she gave a big dramatic sigh, he had to bite down harder.

She walked into the study.

"Well? Where are you?" she demanded.

He raised his arm so she could see it over the couch. She walked around the huge sofa, and stopped to stare at him.

"Is there a problem with the couch?"

"No."

"Then why are you sitting on the floor?"

He shrugged. "I like it."

"Whatever. What do you want?"

"Come here."

"I am here."

He patted a spot right next to him. "Here."

Grumbling curses, she stomped over to the front of the couch and sat on the floor. But she still kept her distance.

"What?" she asked.

He grabbed the loop on her denim cut-off shorts, quickly snatching her over to his side. Just as quickly he released her before she could start hitting him.

"Now, that's better."

"What do you want," she bit out between clenched teeth.

"To talk."

"About?"

The temptation to say—while staring deeply in her eyes, of course—"About us" so that he could watch her lose her mind, almost overwhelmed him. But he really did have a purpose here. His purpose became clear as soon as he pushed her up against the car last night. His no-human rule didn't matter anymore. Nor did it matter she had a whole Pack of hounds protecting her. Or that the woman made being mean a lifestyle choice. He wanted her. More than he'd wanted anything before in his entire life. First, though, he would have to find a way around the wall of ice she built up.

Tigers were all about waiting for their prey, though. She would be no different.

And when they had their fill of each other, when he'd fucked her senseless and could no longer remember his name, he'd send her back to her pound puppies and he'd go back to looking for the right tiger females to bear his cubs.

"I wanted to discuss our conversation from last night."

She sighed. Another big, dramatic sigh. "There's nothing to discuss. Really."

"See, but I think there is."

And another sigh. "Fine. Let's just get it over with."

Good. He got through the hardest part. Getting her to sit and listen being a major triumph.

"So, I was thinking…"

She opened her mouth to say something, but seemed to think better of it. "Too easy," she muttered.

He kept going, "…about what you said. And I wanted to ask you if you're okay with not wanting to be touched?"

She frowned in confusion, then shook her head. "Yes. I'm fine. Can I go now?"

"No. We're not done." He worked hard not to smile. When this cranky, she reminded him of a snarling kitten. She didn't make it easy but she made it fun. "You see, I think it's about control for you?"

Her head snapped around to glare at him, her eyes dangerously narrow, and he knew in that moment he'd been absolutely right.

Oh, baby, this is going to be fun.

"What?"

"Well, I just thought you didn't like to touch or be touched. But you don't like anyone touching you, but you can touch anyone you want. So it's about control and trust for you."

Once again she opened her mouth to say something and, again, apparently changed her mind. Instead, she growled, "What do you want, hillbilly?"

Got her! "To try a little experiment."

No. No. No! She did *not* like the sound of that. The last experiment she'd become involved in she'd lost all her hair for three weeks and had beaten Miki Kendrick within an inch of her life. She was twelve at the time, and she'd grown intelligence-wise since then.

So, she would not be tripping down experiment lane with this big idiot.

"I'm leaving."

She went to stand up, but he grabbed the belt loop on her shorts and yanked her back down.

"Because what I'm thinking is," he continued without missing a beat, "we give this a try. See if it works. If not, we never discuss it again."

That sounded reasonable and a quick way out of this hillbilly nightmare.

"Will you leave me alone if this doesn't work?"

"Yes."

"Will my hair be involved?"

"Um...not unless you want it to be."

"Fine. Let's get this bullshit over with then."

"Good." He jumped to his big tiger feet. For a large man, he was quite spry.

He pulled off his T-shirt and went for his jeans as he began walking around the couch.

"What are you doing?" She didn't bother to hide the panic.

"This experiment requires me to get naked."

He disappeared behind the couch.

"No! No! No naked required!"

She tensed, ready to bolt at the first sign of his massive cock. *Damn him.* If she saw it again, she really wasn't sure she'd be able to keep her mouth off it this time. She didn't know what he thought he was playing at, but she'd be damned if she'd play along.

But when he came around the corner at the opposite end of the couch, she found she couldn't move. She pushed herself up against the sofa and let out a whimper.

What the fuck *was* he playing at?

The son of a bitch had shifted. He had to be ten feet long from nose to tail and his paws were as big as her head!

She'd just begun to hyperventilate when he lay down. She wondered if she'd make it to the exit in time if she bolted now, when he suddenly rolled onto his back. And, like an enormous kitten, he brought his paws up and swatted at the air.

Then she suddenly understood. Understood what the hell he was up to.

She laughed. *Crazy fuckin' hillbilly cat.*

Angie covered her mouth to stop from laughing and stared at him for a good while. He didn't move.

He waited for her to make the first move. She liked that. It made her feel in control, even though her rational mind knew better.

Leaning over as far as she could without moving her lower body any closer, she carefully slid her hand across his paw. The pads were rough against her fingers.

So weird. So freakin' weird.

Unable to stay away, she scooted closer to him. When would she ever get a chance again to be this close to a tiger and not have to worry he'd bite her head off?

She ran her hands over his flank and across his chest. He closed his eyes and made that puffing noise again. *That must be his happy noise,* because he looked quite comfortable at the moment.

Angie moved a little closer, until her knees touched his side. She petted him on his big barrel chest for a few more minutes. Then she became braver.

"Turn over." He obliged immediately and she leaned into him, running her hands over his back and digging into his fur. She rested against him, taking a big sniff. Sara did that all the time with her dogs. She said they had a "puppy smell" she loved. But Angie only smelled Nik. She had to admit, though, she *really* liked how he smelled.

She crawled onto his back, laying face down across the fur. She stretched her arms out, her fingers rubbing his head and marveled at the fact her feet didn't even come close to his tail. She sat up, her legs straddling his mid-section.

I could ride this motherfucker to Utah.

She slid off his back and crawled forward, grasping one of his paws. She held it up against her hand. It completely dwarfed her long fingers. She smiled. Oh, yeah. This had to be one of the coolest things *ever*.

His enormous head nuzzled her gently under the chin. Without even thinking about it, she nuzzled him back. He puffed air out and then he purred.

"Stand up a sec." She wanted to see how tall he stood on all fours. He pushed himself up and, still smiling, she reached up and ran her hands over his face. His black markings were so striking, she wondered if they meant anything. Why did tigers have them? And the white hair that rested behind his ears as human now formed perfect circles on the back of his tiger ears. But why? All sorts of questions raced through her brain. Miki-type questions.

He walked forward, nudging her with his head. She leaned back, resting on her elbows, as he towered over her. He lowered his head and she reached up with both hands, grasping either side of him. She let her weight hang off him as she rubbed her fingertips in lazy circles through his fur and his eyes closed.

She became so lost in what he allowed her to do, it took her a minute to realize he'd begun to lower himself onto her. The thought of seven hundred pounds of tiger flesh, sitting on her size-twelve body, did not give her ease. But before she could go screaming into full-blown panic, Nik shifted again. Just like that. He went from tiger to man in a few seconds, and suddenly Nik the man was on top of her. Specifically between her legs, his gold eyes burning into hers.

His arms braced on either side of her body, he didn't attempt to bring himself any lower. Instead, he waited for her to once again make the first move.

Damn. He didn't mean to shift like that. This exercise in touching was supposed to last until she became completely comfortable with him, but hopefully before she had to return to her people. Yet he never expected her to respond so immediately or eagerly to him as tiger. And having her hands all over his fur, only made him yearn for those hands on his flesh.

Now here he lay. Between her thighs. Completely naked.

The only thing between him and her amazingly hot pussy, a pair of denim shorts he could tear off in seconds. Of course, his dick decided at that moment to stand up and say "hey, y'all".

Great. Now she'd never trust him. *Stupid, stupid hillbilly!*

Angie stared up at him. A range of emotions passing over her face. Anger. Distrust. Fear. Then a shudder passed through her body. He knew he should move. Get off her. But he wanted her to tell him to go. He *needed* her to tell him to go.

She didn't.

First, her fingers moved deeper into his hair, tightening the strands around them. Then, using him as leverage, she pulled herself up until their mouths were barely centimeters apart. So close their breath mingled and he realized she'd begun panting. Soft, quiet little pants.

"Angie," he whispered against her mouth. She gave the tiniest whimper, seconds before her lips touched his.

He should hold back. He really should—but he didn't. He couldn't. Not with the sweetest mouth God ever created at his disposal.

Nik kissed her back. Hard. He used one arm to pull her flat against him. The other he braced flat against the floor to keep them right where they were. He didn't want anything breaking this spell.

He slid his tongue past her teeth and rubbed it against the inside of her mouth. She shuddered again, and her tongue touched his. He groaned and sucked the sweet muscle into his own mouth. He wanted to taste her. Wanted to know what that tongue of hers could do.

He settled the weight of his lower body against her and, in response, she spread her legs wider.

It suddenly hit him. She wanted him. *Holy hell!* She wanted him as much as he wanted her. He forced himself to remain calm. He wasn't going to blow this. He rocked his hips into her and she rewarded him with a groan. He slid the hand that held her up under her T-shirt, rubbing her back in slow circles. She didn't try and pull away, instead, it made her hotter. He could smell her desire. Feel the way her entire body pulsated at his touch.

There were so many things he wanted to do to her, he didn't even know where to begin. She held herself against him with her arms. So, he dragged his fingers across her flesh until he hit the lace of her bra. He snapped the clasp at the front and moved that damn annoying piece of material out of his way. His hand molded itself to her breast and squeezed.

She finally pulled her mouth away from his, but only to let out a soft groan as her head fell back.

He couldn't stand it anymore. He lowered them both to the floor. He needed both hands for this. For her.

Lowering his head, he pushed her T-shirt up, and ran his tongue over and around her nipple, loving the feel of it against the sensitive muscle. He played with it at first, making her crazy. She gripped his head hard and tried to force his mouth on her while her entire body squirmed beneath his. But he kept playing with her for as long as he could handle, which, to be very honest, wasn't very long. He finally needed her in his mouth as much as she needed him to be there.

He held her nipple between his teeth, holding it still while his tongue teased it a few more times. Until he sucked on it.

Angie's whole body jerked, her back arching off the floor. "God, Nik!"

She said his name. His real name. And he knew, based on her body's reactions, he could make her come by doing exactly what he was doing now. And he wanted to make her come. He needed to feel her fly apart beneath him.

She would, too. He was going to make sure of it.

"Nikolai?" He frowned. He just got her to use Nik, he somehow doubted she was ready to dive into his Christian name. "Nikolai, darlin'? Could you tell me where that sweet little girl is at?"

His head snapped up in time to see his mother come swinging around the couch.

"*Holy fuck!*" Angie scrambled out from under him, yanking her shirt down. "I...uh..." She glanced between mother and son. Then, with a groan of pure embarrassment, she bolted. Over the couch and out the door. Kind of like a gazelle.

Still lying stomach down on the floor, Nik reached up and grabbed a blanket from the couch. He snatched it down and covered his ass with it.

"What the hell are you doing here?"

"Ah, ah, ah. Don't talk to your mother that way. I know I raised you better than that." His mother nodded toward the door. "I'm here to see Angelina. I need to talk to her. So why don't you go get her."

Through gritted teeth, "I can't exactly get up right now."

His mother cleared her throat, but she couldn't hide that damn smile. "I see. Well, why don't I wait in the kitchen and when you're ready, send her my way."

"You're not leavin'?" Damn, did his voice actually crack on that question?

"No. I'm not. So get yourself together there, boy." She headed toward the door, muttering, but he could make out every word.

"I swear. One second you're like me and the next...you're like your daddy."

Angie couldn't move. She simply stood there. Her head resting on the door, her hands braced against the hard wood. She'd torn into her room and slammed the door after her. She laid her head against the heavy wood, trying to get herself under some kind of control. But that wouldn't be happening anytime soon. Not when her clit kept pulsating like that. Over and over. *Thump. Thump. Thump.*

She knew what it wanted. It wanted her to get her fat ass back downstairs and finish what the hillbilly started. But she couldn't. His *mother* had walked in on them. For the first time in her entire life, she felt like a teenager. She never felt that way before, even when she was one. His mother had found them on third base and rounding into home.

She took a deep breath, but it went in shaky. Like she'd run for her life. Hell, maybe she had. The poor rodeo clown received a full-on bitch slap when he tried to hold her hand in public. The look of horror he gave her still stuck in her mind. But Nik had been all over her and she didn't care.

In fact, she still didn't care. The only thing she cared about was that goddamn thumping.

Thump. Thump. Thump.

Really, who knew a clit could make that kind of racket? Christ, could the neighbors hear?

Could his mother?

A soft knock at the door almost had her diving out the window.

"Angie, sugar. Open the door."

She almost screamed, "Are you fuckin' nuts?" But, instead, she took another shaky deep breath, and pulled the door open.

The hillbilly stood there, a brown blanket wrapped around

his hips.

"Can I come in?"

She was staying in his house and he was asking her if he could come in.

Only in the South.

Angie nodded, not sure if she could create an intelligent sentence if she decided to speak, and stepped away from the door. She went and sat down on her bed, then jumped back up again.

Sitting on bed...not good.

Nik closed the door and slowly walked over to her. When she stepped back, he stopped.

"You okay?"

She finally spoke, unable to hold it in any longer. "In less than twenty-four hours, your mother has seen me break a man's nose, hit him with a chair, and molest her son. No, I'm not okay."

Grinning, Nik took a step toward her. She jumped back, slamming into the bed. She held her arm up. "Stay!"

He laughed. "Aw, sugar. That only works with dogs." Then he was right there. Right in front of her. She put her hands down at her sides to prevent herself from rubbing that amazing body all over.

"It's not a big deal. Really. My momma don't care."

"I do. That woman probably thinks I'm a whore. A dangerous, psychotic whore."

"Naw. Daddy has twenty-eight stitches where Momma mauled him one time. Trust me. In my family, this is nothin'."

He couldn't believe how beautiful this woman was. She

wore no makeup, her thick hair still damp and tangled from their roll on the floor, her clothes a simple T-shirt and shorts. Yet to him she was ten times more beautiful than she had been the night before when she'd gotten all fancy. At some point, he'd tell her never to wear makeup again. She didn't need it. It actually stole some of her natural beauty. And she was a natural.

One of his hands held the blanket. The other reached up to touch her face. She took another step back. Or, at least, she tried to. But the bed got in her way.

Nik waited until she stopped moving, and he lightly touched her cheek. To his surprise, she didn't swat him away this time. Instead, she closed her eyes and made that sexy little whimpering sound.

"Okay." Her eyes snapped open and focused on him. "Let's get this over with."

"Get what over with?"

"You. Me. Let's just fuck and get it over with."

She had to be *the most* entertaining female he'd ever met in his damn life. Where the hell had she been hidin'? Were all the women in Texas like this?

"What?"

"Look, hillbilly, I want you. You want me. Let's just bang this out and go on about our day."

Nik shook his head slowly. "No."

She frowned, then nodded in understanding. "I see. You don't want me."

"Sugar, you must be kidding." He grabbed her hand and wrapped it around his cock, the blanket the only thing between them. "Feel that? You did that. You *keep* doin' that to me."

"Oh." She stared down at where her hand connected with

his body. Then those beautiful brown eyes snapped up to his. "So what's the problem?"

"There will be no banging out anything." He stepped even closer to her. "When we do this—and we will do this—I don't plan to rush a goddamn thing. We're not something to 'get over with'."

She stared up at him, brown eyes wide, "We're not?"

Since she seemed quite content to keep a healthy hold on his growing erection, he moved his hand back up to her cheek. He brushed the smooth skin with the tips of his fingers—and she let him.

"Nope. We're not. We're going to take this slow and easy, sugar."

"We are?"

He pressed his body against hers, her hand caught between them. "Oh, yeah. We are."

"Why?"

And she meant it. She had no idea why he wouldn't just throw her down on the bed, come, and go on about his day. That Nik had no intention of rushing anything where Angelina Santiago was concerned. This was a woman you savored. Enjoyed. Fucked. Hard, long, and as often as possible.

No. She'd have to forget about "banging out" anything.

He had other plans. Bigger plans. And they all involved her coming all over him.

"Because, sugar—you make me purr."

She had men say many things to her over the years. Some nice. Some sweet. Some thoroughly disgusting. But no one had ever told her she made them purr. And she never knew it would have the kind of effect on her it did.

132

Angie wrapped her hand tight around his cock and squeezed. Nik closed his eyes, leaning down until his forehead rested against hers.

"Damn, darlin'. That was plain mean."

"I don't like to wait, hillbilly." She really wanted to beg. She wanted to scream, "Please don't make me wait!"

But, dammit, a girl had her pride. Didn't she?

He smiled, even though she got the feeling she might be killing him. "But you're gonna wait." And it was an order. A delicious order she felt all the way to her toes. "You'll wait for me."

In the big scheme of things, it wasn't like she really had a choice.

"Damn cat."

He chuckled, his free hand playing along the bottom edge of her T shirt. The air changed around them. Going from playful to serious in a heartbeat. He tugged on the shirt.

"Pull your shirt up."

Normally, she'd ask what the fuck for. But they both knew that wasn't going to happen now.

Unwilling to release his cock anytime soon, she gripped the end of her shirt with her free hand and brought it up over her breasts. She'd never had time to fix her bra, so they were bare, the nipples hard.

Nik tucked the blanket he wore into itself, so that it stayed on his hips. Then he took both his hands and ran them up her ribcage, his fingers gliding along her flesh. The thumping became more desperate. Like a dog banging his tail, waiting for a treat.

Thumpthumpthumpthumpthump...

Nik's big fingers circled her breasts and both she and Nik

133

let out a shuddering breath. She no longer found his hands on her annoying. Not in the least. She had the distinct feeling she could easily get used to this. Used to him touching her, fondling her, making her squirm.

He gripped each of her nipples between thumb and forefinger. Her squirming intensified, the ball of her right foot pushing into the floor.

He rubbed his lips against hers, but he didn't kiss her. She wondered if he was afraid to. Afraid he wouldn't be able to stop.

With a deep sigh, he released her breasts, and grabbed hold of her bra. Gently, he re-hooked the lace over her, took the T-shirt from her hand and pulled it back down. He still had his forehead against hers and she watched him struggle with his decision to pull away.

Finally, and with obvious reluctance, he stepped back, unwrapping her fingers from his hard cock.

"We're not doin' this now." He brought her hand to his mouth, turned it over and kissed the inside of her wrist, right below her palm. He ran his tongue along the veins. Once he had her squirming again, he stopped.

"Slow and easy, sugar. That's what the South is all about."

"I'm beginning to hate the South."

Jesus Christ, who knew a girl could get so wet? Her panties must be sopping. She'd have to change them before she went anywhere or she'd catch her death of cold.

"You need to go, sugar. My momma's waitin' downstairs for you."

"You must be kidding."

He shook his head, his black hair falling in front of his gold eyes. "Nope. And it must be important for her to come traipsin' onto my territory. So, don't keep her waitin' long."

He let her hand go and stepped away from her.

"Where are you going?"

"The lake. I need to go to my lake—it's cold water. Nice and cold."

He backed up to the door, his eyes never leaving hers. The thick blanket around his waist unable to hide the hard-on pointing out at her, he grasped the handle as soon as he reached it and opened the door.

Nik stared at her for a moment. His eyes sweeping down and back up her entire body. When he returned to her face, he shook his head. "Damn, girl."

Then he was gone. The door quietly closing behind him.

Angie went to sit on the bed, but crash landed on the floor instead.

She didn't even feel it.

Chapter Nine

One more shower and a fresh round of underwear and clothes later, Angelina walked into Nik's kitchen to find his mother sitting at the table reading the newspaper and drinking coffee. Her long legs were crossed and she had the paper open to the business section.

Without looking up, "I certainly hope I didn't embarrass you too much, my dear."

"No, no," Angie lied. "Not at all." She reached into one of the cabinets, grabbed a mug and poured herself a cup of coffee.

"I received a rather interesting call this morning," Nik's mother continued.

Angie debated whether she should repaint her toenails. Something not so dark. "Oh?"

"From Vicki Löwe."

"Really?" Although, pink didn't look too good against her skin. So, maybe she should stick with the dark reds. Also she really needed to check on Sara's party plans. Just because she'd been kidnapped and Miki attacked on campus, didn't mean that Sara's goddamn birthday party wouldn't go off without a hitch.

"She thought maybe I had information on the past, but I really don't because that would require me to care."

So the question became, did she want to go with closed-toe or open-toe shoes for the party?

"I don't like worrying myself with everybody else's crap."

Angie finally turned and looked at Nik's mother. Nik really did look like her. "Is that right?"

"I have enough things to worry about, wouldn't you say? And back then I spent most of my time avoiding Boris. But I do know someone who understands that knowledge is power. And the woman does like power. You should meet her. Preferably now while I'm still in the mood."

Angie sipped her coffee. She really didn't feel like getting dressed. Again. But this truce idea had her intrigued. What if she could get Sara and Löwe together for a truce? Would that make Miki's baby any safer? Maybe calm Sara the fuck down a bit. Really, it was worth looking at a little more.

She still sighed out her answer, though. "Fine. I'll go."

"Now, darlin'. I know I'm pulling you away from playing grab ass with my oldest boy on his nice hardwood floor..." Angie barely stopped herself from spitting out her mouthful of coffee. "...but if he's anything like his daddy, trust me, he'll still be here when you get back."

CB&C3

Nik pulled on his T-shirt as he checked Angie's room. Nope. She wasn't there either. His mother and her Jeep were gone. So where exactly did his little hellcat go?

It wasn't until he looked around the entire kitchen that he found her note tacked to the refrigerator.

Off with your mother. I'm looking forward to bearskin rug stories.

–Angie

The smile spread across his face as he stared at her note. *She is such a cutie.*

CR∞BO

Angie stared at the shack Nik's grandmother, Broyna Vorislav, lived in. "My God, he lets her live here?"

"She won't move. Trust me, Nik's tried."

After a moment, Angie understood why. She could feel it sliding through her feet and up through her legs. This was a place of power.

"She lives on a burial ground." Angie shuddered at the thought. Her grandmother, a witch of some power, would never desecrate a place of the dead. But she'd told Angie lots of stories about many witches who would.

Seemed Nik's grandmother was one of those.

Natalia looked at her in surprise. "How did you know that?"

"God, woman. Can't you feel it?"

"Not really."

The screen door opened and what had to be, Angie guessed, the oldest living woman on the planet limped out onto the porch.

"What you want?" The woman glared at Nik's mother like she carried the plague.

"*I've brought someone to see you,*" Natalia yelled.

"I ain't deaf."

"*Of course you're not,*" she continued to yell. Angie knew immediately Natalia was fucking with the woman. "*Now this young lady has a few questions for you!*"

The old woman let loose a roar that shook the surrounding woods.

"I think she wants me to leave, Angelina. Will you be all right?"

Angie looked at the older woman. She had a small hump on her back, gnarled hands, and a black patch over one eye. *Good God.* That's why Natalia kept calling her O-E-G. *One-Eyed Grandma.*

Sara's furry ass really better be worth this bullshit.

"Sure. I'll be fine."

"Great. I'll come back for you in a bit." She looked back at the old woman. "*Talk to you soon, Mother Vorislav!*"

She turned away, giving Angie a big wink, and left her alone with the scariest being Angie had ever met.

She looked up at the woman. The big cat stared at her for several long seconds, then she nodded toward her shack.

"Well, you might as well come on in."

CB80CB80

Since his mother must have taken her shopping in town, like either of those women needed more clothes, Nik decided to get some work done. He grabbed his laptop, his cell phone, and sat out on his porch with a pitcher of sweet tea Kisa had left for him. He answered messages, sent out emails, bought an apartment building in Paris and a resort in the Cayman Islands.

He was just contemplating a nap or some fresh elk, when his phone rang.

"This is Nik."

"It's Zach."

Nik frowned. "Who?"

"Zach Sheridan."

Nik searched his brain for who this was, but he'd always been lousy with names of people he didn't give a damn about.

"You have our female and our families almost killed each other at my sister's college graduation."

"Oh." *The dog.* "Hey."

Nik felt his entire body clench. They couldn't be coming for her this soon, could they? The thought of giving Angie up to anyone put Nik into an almost full-blown rage.

"How is she?" the dog asked.

"She's great. She's with my mother."

"Your mother? What's next? Thanksgiving dinner at your house?"

"Why are you calling?"

The wolf chuckled. "Christ, she's right."

"Who's right? About what?"

"I got a call from my sister last night. She seems to think I should leave Angie with you as long as I can manage."

Alek. What his fascination with this man's she-wolf sister may be, Nik would never understand. But damn if he didn't appreciate it at the moment.

"And how long is that?"

"Three days, tops, redneck. To be honest, we could use the extra time. But my female has stopped speaking to anyone, including the psychopath. Which is making us all very nervous."

Nik bit his flip remark back about dogs not being able to control their bitches. As tempted as he was to mess with the pooch, Nik couldn't afford pissing him off. Not when Zach was giving him exactly what he wanted. More time with Angie.

"So, you've got three days. But on one condition."

"Which is?"

"Keep your hillbilly brother away from my sister."

If Alek wanted her, he'd have her. No matter what Nik did or didn't do. But he wasn't above lying to a dog.

"I'll see what I can do."

"You do that, hick."

CB&>&O

Exactly how the old crone roped Angie into helping cook dinner was beyond her. In less than ten minutes of entering her house, the woman had her seated at her kitchen table and working. She snapped the green beans while Broyna fried up a shitload of chicken and rolled out some biscuits. Clearly she expected more company or she really thought Angie could pack it away.

"So you're with my Nikky."

Angie almost choked on her iced tea. "No. I'm staying with him temporarily."

"In his bed?"

Angie put down her glass. "No." She wasn't lying. At least, at the moment, she wasn't.

"But ya wanna be. In his bed."

Angie simply didn't have the patience of Sara when it came to old women. Her grandmother had been a saint. A lovely woman who raised Angie even during those really dark high school years when all that pent up rage toward her parents found an outlet in random acts of violence. To this day, it still cut Angie how much her violent years hurt her grandmother.

But other than that, she didn't buy into the whole respecting one's elders thing. Of course she blamed that on Sara's grandmother. The whole town still talked about the time Angie decked Lynette Redwolf when she found the woman hitting Sara with a broom. If it hadn't been for Miki and Sara holding her back, she probably would have killed the old bitch.

"Look, old woman, what I do or don't do with your *adult* grandson is my own goddamn business."

"You're an ornery, big-boned gal, ain't ya?"

"And you're a cranky old bitch. So I guess that makes us like sisters."

Chuckling, the old woman turned back to her chicken. "Well, my Nik's in for a time with you."

She moved the pieces of chicken around a bit, put the top on, and limped over to the table. She sat down heavily, a sigh easing from her thin lips.

"So what do you wanna know?"

Finally. "The war between the Magnus Pack and the Withell Pride. Know anything about that?"

"Sure."

She said that awfully quick. "Maybe I should re-phrase. Do you know anything I'll actually find interesting?"

The old woman leaned across the table toward Angie. It took all of Angie's ice-like demeanor not to shy away from her. "Did ya know that those two bitches were friends?"

"What two bitches?"

"Annie Withell and Kylie Redwolf?"

No. She didn't know that. And Sara definitely didn't know that.

Grinning at her like she knew Angie would taste good with ketchup, Broyna took the bowl of beans and motioned to the section of the table where she'd already started the biscuits. "Go finish up them biscuits and I'll tell ya some interesting things about them stuck-up lions and crotch-licking dogs."

Angie rolled her eyes. *Tricky goddamn cats.*

CB © BO

Nik sat on his front porch, his feet up on the railing, a copy of *The Portable Mark Twain* on his lap. He watched his brothers drive up toward his house in Alek's Chevy pickup. One of the few vehicles both men could comfortably fit in together. Behind the truck, his sister and cousin were in Reena's Porsche.

They pulled to a stop in front of him. Ban stuck his head out the window.

"You better come on. We gotta rescue your girl."

Nik swung his feet off the banister, a low growl emanating from his chest. "What the hell are you talking about?" Already his mind tore through all the different horrible scenarios.

"Momma left her alone—with One-Eyed Grandma."

"Shi-it!" Nik jumped over the railing and dived into the cab of Alek's truck.

It was worse than he thought.

Chapter Ten

"Put this outside."

With an annoyed sniff, Angie snatched the jug of iced tea out of Broyna's hands. "Any other orders, Mein Fuehrer?"

"I'm sure I'll think of something," she cackled.

Angie stomped outside, the jug between her hands. As she walked to the porch stairs, a honey Porsche and a sweet pickup truck drove up. As the vehicles came to a stop, Nik jumped out of the back of the truck.

As soon as he saw her, he stopped. And stared. His gaze flickering across her flesh as if she were naked. And her body immediately responded.

The jug slipped from her hands, and she immediately tightened her grip. That's when she realized Kisa had taken it from her.

"Afternoon, Angie." Kisa placed the jug on the long picnic table they'd set up outside before walking into her grandmother's house. The rest of Nik's kin moved past her, none of them bothering to hide their smirk. She wanted to be angry. Wanted to believe they were sitting around having a good laugh at her expense, so she could stop feeling this way about the man. Especially when she knew he could never return it. Not really. Yet she knew better. Nik hadn't said anything to them. He didn't have to. Their lust hung off them both in great slabs of heat.

Once all his siblings were inside, Nik motioned to her with a tilt of his head. "Come here."

"Not on your life," she whispered with a hard shake of her head. "I've had enough of your family finding me in difficult situations with you."

His smile spread across her like a sunrise. "If I have to come get you, I'll make sure they find you in a *very* difficult situation. Now, come here." His growl slid down to her stomach and right between her legs.

She glanced over her shoulder at the front door. She could hear laughter and chatter from inside the house. She walked down to him, but stopped on the last step.

"I'm waitin'," he sighed.

She folded her arms in front of her chest. "You come the rest of the way."

"Why?"

"Because I'm worth every step you'll take."

Hot damn. He did love a woman who didn't make it easy. He walked over to the steps and stared down at her. Such a sassy little thing.

"Now what?"

He leaned in, sniffed her neck. "I know, how about anything?"

"You had a shot at anything this morning, and from what I remember you blew it."

A *damn* sassy little thing.

"Well, there's anything, sugar," he licked her neck and she

145

gave that sexy little whimper. "And there's anything."

"My friend warned me about you cats."

"The dog?"

"No. The genius."

"Interesting friends." He grazed his thumb across the pulse point on her neck. "Did ya miss me today?"

She slapped his hand off. "Yes. I pined all afternoon. Can't you tell?"

"Hey, girl," O-E-G yelled from the house and Angie's eyes rolled back in her head with serious annoyance. "Get your butt back in here. We ain't done."

"I'm so close to killing her."

"I'll go hide the steak knives."

Angie reached across the table to put down a bowl of green beans and both Nik's brothers leaned over a bit to get a good look at the long legs stretching out from her shorts.

He slapped both of them in the back of the head. "Stop doing that. Now."

"A man can appreciate a view," Ban joked.

"A man can also lose both his eyes in a tragic tiger mauling."

His brothers snickered and he felt his annoyance grow. Hard not to let it happen when he was as horny as a dog. Just watching her move had his mouth watering. Classy. Sweet. Funny. A real lady.

Angie evaluated the table, then stepped back. *"Dinner!"*

All three brothers jumped. A real lady who could out-scream a football stadium.

His parents showed up as the rest of them made their way

to the table. His mother stormed out of Boris's pickup truck, slamming the door behind her. She looked angry as hell, but she still had a hickey on her neck.

"Good," Boris boomed. "I didn't miss Momma's fried chicken." He smiled at Angie. "Best fried chicken in the entire South."

Boris stood at one end of the table while Nik helped his grandmother into a chair on the opposite end. His father pulled out a chair for Angie and then another for Nik's mother. Angie sat while Natalia slapped Boris's hand away, re-adjusted the chair, and sat down. The fact his mother agreed to stay for dinner at his grandmother's house was quite a feat for his father. No wonder the old man beamed like he bought another company.

Nik settled his grandmother and walked down to the seat beside Angie. Ban already took Nik's seat next to Angie, so he grabbed the chair his brother sat in, lifted up both, and moved him closer to Reena. He grabbed another chair and sat down beside her.

Angie shook her head. "And to think I used to wish I had brothers and sisters."

"What do you mean? I love my family."

Angie simply snorted in response.

Nik pushed a stray hair behind Angie's ear. "So, sugar, why exactly are you here?"

"Spending quality time with the Clampetts really can't be beat."

His hand strayed down to her bare leg, caressing it under the table. He loved that she jumped at his touch. "Still think you're better than my family?"

"Oh, honey. I don't think I'm better than your family." She

lifted his hand and placed it on the table. "I think I'm better than you."

Nik smiled as his father slammed his fist down on the table.

"I *do* like this girl!"

Well, Angie had to admit it. She *liked* these people. They were funny and interesting. They kept her laughing all through dinner with stories of their other relatives and the people from town, shifter and human. Broyna said very little except for the occasional snide remark about a cousin or local. She seemed simply to enjoy having her grandkids and son around.

Angie found none of this surprising. Southerners always did tell the best stories. Of course, they were also the ones with relatives named Big Earl and Jackie Ray.

After dinner, things slowed down a bit. The family wandered from the table, Ban and Alek helping their grandmother back into the house. Reena and Kisa went off to talk to Natalia while Boris stepped away to check his messages on his cell phone.

All of which essentially left her alone with Nik.

He grabbed hold of the chair by its legs, turning it, and her, around so she faced him. He pulled the chair in close to him, so that his big legs ended up bracketing hers.

She expected him to say something, but he didn't. He simply stared at her face. After two minutes of that, she grew considerably uncomfortable.

"What?"

"Nothin'."

"Then stop staring at me. You're freaking me out."

"Everything freaks you out."

"Not true. I have a very high tolerance for weirdness. I have a high tolerance for you, don't I?"

"And my family."

"They're nice." She always wondered what it was like to come from a big family. Angelina didn't know. Her parents were never close to their few siblings and other relatives. And once they dumped her off in Texas it was like she no longer existed to the rest of her family.

Nik rubbed her legs with both of his hands, stopping to touch a rather long, simple scar cutting across her right knee.

"How'd ya get this?"

She glanced down at it. "Knife fight."

"A knife fight?"

"Yup...well...I didn't have a knife. I'm not really good with knives."

"I see."

"I had a baseball bat."

She looked off down the path that led to the house. Headlights headed their way in the murky light that came before it went pitch black.

"I guess you learned to use that from the baseball player."

"Nope. He taught me to pitch. The head of the motorcycle club I dated when I was sixteen until Marrec found out—he taught me how to use a baseball bat. I don't think he expected me to use it on him, though."

She glanced at Nik. "Hey, don't look at me that way. He's back on solid food."

"You gonna tell me what happened?"

"What's there to tell? He was mean to my friends. That's all I needed to know."

Nik grunted and, for some unknown reason, seemed satisfied with her answer. Maybe it was a shifter thing. She'd stopped telling her dates that story long ago. They'd go to the bathroom after dinner and never return.

"Someone's coming."

Nik nodded, but he seemed eternally interested in her legs. "I know." His big hands wrapped around her knees and she marveled at the size of them. "Do you have a boyfriend, Angelina?"

Why did the men in his family insist on asking her that question?

Angie thought back on the rodeo clown. He'd wanted to be her boyfriend. At least, he did in the beginning. Like all the others, however, he soon realized her friends were the most important thing to her and she really didn't want anyone touching her unless it involved fucking. That last bit seemed to be the biggest problem for the cowboy. She had no idea why. He still would have gotten laid. Instead he got needy and possessive. She hated that.

"No. I don't have a boyfriend."

"Good." He squeezed her knees.

Suddenly, the man's hands were on the move, sliding up her legs, his thumbs disappearing between her thighs. Angie jumped, practically off the chair, and a little whimper escaped her throat. Her hands grabbed his wrists and he stopped moving. But she knew he could have kept going if he wanted to. His arms were like big, thick steel rods.

"I felt you underneath me this morning, Angie. I don't think anything's ever felt that good before."

Angie glanced around. No one seemed to be paying them any mind. But she didn't know how much longer she could keep this calm thing going. With just words the man made her
150

desperate to come.

"How you moved, your responses...sugar, you make me hurt in all the best places." He rubbed the inside of her thighs although he didn't move any farther toward her crotch, and she was grateful. She didn't think she would have been able to stop him. Not because he would have forced himself, but because she knew she wouldn't want to stop him.

"God, woman," he whispered. "I can't wait to get inside you. To feel your pussy clench around my cock when you're coming. To hear you say my name like you did this morning when I had your breast in my mouth."

"You really need to stop now."

He finally looked into her face and whatever he saw, he seemed damn happy about. He let out a breath and Angie swallowed in response. "I'm so glad I'm not feeling this way by myself," he murmured.

She gave a desperate chuckle. "What? Are you kidding?"

"Hey, Nikky boy!" Nik glanced over and Angie realized the vehicles that had been heading toward the house had parked and a load of relatives or neighbors were already out and socializing. She hadn't even noticed. A young man, clearly another shifter based on his size alone, waved at Nik.

"Hey, Cleats. Be with ya in a sec."

Nik turned back to Angie.

She cleared her throat. "We...uh...better...ya know, your relatives and all." Well that made absolutely no sense.

"Yeah. We better. But, sugar, you need to let me go." She blinked, not knowing what he was talking about. "You're starting to draw blood." He gazed down at her lap and her eyes followed his. She still had a death grip on his wrists, but her nails dug into his flesh and she could see blood starting to form on his skin.

"Oh, God!" She yanked her hands away. "I'm so sorry."

He grabbed her hands back. "For what? For telling me you want me in no uncertain terms? Sugar, don't ever be sorry 'bout that."

He squeezed her hands, gently laying them back in her lap. "I gotta go make nice with the kin or Daddy will never hear the end of it. Which means *I'll* never hear the end of it."

Nik stood up, glancing around. He glowered and Angie again followed his gaze. The females were chatting and giving each other hugs. But the males were staring at her. For the first time since she found out exactly what Sara was, Angie felt uncomfortable around shifters.

Nik leaned down, his hands on both sides of her face. "Sorry, sugar, but this one can't be helped." He kissed her. A hard, demanding kiss that made her grip his wrists again as he practically yanked her out of her chair. His tongue slid inside her mouth and curled itself around hers. She'd never been with a man who could make her lose all sense of herself. Not when she kept such a rigid leash on her control. But with Nik, she forgot where she was, who else was around, or why the fuck she was there. All she knew was that Nik was the most amazing kisser she'd ever had the pleasure of meeting and that his grandmother's fried chicken probably *was* the best in the South.

He finally pulled away, slowly lowering her back in her chair. "In case any of my kin get any funny ideas." He winked at her, then walked off to greet the others.

Angie, staring down at her lap, rubbed her lip, and tried to be calm and rational about all this. Not really working, but a worthy attempt nonetheless.

When she felt confident she wouldn't embarrass herself,

she finally looked up—only to face pretty much all of Nik's female relatives. They sat on and around the table, while two took the time to clean off everything and bring it back to the house.

She sighed. "Aw, hell."

Nik slapped one of his younger cousins on the back as way of greeting, sending the poor kid flying into Alek.

He winced. "Sorry 'bout that."

Alek helped the kid to his feet. "Don't take it personally, Jimmy Ray. Nik's feeling a little primal right now."

"Shut up."

But his brother was right. Angelina brought out his most base instincts. She turned him into that tiger protecting the female with the cubs he knew were his.

Christ, she brought out the Boris in him. He shuddered at the thought, but he knew. Hell, now everybody knew. But if he'd just wanted to get in her pants, he would have fucked her by now and sent her back to her Pack in the family jet. He sure as hell wouldn't be *waiting* to fuck her. Waiting for the right moment. Waiting until she was so crazy in lust she'd never be able to simply walk away from him.

He mentally shook himself. He wouldn't go that far down Boris-lane. If his father wanted to be trapped with one female his whole life that was down to him. Nik just wanted this to be memorable. Of course, Angie'd already made it that way.

A knife fight?

"By the way," Nik announced to his brothers as he caught the beer Cleats chucked at him, "I got a call this afternoon."

"Oh?" Alek took the beer Ban handed him.

"Yeah."

153

"And?"

"I'm supposed to keep you away from his sister."

The three brothers stared at each other. Then they burst out laughing.

"Can I help you?"

An older woman leaned forward and Angie waited for it. The interrogation. Or the "scare off". Whatever. She could handle it.

"So, what would you put me in?"

Well this has gone suddenly weird. "I'm sorry?"

"I think Chanel. But my sister thinks Dolce & Gabbana."

"I thought Dolce & Gabbana only made shoes," one of the younger females tossed out.

"No. They don't only make shoes. What is wrong with you?"

Good God. They wanted to know about clothes.

Angie shook her head. "Um...I'd put you in Marc Jacobs."

"Really?"

She smiled to keep from laughing hysterically. "Definitely."

Chapter Eleven

Nik couldn't believe she'd fallen asleep in the back of his brother's pickup truck. That was awfully "down-home girl" for his little hellcat. But that's where he found her when the impromptu party began to break up. She had the sweatshirt he'd been wearing over his T-shirt wrapped around her like a blanket. He pushed her hair off her face. She didn't swat him away this time. Instead, she smiled in her sleep.

Alek gripped his brother's shoulder. "You ready to go?"

Nik agreed by quietly climbing into the back with her. He carefully pulled Angie into his arms, careful not to wake her. She cuddled into his body and sighed as one hand gripped his T-shirt.

They got home far sooner than he would have liked, although he knew his brother took his time. Alek opened the rear door, allowing Nik to get out of the vehicle like a normal human being.

Nik picked Angie up in his arms and jumped out of the truck. He nodded at his brother and went into his house as Alek pulled off. He carried her up the stairs, and to her room.

The cleaning people must have come by because the bed had been changed and made. He used one hand to pull the comforter and sheets back, then carefully laid her out. Slipping off her white Keds, he stopped to rub her chilled feet before carefully unwrapping the sweatshirt and pulling it off her. He tossed it on the floor, and dragged the sheets and comforter back over her still body.

Crouching down beside her, he stared at her face. Damn, but she sure was pretty. He leaned in and kissed her on the cheek.

"Night, sugar," he whispered softly.

He walked back to the door, shut off the light, and closed the door after him.

Angie lay in the darkness for what felt like forever. *What in hell was that anyway?*

She thought for sure he'd try and cop a feel while she was asleep. Actually, she kind of hoped he would. But he didn't. Nor did he have one of his brothers simply dump her ass in the bed while he went off to do whatever tigers do after a certain hour.

But a chaste kiss goodnight? What the hell *was* that? What exactly did that mean? And when exactly did she start analyzing anything anyone did or said? Especially a man. Normally that stuff didn't mean shit to her. Miki did the analyzing. Sara did the obsessing. And Angie worked hard trying to prevent the two of them from driving themselves into a mental institution.

Add in that the long, revealing conversation with the females of Nik's family had confused her even more. Tigers were notorious players. Both the men and the women. The majority of them didn't want anything beyond the fucking and the kids. The women had their own lives, their own careers, their own homes.

They considered Boris a freak of the highest order. A tiger who clung to one mate no matter how hard she fought. They didn't seem to like Natalia too much. Thought she was a rich snob, like Broyna did, but they didn't think she was any different than the rest of them when it came to sex and relationships. But as soon as Boris saw her, when they were only twelve years old, he decided she would bear his cubs and be his mate. By the time he was twenty-one, he'd already gotten Natalia pregnant with Nik. Ban came a short time after. And finally the twins. Due to complications during the birth of Alek and Kisa, Natalia was unable to have any more children. The family felt certain, or at least hoped, that Boris's obsession with her would end. That he'd move on to other females that could still breed.

He didn't. He had four children and seemed more than happy with that. He never left her. Never gave her up. Terrified any male who got within sniffing distance. And although their days consisted of her telling him to get the hell out of her life, they spent their nights together in the same bed.

Everyone, however, hoped his children would be more like the rest of them. Yet after the way Nik kissed her in front of everybody, they now seemed pretty confident he took after his daddy.

Angie, however, didn't feel nearly as confident about Nik's feelings toward her. He wanted her, but that could be because she was simply a fresh pussy in his house. But his wanting to wait for sex and his incredibly sweet goodnight kiss kept confusing her. Although he made it perfectly clear his kind wanted nothing more than a fun romp in the hay, Angie couldn't help but feel something very different might be going on here.

What concerned her more than anything? That she cared. She cared whether Nik might be falling for her. She cared whether his family liked her. Hell, she cared whether the man was happy or not. Her. Angelina Santiago.

Angie cared when she never had before, and that absolutely freaked her the fuck out.

Nik checked the house. Now that he had Angie staying with him, he didn't like taking any chances with her safety. Once he felt it was secure, he shifted and headed out to check his property. He knew his brothers were around, too. They'd taken it upon themselves to make sure his grounds were safe.

It didn't surprise him they felt as responsible for her as he did. Because they were. They'd taken her from Marrec's Pack. But he couldn't be angry with them anymore. Not really. If it hadn't been for them, she wouldn't be here. Sleeping in his house.

He owed his brothers for this one. He owed them big.

Angie, unable to sleep, rolled out of bed. She took a quick shower, put on a long T-shirt, and headed to Nik's office on the first floor. She opened the glass doors that led outside. The fresh smell of pine assaulted her and she suddenly felt like one of those women in the floor-cleaning commercials. "Shifters— now with a pine-fresh scent."

She laughed and went to his desk, searching out another magazine, thinking she could read a little while before heading back to bed. She grabbed an issue of *GQ* and plopped down on the couch. She liked how Nik had this room set up. With a desk and seriously comfy leather chairs. But also another enormous couch like the one in his living room, facing a set of French doors, looking out over his backyard. She wondered if he spent a lot of time in this room. She wondered if he lay on this couch as a tiger. It had to be one of the biggest, sturdiest couches she'd ever come across. Also the most comfortable.

Instead of turning a light on so she could read the

magazine, she continued to stare out into the Carolina night and enjoy the couch. Before she knew it, she was out cold.

Nik shook his head and trotted back home. If his brothers wanted to chase rabbits like a couple of cubs that was on them. He had a warm bed waiting for him and the delicious smell of Angelina Santiago to keep him company. Much better than rabbit.

The three of them had done a complete sweep of the area first, and his markings were still strong. Any that weren't, he refreshed. As he approached the house he saw that his study door stood open. He knew he left it closed.

He burst into a full-out run, coming to a sliding, crashing stop when he saw Angelina asleep on his couch. She must have woken up after he put her down for the night. She'd showered and wore a T-shirt. He padded closer to her to make sure she was okay, and she suddenly moved in her sleep. Her T-shirt rode up a bit. Enough for him to see she wore no panties.

His big tiger head crashed to the floor, his paws covering his eyes. *What is this woman trying to do to me?*

Angie woke when she heard cardinals singing outside the study doors. Still slightly dark out, she realized she'd slept the rest of the night in Nik's study. She wanted to be out of there before he woke up since she was half naked. She tried to move and realized something pinned the entire lower half of her body to the couch.

She took a second to let her eyes become accustomed to the lightening darkness and propped herself up on her elbows to look down the length of her body. That's when she saw him. His huge tiger head resting on her lower abdomen. His giant forearms spread across her legs, pinning her to the spot. The rest of his furry body comfortably situated between her thighs and across the couch.

She figured this could be the one thing that pushed her back into therapy.

Nik's eyes slowly opened. He looked around the room, then his big head turned to look at her. His gold eyes blinked.

Too weird. Too weird. Too weird. Even for her.

As she tried to scramble out from under him, he shifted. Back to human. Suddenly she had Nik the man between her legs. And now she didn't want to go anywhere.

His arms tightened around her thighs, holding her in place. Apparently he didn't want her going anywhere either.

His head dipped down and he nuzzled her exposed sex. He glanced back at her, watching to see her reaction. She didn't move. Or breathe. Or do anything, but grasp her bottom lip lightly between her teeth. Of course the hillbilly didn't need much more than that.

His head lowered again and Angie realized she held her breath. What if Nik just gave the appearance of being a hottie in bed? She had that happen before. The guy who taught her how to water ski promised to make her legs shake. She ended up walking out halfway through it. What if Nik were the same? What if he bored her senseless? She refused to fake it. Faking it was not in her DNA. Then what? Would he throw her out? Beg her not to tell? What if...what if...*holymotherfuckingshit!*

Her elbows went out from under her and she dropped back onto the couch. His tongue took another long swipe and Angie's toes curled. The tip of his tongue flicked her clit, but thankfully his big arms were still holding her down, otherwise she would have flipped right off the couch. He didn't concentrate on that though, but a mere tease of what was to come. Instead, he took his time exploring every inch of her pussy with that rough, flat tongue of his. Even sliding inside her and fucking her with it.

No. She wouldn't be faking anything this morning. She wouldn't have to.

Nik adjusted her legs so they rested on his shoulders and he moved up a bit, lifting her ass, giving him deeper access into her body. His hands reached under, gripping her cheeks as Angie reached up and gripped the arm of the couch. She arched her back and he continued tongue fucking her, while his fingers squeezed her ass.

Her head fell back, her body arched even more, while Nik returned to her clit, rubbing it with the flat of his tongue. Her hands released their grip on the couch and, instead, dug into Nik's thick hair.

Angie's entire body began to shake, and she knew she probably ripped hairs from his head as her orgasm ripped through her. Swiftly followed by this long, low purring sound she'd never made before.

Nik growled in response and kept right on going. Working his tongue around again until her shoulders left the couch and her entire body clenched violently, clasping him tightly to her. Any other man might have gotten his neck broken but, instead, Nik purred, stretching out her orgasm for what seemed like forever.

She finally couldn't take anymore, but unable to actually form coherent words or thoughts, she yanked on his hair to get him to back off. His wet, grinning face rose from her lap and she knew she'd never seen anything so beautiful before.

Nik pulled himself out from the grip of her legs, nipping the inside of her thigh before dragging himself up her body until they were face to face. He hovered over her for a bit, his arms on either side of her. After a moment, he leaned his head down to kiss her.

Angie moaned into his mouth, her own taste giving her one last shudder. After he thoroughly and slowly explored the inside of her mouth, he pulled back, his smile still as wide as before.

"Mornin', sugar." He kissed her nose, then slid off her, and walked out.

Angie pushed herself up on her elbows, staring at the door he'd just left through.

For less than a split second she wondered again if maybe he didn't want her. But she saw that bobbing cock bouncing out the door, harder than a plank of wood. She didn't believe for a second he wasn't ready to fuck her.

So what the hell is he waiting for? And exactly how much longer could she hold out?

Groaning, she turned over and buried her head into the couch cushions. Then she screamed.

Chapter Twelve

The phone rang again, and Angie reached over, snatching it off the side table. She would have to change that ring. After getting two orgasms pumped out of her, she'd gone back to bed, and she found her phone ring damn annoying at eleven in the morning.

She flipped it open and, without lifting her head from her wonderfully firm pillow, answered.

"Yeah?"

"Hey. Hey. I've got her. Hi, baby."

Angie sat bolt upright in the bed. Now she was wide awake.

"Mom?"

"Yes. Hi. I've got your father here, too."

Okay, what the hell was happening? First this morning's antics with Nik and now this.

"Is everything okay?"

"Oh, yes. Yes. But I was going through my day planner this morning trying to find where I'd stuck some notes when I noticed that we missed your birthday. So we wanted to call and wish you a happy birthday."

Angie closed her eyes. "My birthday? That was three months ago."

"Well, better late than never."

Angie would prefer never. She didn't know why, but no call at all would have been easier than these months or even years later calls that both her parents insisted on. Could they truly be trying to prove they somehow cared?

She already knew they didn't care. Not about her. Both of them being archeologists, maybe if they had to dig her up in the Sudan, they'd care a little more.

Yet caring about humans just wasn't in their nature. It never had been.

She felt herself go icy all over. Her heart hardening against the pain. Her heart hardening in general. Before she learned how to do this, she used to do the stupidest shit. It amazed her every day both Sara and Miki stuck around during those ugly times in junior high and high school. Those two women, mere girls at the time, washed the blood out of her hair, put antiseptic over her cuts and bruises, and hid any evidence. They kept reminding her they were her family now and that they loved her even as they pried the blood-covered two-by-four out of her hands.

"So," her mother struggled with conversation, "how's it been going?"

What should she tell her? *Well, my best friend's a shapeshifter and my other best friend is in love with one and having his baby. Plus a pack of hyenas tried to kill me. And who knows what the hell the lions are doing. And I'm temporarily living with a tiger who seems to have the hots for me. And you?*

She didn't, however, want to talk to her mother. Yet she couldn't bring herself to hang up the phone either.

"Fine," she finally got out.

"Anyway, there was one other thing."

She should have known better. There had to be a reason her parents suddenly called her out of the blue.

"What do you want, Mother?"

"I merely needed some information on your grandmother's estate."

"You know I don't deal with that. Uncle Ernesto's handling everything. Has been for years." Her grandmother had given Angie a good portion of her money when Angie graduated college. The old woman knew then her daughter and son-in-law would make it difficult for her granddaughter. Universities didn't pay much and it cost a lot to keep some of their digs going. When her grandmother died, the will gave control over to Angie's uncle who still lived in Brazil, but Angie already had her money and never expected any more.

"You're much better with him than I am."

"He's your brother."

"Yes. But he enjoys speaking to you."

"What are you asking from me, mother?"

"Well—"

Angie jumped a little when big fingers gently pried the phone from her hands. She looked up to see Nik staring down at her.

"This, sugar, is called the power of the hang up." He closed the phone with a snap. "Now, how about some breakfast?"

She didn't say much, even as she followed him down to the kitchen. But she wouldn't let him near her either. She shied away from his touch worse than when she first arrived. Damn parents. He'd gotten so far with her and they'd pushed him back about twenty feet. If he didn't know better, he'd swear what happened just that morning with her groaning and coming like an express train never took place. But he knew it had. His head still hurt from where she'd ripped hair out of it.

Hell, how do parents forget their kid's birthday? Maybe a father, but a mother? Didn't she have to push Angie out of her? Usually women remembered that stuff, and most never let a body forget it. At least his mother never did. Especially when she found guilt such an effective method of getting what she wanted from him and his brothers.

His parents always celebrated their kids' birthdays together, too. One of the few things they willingly did as a couple. From the party he had with a cowboy theme, to the party the twins had involving a clown they scared to death and chased into the woods because it was fun to watch him scream, his parents made sure each and every one of their children felt loved and protected.

The tiger females who raised their kids on their own made sure their children understood this. No matter how many daddies were involved.

Now he understood why these two women Angie kept talking about were so important to her. They were the only family she really had. Even a pack of dogs as kin was better than those people she'd been talking to.

While she ate, he went back to her room and retrieved her phone. He ran through her phone book until he found what he wanted. He pressed the Talk button and waited.

After three rings, "It's fuckin' eight in the morning so this better be fuckin' good."

Good God.

"Uh...is this Miki?"

"Yeah."

"This is Nik. Nikolai Vorislav. I have Angie."

"Oh, yeah. The hillbilly kidnapper. She's okay, isn't she?"

"Yeah. Yeah. She's fine."

"Then what do you want, Jethro?"

He took a deep breath. It was one thing to take insults from Angie, who made his cock hard from simply crossing and uncrossing her legs, but he wasn't about to take it from some dog-loving bitch. "Her parents called today."

"Why did *they* call?"

"I think to wish her a happy birthday."

The pause lasted a good thirty seconds, then, "You've gotta be fucking kidding me? Her birthday was fuckin' three months ago. *I swear to God these people are fuckin' idiots!*"

Wow. What an interesting young lady. With such a colorful and loudly expressed vocabulary.

"Could you put her on?"

"Yeah. Hold on."

He returned to the kitchen and handed Angie the phone. She looked at it with dread, like she expected it to be her parents again. Although he had a feeling she wouldn't hear from them again for quite awhile.

She took the phone from his hand. "Yeah?" She scowled. Then she smiled in relief. "You're such a bitch. I never said that. No I didn't. No I didn't. No. I did *not.*"

Nik shook his head and walked out of the kitchen. He expected her friend to soothe her, make her feel better. Not start a fight with her. But as Angie put her feet up on the table and barked, "You're so full of shit, Kendrick!" he realized that was exactly what she needed.

Forty-five minutes of arguing over everything from whether Angie promised to call the night before or not, to the planned gift they arranged for Sara and whether Zach would play along, to Miki stating that if she had a boy she was naming him

Bartholomew, went a long way in making Angie feel a part of something again.

"So basically you're going to tattoo 'kick me' on his ass."

"What does that mean?"

"You name a kid Bartholomew and you're condemning him to a life of torture. You remember those days, don't ya, Mik?"

"You sound like Conall."

"Well at least one of you has some goddamn sense."

Angie let out a breath. The tension and ice she'd felt after the call from her mother had been argued out.

"So, what made you call?"

"I didn't. Tigger the hillbilly called me."

Angie swung her legs off the table and sat up. "What? Why?" Christ, her nipples hardened at the mere mention of the man. Was that sort of thing even normal?

"I'm guessing he was worried about you. You can get pretty scary after one of those out-of-the-blue calls from your parents. Me and Sara used to call those your 'episodes'. Of course, if he's worried that means only one thing—"

"Shut up, Kendrick."

"Someone's in love."

"Shut. Up."

"I haven't had a chance to add shifters to The List. You could get him in under the wire."

"Would you let it go?"

"I could...but where's the fun in that?"

Angie sighed and ran her hand through her hair.

"So, Santiago..."

"What?"

"You like him?"

She shrugged. "I don't *dislike* him."

"Well, for you that's almost marriage."

"Very funny." She wanted this conversation to stop. Now. "Look, could you put Zach on?"

A long pause followed that request. "Why?"

Angie let out an annoyed sniff. "Just put the man on, would you please?" Good a time as any to let someone at least remotely sane know about the proposed truce and the truth about Sara's mother. *Especially* the truth about her mother. Sara never knew her mother, and her father had worshipped his mate. So all Sara ever heard were the good things about Kylie Redwolf. Finding out the woman and her lioness buddy went after hyena territory like Donald Trump with a little Gambino Mob family thrown in for color wouldn't be easy to get across to her friend. They'd murdered that hyena, at least that was how it seemed. They weren't human when they did it, but they'd hunted down and murdered the Matriarch of the Leucrotta Clan—and Dianne Leucrotta's mother. Who killed the lion and who killed the wolf afterward, no one really knew. But Kylie Redwolf's hunger for territory put her on that path and everything fell apart from there.

So Angie needed Zach's perspective, his calm demeanor...

And his ability to physically hold Sara down when she snapped.

CRSCRXO

Angie found Nik's note tacked to the inside of the front door.

*Had to go into town for business. Try and stay out of trouble.
My brothers are around somewhere, so you're not alone. And
please feel free to put on another pair of shorts for when I get
home.*

—Nik.

She smiled as she thought about Nik's eyes on her last
night at the party. He did seem to like her legs, especially when
she wrapped them around his neck.

The knock at the front door caused her to jump back three
feet. She took a deep breath. When did she become such a
jumpy mess?

"Yeah?"

"It's us, Angie."

Well, now she had a Carolina "us" and a Texas and
California "us". *How cool am I?*

She opened the door to find Kisa there. "Hey. What's up?"

"Nothin'."

Angie stared at the woman. "You wanna go shoppin', don't
ya?"

Kisa crinkled up her nose in an adorable way. "Yes, please."
She stepped back and motioned to Reena. "We brought Daddy's
pickup. The real big one."

"Why?"

"For all the clothes!"

Angie grinned. "Of course."

CB𝕤𝕠BO

Nik never understood why his father insisted on doing business like this. Sitting in a restaurant and signing important contracts between orders of chitlins and pigs feet. What made this time worse...his father seemed to have an agenda.

"So, boy, are you taking good care of your little house pet?"

"Don't call her that, she's completely safe at my house, and I'm not having this conversation with you."

"You can't play with this one, ya know. She's special. There's something about her that says she'll happily kill you in your sleep."

Nik smiled, even while he kept his head down over the paperwork in front of him. "You like her."

"Don't you?"

"I don't *dislike* her."

"Hell, boy, for you that's marriage."

"I thought we were here to work?"

"Don't blow this by being a chump. A woman like that comes along once in a lifetime."

He sure hoped so. He didn't think he could handle more than one Angelina Santiago. Face like an angel. Body like a demon. Mouth like a Bronx trucker.

But he never planned on keeping her. He wasn't his father. At least, he kept reminding himself of that over and over again. Still...a woman who practically snaps your neck when she's coming was *not* a woman you tossed aside easily.

"Look, old man, I refuse to discuss my life with you. Now or ever. So let it go."

"All right, if you want your future slippin' away from you 'cause you ain't got no sense—"

"*Why can't you be normal?*" Nik didn't mean to nearly yell it, but his father's pushing had finally gotten the best of him. "Why can't you be like everybody else? Have yourself more than one female. Have yourself twenty! Why are my brothers, my brothers? And not my half brothers? The only ones who should be from the same mother are Kisa and Aleksei because they're twins."

"Being normal is boring." His father looked around at the greasy diner he always insisted on going to. Full of shifters, mostly tigers but a few Pack and Pride, they all openly stared. Most likely hoping for a full-on fight between the old tiger and the younger one. Old tigers never went down quietly. "These people are boring. Your momma, though...that woman has never been boring. Crazy. Mean as a snake. Snobby as all hell. But never borin'."

"And what makes you think Angelina is never boring? Right now she's back at my house reading *Vogue*—again—and whining about how there's no TV. Does that sound interesting to you?"

"Really?" His father nodded toward the window. "Isn't that her in one of my pickup trucks?"

Nik's head snapped around. Sure enough, Angie—most likely one of the most dangerous drivers in the Carolinas from what she'd told him—was behind the wheel of his father's Chevy Dually pickup.

"And ain't that your sisters next to her?"

Nik rubbed his eyes. *I leave the house for five goddamn minutes and all hell breaks loose.*

"See, boy? Never borin'."

ೞ೮ೞ೭೦

"What do you think?"

Angie sipped her champagne. She debated whether to be kind.

Nah.

"I wouldn't, hon."

"Really?"

"It makes ya look dumpy...and fat."

The lioness turned and stormed back to the dressing room.

Reena, a little tipsy on all that champagne, stretched out on the couch. Her head rested against Angelina's side and Angelina felt the urge to toss her off the couch. She didn't have the heart to be so bitchy, though. Not today.

"You know, Santiago, you should feel damn proud of yourself."

"Oh? And why's that?"

"Because this is the first time Fallons Department Store ever had tigers, lions, she-wolves, a couple of cheetahs, and a few bears all in the same place without beatin' the hell out of each other."

"I thought these places were neutral ground for you shifter types." She liked this place. It reminded her of Neiman Marcus or Bloomingdales. Big, spacious, with all the great designers.

"They are. Humans shop here, but it's run and owned by shifters. Still, we can usually smell each other. The lions stay away from the tigers. The hyenas away from the lions. Etcetera, etcetera. This is the first time that I can recall this level of inter-mingling."

"How many of these stores are there?"

"All over the states and Europe."

"Cool." Maybe she could drag Sara's ass to one close to the Pack den and get the woman some hot clothes without the Harley-Davidson logo on them. "I find out something new every day."

Kisa sat on the couch. "Like what else?" The more Angie talked to her, the more Kisa opened up. Like a turtle sticking her head out of her shell.

"Well, I had no idea Manolo Blahnik made size thirteen shoes."

"Well, they don't make them openly. But the bears and wolves have huge feet," Reena whispered.

"We heard that," one of the bears growled.

Angie stood up, laughing as Reena's head slammed against the couch. "Sorry."

She headed off toward the bathroom, stopping several times to dissuade two women to never wear orange again and to urge a wolf to consider waxing her brow into two distinct ones.

She reached the bathroom, her hand on the door, when her hackles raised off her neck. She remembered feeling that way before—when she'd turned around to find a hyena female standing behind her outside her shop.

Angie turned slowly. A different female stood behind her this time, but a hyena just the same. She could tell the difference now.

The woman didn't speak, but she bared her fangs. A whole mouth full of them. Little, needle-sharp fangs that could easily tear the flesh from Angie's body.

What a pleasant thought.

The hyena took a step toward her and Angelina tensed her body, ready to start hurting anything that got near her. Most normal people would run. But Angie didn't run unless someone told her to. Otherwise she stood around and started swinging. Since neither Sara nor Miki were there to tell her to run that meant one thing, and she balled up her fists preparing to let them fly.

"Is there a problem, Angelina?"

Sahara Lyon stepped around the corner, a she-wolf female beside her.

"We thought we smelled somethin' funky," the she-wolf grumbled. "So we decided to come check."

The hyena female stared at Angie. She knew that look. The look of someone desperate to kick the living shit out of her. She'd seen it more than once over the years. And Angie bet her face mirrored the exact same sentiment back to the hyena. She could almost taste the beating she'd planned to give her. She could practically feel the flesh and bone give as she laid into her.

"What will you do?" Angie whispered. "So close and yet you just can't get near me."

The female took another step toward her and Angie thought she might have goaded the dumb bitch into a fight. But to Angie's eternal surprise, Kisa stepped in front of her. Big tiger fangs bared. She opened her mouth wide, a tiger growl ripping through the store.

Angie glanced at Sahara who shrugged in mutual surprise.

Kisa grabbed the woman by the throat, yanked her close, and then threw her. The hyena flew over several racks and into a few other hyena females. Racks hit the floor, glass broken, clothes damaged. Angie winced. *Well this is gonna cost.*

The hyenas picked up Angie's challenger, not even stopping to brush the glass off, quickly moving toward the escalators as Kisa walked back to Angie. "I think I'm going to get that blue dress I tried on."

"You do that, Kisa. It looks really good on you."

The tigress walked off and Angie glanced at Sahara. "Okay. She's a little scary."

"A little?"

C3 ଅ ଅ

Nik stood on Main Street next to his brothers. "When did you first see 'em?"

"Just today."

Male hyenas. Weak, subservient bastards. Probably from one of the Raleigh Clans.

Nik watched them skulking down the street, trying to fit in. But every shifter in town watched them walk by and smelled that they didn't belong. Hyenas didn't live this far away from a city. Which really wasn't very surprising. One breed at a time they'd happily fuck with, which was easy enough to do in a town like New York or San Francisco. But two, three, six breeds all managing to live together in a small town in the middle of nowhere? No. Hyenas stayed near the big cities where they felt safer and could do more damage, usually steering clear of the small shifter-filled towns.

"What do you want us to do?" Alek asked.

"Do what the South is famous for. Run their asses out of town."

His brothers grinned.

Chapter Thirteen

Nik threw open his front door. *"Angie?"*

"Kitchen."

He froze. *Kitchen?*

Nik walked toward it with trepidation, but as he neared, he smelled food. And it smelled really good.

He found Angie sitting at the kitchen table, her feet up on the sturdy wood. The latest copy, he assumed, of *Mademoiselle Magazine* open on her lap. The relief he felt at seeing her safe practically knocked him back out the door. When his brothers pointed out the hyenas in town, he immediately feared the worst. And seeing female wolves and lions hanging out in front of Fallons Department Store simply confused him.

"What's that smell?" He liked that he didn't have to start every conversation with the usual pleasantries. In fact, he got the feeling Angie hated pleasantries.

"My kick-ass spaghetti with meat sauce."

"You can cook?"

She glared at him. "Yes. I can cook. I often choose not to, but I *can* cook."

He folded his arms in front of his chest. "So why have you chosen to cook for me?"

"You know, to thank you for your wonderful hospital—"

"Angie."

"All right, all right!" Wow, that didn't take much turning of the screws to get her to break. "I went into town with your sisters and there was a small problem with hyenas and Kisa. Then a fight with the lions and the bears, and then the cheetahs pissed off the wolves...anyway, Fallons will be charging about two grand to your personal account."

Nik forced himself not to smile. "You rack up two grand on my account and all I get is your lousy spaghetti?"

He barely ducked that magazine in time. "My spaghetti is *not* lousy." She swung her feet off the table and stood up. "And you're going to eat it and you're going to goddamn love it!" She pushed past him.

"Goddamn hillbilly," she muttered while stomping to the stove. She had on shorts. *Nice.*

"Well sit your hillbilly ass down."

He pulled his chair out and dropped into it. "It's ready?"

"Nearly." She dropped a plate in front of him. "But to get you started, here's salad."

She turned to walk away, but he grabbed her wrist and yanked her onto his lap.

"Where you goin'?" Somehow he knew there was more to this story.

"Get your cat paws off me." She laughed, struggling to pull away from him.

Nik wrapped his arms around her waist and held her tight. "Now, what aren't you telling me?"

"Nothing."

"Don't lie to me, Angie."

"I'm not." He slid his hand between her legs, and she grabbed onto his wrist. "Don't you dare!"

"Then tell me."

"There's nothing to tell." He pushed his hand farther up her leg. "Okay. Okay!"

Angie took a deep breath, but still refused to release his wrist. "There was a slight fender bender with your daddy's truck, but it was your sister's fault."

"How much is that going to cost me?"

"I don't know."

His hand moved up another inch.

"I don't!" She pushed at his arm. "But your daddy said he'd let ya know."

"Maybe," he ran his tongue up around her ear, before pulling back, "you could work all that money off. Ya know. In trade."

"Oh, get a grip, hillbilly. You know I'll pay you back for all of it."

He licked her neck. She pinched his hand. He bit her neck. She punched his arm. He slid his hand up and down her calf, simply enjoying the feel of her soft flesh beneath his hand and she snarled, "Look, hillbilly, unless you're going to fuck me, stop freakin' touching me."

Nik stopped because he wasn't sure he heard her correctly. "What?"

"I don't like to be touched unless it leads to fucking. And, then, only if it's the important areas. Otherwise, get your hands off me."

"You're kidding right?"

"No."

He decided to test her, running his hand behind the back of her knee.

With a growl, she pulled back and he let her go. Unfortunately, she lost her seat and fell back off his lap, dropping to the floor.

Her ass hit the tile, then her head. Nik winced in sympathy.

"You okay, sugar?"

"Oh, fuck you."

"Now that's just rude."

"You know..." She struggled to sit up, so he grabbed her T-shirt and yanked her into position. She slapped at his hands. "You are a very distracting man."

"Why, thank you kindly."

"It wasn't a compliment, Cleatus."

"I'm Nik. Cleatus is my second cousin twice removed. We call him Cleats for short."

Angie buried that pretty little face in her hands and sighed.

She really could just kill him. True, she'd go to prison for at least twenty-five years, but it might be worth it.

He crouched down in front of her, grabbing her ankle and pulling her toward him.

"Hey!" She slapped at his hand. "What are you doing?"

"You took a nasty fall there. I wanna check the back of your head."

"My head's fine." She tried to scramble away from him again, but with grim determination, he snatched her back, pulling her tight against his body.

"You're not going to make me tie your hands behind your back so that I can do this, are ya?"

He meant it jokingly, she knew he did. But her mistake? Turning away, her breath coming out in a rush, and her nipples getting hard. All at the same time.

What could she say? The idea of being tied up and at this hillbilly's mercy sent all sorts of dirty, erotic images slamming through her tired, slightly tipsy-from-the-champagne brain.

He didn't miss any of it. His hands tightened at her waist and for someone who went running as a tiger for miles and miles every night, he seemed to have a sudden labored-breathing problem.

"Let me go, Nik."

"I really don't want to."

"Nik...let me go."

He did. Slowly. His fingers taking an achingly long time to release her. Once he did, she scooted back from him a bit.

"Angie—"

"Don't get any weird ideas here, hillbilly." She wanted to back away from him, but then again she really didn't. "It's not what you think. I'm not into any of that weird shit."

"I know. I know exactly what you want." He nuzzled her chin. "You like to play." How come she suddenly felt like one of those squeaky mice someone gives to their cat? He leaned in closer and she closed her eyes. He smelled so good and her entire body tingled at his scent. "I've been waiting a long time to meet someone like you, Angelina Santiago."

She felt his tongue against her lips and, with only a moment's hesitation, opened to him. He groaned, his mouth claiming hers. His hand sliding behind the back of her, pulling her close.

So now what? She had an uncontrollable tiger by the tail. *And what the fuck do I do with that?*

Anything she needed. Anything she wanted. Absolutely

anything—as long as he could bury himself inside her until the end of time.

Angie pulled out of their kiss. "My sauce...I...I need to finish it."

Nik rocked his weight back on his heels and held his hands up, palms open. She had that feral alley cat look she sometimes got. He wouldn't do anything to push her away. Not now. Not ever. "Okay. Not a problem. I've gotta finish up some work in my study and then I'll come back and eat when you're ready."

Together, slowly, the pair stood.

"I'm gonna go in my study now." He spoke slowly so as not to startle her. "If you need me—"

"Yup. Yup. I know where you are. Now go away."

He backed out the door. Once he was in the hallway, he heard her give a seriously sexy and frustrated sigh and start cursing like a sailor. After that, a lot of pot banging.

But she didn't leave. And that was all he needed to know.

ౠ

She couldn't even taste the food. And that had to be the longest, most uncomfortable dinner she'd ever sat through. Especially when she kept thinking of Nik naked.

Thump. Thump. Thump.

"My brothers will be here soon."

The last bit of spaghetti she brought up from her plate stopped, hovering right by her lips. "Why?" Well she'd filled that question with an aura of intense distrust. So much so that Nik leaned back in his seat.

"Hunting usually. But tonight we'll be checking to make

sure the property is safe. That you're safe."

"Oh."

He pushed his chair back from the table, stood, and leaned against it. His big hands resting against the thick wood. "And maybe we should get some things clear."

"Clear?"

Without responding, Nik picked up the table and moved it out of his way. Angie watched him, mesmerized. That thing had to weigh a ton. A fine, fine piece of antique furniture she'd been silently wondering the cost of for two days. Twenty thousand easy, and his family used it like he'd picked it up at a flea market for twenty bucks.

Nik walked up to her, took the fork from her hand and tossed it across the room into the sink. Before she could move, he gripped her under her arms and lifted her out of the seat until they were eye level.

"Yes. We need to make some things clear. I don't share what's mine. So you have no worries about my brothers. Ever."

Too stunned to respond, Angie stared at him.

Nik grunted. Seemingly satisfied with her lack of response. He carried her over to the sink and set her down. *If he's expecting me to do the dishes, he can forget it. I cooked the meal, he can damn well clean it up.*

But Nik seemed pretty disinterested in the dirty dishes and the mess she'd made on the stove. Instead, he grabbed her hands and spread her arms out away from her body and across the counter. He leaned into her, trapping her against the stainless steel.

He stared at her for what felt like forever. Looking down at her face, her arms pinned against the counter. God, his body felt good. Just one, *hard*, long piece of flesh.

And, for the moment, all that flesh belonged to her.

A hard bang against the glass doors leading into the backyard startled her away from Nik's gaze.

"I think they're here for you."

He smiled as his two brothers pressed up against the glass. They stood on their hind legs. Big paws sliding over the smooth surface, long tongues hanging out. They were so adorable and goofy, she found it hard to believe they were deadly predators.

Nik snarled and bared his fangs. After responding growls, the two brothers ran off.

"I'll be back soon." He kissed her and Angie's body throbbed to life. She didn't want him to go. She never wanted him to leave. *She* never wanted to leave.

Nik pulled back slightly, his lips still against hers. "The spaghetti was great, by the way."

Spaghetti? "Uh...thanks."

"Now what are you going to do while I'm gone?"

Masturbate until my hand falls off? "Shower. Sleep. Put the dishes in the sink so you can wash 'em later."

His lips smiled against hers. "Good. But don't get yourself off."

"What?" *Oh, God! The hillbilly can read minds. Damn witch one-eyed grandma genes!*

"You heard me, sugar. Don't you dare make yourself come." He rubbed his mouth against hers. "That's my job now."

Gee. What's that puddle at Nik's feet? Why, that's Angie Santiago. She used to be an ice princess, now she's just a sopping mess.

"Ya hear?" Funny how controlled he sounded. 'Cause he

didn't feel like he had any control. He felt like if this woman twitched even once, he'd come all over the floor.

Oh that would be classy, Nik.

"Yeah. Yeah."

He let her go before she squirmed in his arms and he lost it. But he did give her a quick kiss on her neck. "Good."

He walked out, slamming into the two idiots right outside the house. He barely had time to shift before they tackled him. Nik knocked them both off, batting them with his paws. Christ, you'd think they'd grown out of this. But clearly they hadn't.

Knowing he would make this patrol the shortest of his lifetime, Nik charged off into the woods, his brothers barely pacing him.

Chapter Fourteen

Angie stepped out of the shower, grabbing one of the towels. She couldn't believe this. Horny as she was, she couldn't bring herself to jack off.

What had the man done to her?

She always controlled every relationship she'd ever been in. To the point where one ex-boyfriend referred to her as his "Nazi girlfriend". Rude, but accurate.

Quickly drying off, she yanked a big T-shirt over her head, and started pacing.

Exactly how long was "back soon" anyway? She didn't know how much longer she could wait. Not known for her patience, Angie was ready to go track her tiger down.

Yeah, brilliant, Angie. Go wandering in the woods wearing nothing but a T-shirt, screaming, "I'm ready to get fucked now, Nik!"

Instead of that daring plan, Angie turned out the lights in her room and wandered out onto the balcony. She rested against the railing, looking down at the woods, but seeing nothing except the outline of pine trees and tall grass. A cool breeze chilled her, but she didn't want to go to bed. Alone.

So, instead, she sighed.

Nik skidded to a sliding, slipping halt. His big paws tearing up the leaf-covered ground. A good mile away from the house, he still heard that damn sigh of hers. And the wind brought her lust-filled scent down to him, stopping him in his tracks.

Her scent triggered something in him. Something primal and dangerous. Something he couldn't contain or control. And, apparently, neither could his brothers. They charged past him, heading back toward the house. Back toward Angelina.

Angie watched them tumble out of the woods. She couldn't tell from where she stood on the balcony, which tiger was which. And, at first, she couldn't tell if they were playing or not.

It took her less than a minute to figure out they weren't playing.

Two tigers headed toward the house, a third, moving faster than anything she'd seen before, came up behind them. He slashed the hind quarter of one. Tackled the other, sinking his teeth into the back of its neck.

They rolled, the one on top eventually flinging the other away. Now, thoroughly wounded, two tigers limped off. Back into the woods and away from Nik's house. The other spun around and faced Angie. She stepped back from the balcony. She still had no idea which one this was.

He took a step, then leaped, easily clearing the railing. Angie stumbled back inside. Slowly, he moved toward her, a low, low growl rumbling through the room. Angie held one hand up in front of her. *Oh, yeah, Ang. That'll work.*

She took another step back. And another. "Nice kitty." He snarled and even in the darkness she could see those white fangs. She wondered where the hell she'd left that goddamn baseball bat. If she had it, she could at least go down fighting.

The tiger kept moving forward, even as he pulled himself up

onto his hind legs. Even as his white and orange fur receded back into his body, and his black stripes became the hair on his head.

Nik backed her up until she slammed into the wall, the door a good ten feet away. He slammed both of his hands against the wall, bracketing either side of her head. She stared up at him. His gold eyes still tiger's eyes, his big fangs still visible.

"Nik?"

He closed his eyes. She could see his desperate fight to keep control and she marveled at the energy it took for him to go this far. His fangs receded back into his mouth.

He forced a smile. "I'm going to be okay."

"You weren't okay?"

Nik shook his head. "Not for you. No."

What the hell did that mean? She reached up to touch his face, but Nik reared back. "No!" He took another breath. "I wouldn't do that right now."

"Dude, what are you doing?"

"Trying to keep control."

"Why?" He stared at her like she'd grown horns. "What?"

He leaned into her and just as quickly pulled back. His body shaking, he groaned, "This isn't what I wanted. Not for us."

Finally, she understood. If he fucked her now, it wouldn't be all slow and delicious and Nik in total control. It would be animal fucking, only with two humans.

She remembered when she visited Sara the first time. In the middle of the night, she came down to the kitchen for a bottle of water and discovered Sara and Zach using the kitchen table, most likely not in the way Lou's Furniture Outlet intended. She didn't linger, wanting to give her friends their privacy, but she witnessed enough to know animal fucking when she saw it. Raw. Dirty. Rough.

Score!

"Oh, dude, this could totally work!"

"Angie," he actually whined.

"Nik," she whined back.

"You need to go."

"Yeah, but—"

"Now!"

Frustrated as all hell, she slipped under his arm, and stormed out.

She had to be the craziest damn female he'd ever known in his entire life and if she hadn't left that second, she'd be the most thoroughly fucked one, too.

Nik leaned his head against the wall and let out a sigh of relief. He'd explain everything to her tomorrow. As soon as he could manage, he would call Kisa and she'd take Angie back to her place.

By tomorrow he'd have complete control of himself. He wouldn't be like this. Out-of-control Tiger-Nik. He wanted to seduce Angelina Santiago. Not fuck her up against the wall.

Well...he did want to do that eventually, but not right off the bat.

Nik heard a door open and he snapped to attention. *What the hell?* She hadn't left. She was in his room. He could hear her moving around, muttering to herself and slamming drawers.

What was the woman doing?

After a few moments, she came back in. Stopped by the dresser, dropping something.

"All right, I know you're all worried 'cause I'm much more human than you can ever hope to be, but really, don't let that fool ya. I'm a hearty girl with great taste in shoes. And can I say I had a feeling you'd be well prepared. I have to admit. I like that in a man." She slid back under his arm and stood in front of him.

"What in tarnation are you doing?" *My God. She smells so good.*

"Wow, do you people still say tarnation?" She shook her head. "Whatever. Anyway, I'm not waiting any longer for your pussy-teasing ass. 'Cause now you're just starting to piss me off."

"Sugar, you can't handle me like this." She didn't seem to realize she needed him leashed. Like one of those white Bengal tigers in Vegas. Leashed, restrained, and perhaps even sedated. This was why he didn't fuck humans. Too damn complicated. And they broke real easy, too.

"Handle you like what? All fanged out and cranky?"

"You need to go."

"No. What I need is to get laid. By you." She held up a condom. "Do you wanna do the honors, or should I?"

"I don't think you under—"

"Fine. I'll do it." She ripped the package open. "I'm really good at this. I used to do demonstrations on cucumbers for Miki and Sara, 'cause Lord knows what those two would get up to if it weren't for me. Well, I guess the way Miki is now. All pregnant and unmarried. Just a lot sooner."

Her hand gripped his cock, and he shut his eyes tight. He'd been hard as soon as he shifted back to human. Now it hurt.

And her strong, cool fingers...not really helping.

She rolled the condom down the length of him.

"Angie—"

"That'll work." She gave him one more squeeze. "Now do you wanna do this up against the wall? Or go for it on the floor."

Staring up at the ceiling, "Angelina—"

"Oooh! I know!" She scooted away from him, pulling off the T-shirt she wore. As usual—no underwear. Dammit, why wouldn't the woman wear panties?

"I saw this on the Discovery Channel or PBS or something."

She knelt down at the foot of the bed, stretching out facedown, her arms in front of her, gripping the bedspread. She glanced back at him. "Just pretend I have a tail." She wiggled her ass and her eyebrows at him.

His claws ripped paint and plaster from the walls.

Five more seconds. She would give him five more seconds. If he made her wait any longer, she would drag his sorry ass over here by that huge two-by-four he called a cock.

Angie had never wanted to fuck so badly before. She knew he worried about hurting her, blah, blah, blah. But hell, she took on the girl's lacrosse team that time. Their fault, though. They should have never tripped Sara. Lucky for them, Miki and Sara could pull her back. Otherwise, she would have shoved that lacrosse stick right up the team captain's pasty ass.

Man, he really needed to move that tight ass of his. She was so wet, she was dripping on his nice hardwood floor.

When Angie didn't think she could handle one more second and moved to stand up, Nik's body knelt behind hers. His hand in her hair, snatching her head back. He kissed her and she knew she felt those fangs against her tongue. But she didn't care. She wanted him too badly. And she wanted him just like this.

He pulled away. "Are you sure?" His grip on her hair tightened and she moaned in response, the edge of pain taking her right where she needed to be. "Because once I start, sugar, I may not be able to stop."

She looked up into gold eyes glinting at her in the darkness. Cat eyes. "Let's put it this way, hillbilly—you make me wait one more goddamn second and I'm gonna rip your cock off."

Nik growled, that long low growl he made when she first sat on his dresser wearing nothing but a sheet and talking to Zach. That sound had turned her on then and now it made her absolutely insane.

He pushed her forward against the bed, one hand grabbing firm hold of her wrists while his legs forced her knees apart. Teeth bit into the back of her neck, holding her in place.

Oh, yeah!

His free hand slid to her pussy, two fingers pushing inside, stretching her open. She clenched those fingers tight and he growled again.

"Damn, girl."

His hips slammed into her, his cock forcing its way in. Angie almost screamed, "'Bout motherfuckin' time!" But her ability to speak—kinda gone. Snatched away by her lust and the hillbilly's huge cock.

He pushed his cock in deeper, stretching her impossibly wider until his entire length slid inside her pussy. No preamble. No flowery words. No bullshit whatsoever. Instead, he pinned her to the bed with his body and gripped her wrists tighter, restraining her from doing anything but receiving whatever he gave her. And what he gave her was fucking. No making love. No sex. This...this was fucking. Hard, rough, and exactly what Angie needed. God, maybe what she'd always needed.

His cock pumped inside her as Angie opened her legs more to allow all of Nik in. She writhed desperately under him while she tried to pull her arms out of his grasp. He wouldn't release her and she almost came from that alone.

His other free hand roughly grabbed her breasts, squeezing each one tight and tugging at her nipples.

"Oh, fuck yeah," she moaned.

Well that slipped out, but it kicked Nik's lust up a notch. His cock slammed into her mercilessly as big fingers slid down to her dripping sex and rubbed her clit hard. The pressure brutal. And shit but did it feel amazing.

She always knew she liked it kind of rough, but she had no idea she liked it *this* rough. Actually, she didn't like it...she fucking loved it!

"Fuck me harder, Nik. God, please."

Her body shook with impending orgasm as Nik's fingers stroked her clit. He continued to pound into her and she felt his cock practically double in size as he neared release. She clenched her pussy around him and he growled in her ear.

"Tricky bitch."

"Fuckin' cat." Her orgasm tore through her, ripping her apart, sending her screaming from one rush through another.

He strung out her ride, changing the strokes of his fingers and his cock, until she thought she might black out. She finally clenched him one more time. Hard. He roared a curse, then came and kept coming, jerking inside her until done.

They collapsed against the bed, harsh breaths mingling, sweat dripping onto the floor.

Fangs receded. His eyes shifted back to normal. By coming, he'd put the tiger back in its cage and he realized he had Angelina Santiago, Prada-wearing princess, panting underneath him.

Hot.

Damn.

Never before did he have a fuck like that. And even as he pulled out of her, his cock desperately demanded to get back in.

"Don't. Move."

Angie shrugged in response, her body still resting against the foot of the bed. Nik went to the bathroom, removed the condom, tied it off, and tossed it into the trash. He turned the water on in the sink, cupping his hand under the stream and drinking as much as he could manage. His throat burned from his harsh breathing and it took all his strength to control his raging emotions.

Filling up one of the clean glasses on the sink with cold tap water, Nik returned to the bedroom. He stopped behind her, staring at her long body kneeling on the floor. Her head resting against the edge of the bed. Her hands clutching the bedspread. She sighed again. That little sound she insisted on making, for some unknown reason, drove him absolutely insane.

Good God. I am like my father.

With a grunt of annoyance and lust, he held out the glass of water to her. "Here." She glanced back at him and, with a soft smile, took it.

She drained the water quickly and handed the glass back to him.

"Thanks, hillbilly."

He closed his eyes. She just kept pushing, didn't she? It's

like she couldn't help herself.

He dropped the glass on the side table, knelt down and picked her skinny ass up off the floor. "Come on, hellcat."

"Where are we going," she muttered into his neck as he lifted her off the floor.

"To the bed."

"Why? My knees were so enjoying your hardwood floors."

Rolling his eyes, he tossed her onto the rumpled sheets.

"Hey!"

"Quiet." Nik stretched out beside her. Wrapping his arm around her waist, he pulled her into his body and fell asleep.

CR∞BO

Angie woke up coming. Her arms around Nik's shoulders, her legs wrapped around his waist. She had no idea how long he'd been inside her, fucking her, but man, what a great way to wake up in the middle of the night.

He rolled his hips and Angie's orgasm rolled right along with him. His hot mouth had her nipple and it felt better than the first time he lashed her breast with his tongue.

The last thing she remembered, he'd dumped her off in bed, cuddled up next to her like the giant kitten he was, and proceeded to snore. Not pretty, but a small price to pay for the fuck of her life.

He rolled his hips the opposite direction.

"Ah, Nik!"

He released her nipple with a wet *pop*, lifting his head to look at her.

"You finally awake, sugar?"

"Don't...stop. God, please don't stop."

"No intention. Not for quite awhile, anyway."

Nik the tiger had gotten what he needed. Which left Nik the man. She got the feeling Nik the man had something to prove.

Oh, well, a price she would just have to pay.

His mouth clamped down on hers and his tongue slid around and in, mimicking the movement of his hips. She couldn't help herself. She opened her legs wider, let him sink in even further. She'd never felt so filled before. Especially when he gripped her ass and lifted her just enough so he went in even deeper.

Christ, how could some poor human guy ever live up to this?

Angie pushed her hands into his hair, pulling him back a bit. She had to, she was coming again. This time screaming Nik's name.

"I sure do like that, sugar." He bit the side of her neck and she groaned, her body shaking from her orgasm. "I like how you scream my name. So let's see how many times we can make you do that tonight."

Damn, overachieving hillbillies!

Chapter Fifteen

Those damn cardinals woke her. She used to think they were so cute, now they were getting on her goddamn nerves.

Angie didn't open her eyes but, instead, wished she had her rifle for some target practice. She tried her best to ignore the sound, but she really couldn't ignore the big hand holding on to her breast like it owned it.

Forcing her eyes open, she turned her head and came face to face with a sleeping hillbilly. A hillbilly who looked more than comfortable holding on to her breast, and pushing up against her side.

Is it me? Or is my life getting weirder and weirder?

Slowly, so as not to wake him, she eased out from under his grasp and out of bed. Naked, she walked to the bathroom for a quick shower. The entire time she let the water run over her body, she kept thinking about what Nik had done to her— all night long. She'd only gotten a couple hours sleep at best. And the most interesting parts of her were sore.

The man really did know how to work a girl.

Crap. She liked him. She liked a rich, shapeshifting hillbilly. She liked him a lot and she had no idea what to do with that.

She sighed and dried herself off.

Coffee. That's what she needed. A good cup of coffee always made everything seem simple and easy.

She wrapped a giant white towel around her body, and tiptoed out of the bathroom, heading for the door.

"Where do you think you're goin'?"

She cringed. Well, there went her quiet cup of coffee.

Refusing to turn around, "I was going to get some breakfast."

"But I haven't had my breakfast yet."

If that little fucker thinks I'm making him breakfast...

"Get that ass over here."

She turned around, her breath catching at the sight of him. Man, but he was beautiful. Laid out on the bed, the sheet hanging low on his hips. His messy black hair practically covering those gold eyes. And big arms behind his head like he owned the place.

Oh, wait. He does own the place.

"Why?"

He raised an eyebrow at her response and she raised one right back.

"Don't make me come over there and getcha," he warned.

With a growl she hoped hid her sudden surge of lust, she stomped over to him.

"What?"

Taking one hand out from behind his head, he snatched her towel off.

"Hey!"

He took a deep breath. "Perfect." Settling down into the bed, "Now, bring that pretty pussy over here."

Angie blinked. "What?"

"Right here." He pointed to his face. "I want that pussy right here."

"I am not—"

And there went that damn eyebrow. "Do we really need to have that 'don't make me come over there and getcha' conversation again?"

After all they did the previous night, why this would embarrass her she didn't know. But she'd be damned if she let him know about it. Of course, Angie didn't feel entirely comfortable jumping on the man's face, so she straddled his chest.

"Does that look like my face to you?"

"Well, gimme a sec."

"No. You take too damn long. And I'm starving." He grabbed her ass in both his hands and lifted her up.

"Oh, shit. Wait a minute!"

But he didn't, bringing her body down smack dab on his face. His tongue swiped across her already moist pussy, teasing her clit, and she grabbed onto the headboard for support.

He explored her like he hadn't already done so many times before. And he groaned like she had her hands on him, when in fact she held on to that headboard for dear life.

So many men in her past and none of them made her feel like Nik the Hillbilly Cat did.

As his expert tongue flicked her into another one of those powerful orgasms, she wondered how she would ever walk away from him.

But she'd have to, wouldn't she? He wasn't hers to keep.

The fact she purred when she came, really did make his goddamn day. He could listen to that sound every day, over and over. Add in that he made her make that sound, and he could easily see himself spending the rest of his life trapped between her thighs one way or another.

He'd never thought like that before. Not about anybody. He wouldn't allow himself. But the old man did have a point. A girl like Angelina *did* only come around once in a lifetime.

"God, Nik," she growled as she grinded herself against his face. "Goddammit!"

Her body shook as she came in his mouth. Her legs tightening around his head. He lapped at her gently until she settled into soft groans. Once she stopped shaking, he carefully pulled her off and swung her into his arms as he slid off the bed.

"Now I'm ready to face the day."

"Where are we going," she whispered in his ear, apparently too wrung out to argue with him about anything.

"Shower."

"I just took a shower."

"Well, now you're gonna get fucked in one, sugar." He rubbed his chin against the top of her head. "Besides, I think it's time for you to have a little breakfast, too."

Her arm tightened around his neck. "Good. 'Cause I'm starving."

CB&80

"Angie!"

Angie's eyes snapped open again. Christ, she kept falling asleep at the kitchen table.

"Here, lazy bones. Drink this." Nik put a hot cup of coffee in front of her. If she didn't know where it would lead, she'd kiss him.

"Thanks."

"No problem."

She watched him out of the one eye she could open. He'd only put on a pair of old jeans he didn't bother zipping all the way up. No shoes on those big feet and no shirt.

She closed her eyes again. No one had a right to be that good looking. Absolutely no one.

"You still want breakfast or you want some lunch instead?"

"Whatever's fast. Now I'm really starving."

He chuckled. "Yeah. Me, too. Good fuckin' will do that to ya."

Interesting how when she used that word randomly, Nik looked at her like she was a serial killer. But when discussing the actual act, the man couldn't use the word enough.

Weird hillbilly rules.

He opened his refrigerator and seemed to be debating the pros and cons of its contents. She knew he couldn't find her staring at his ass unless she wanted to end up face down over the table, so she glanced at the French doors, only to see two faces staring back at her.

Both pouting.

She slid out of her chair and walked over, pushing the doors open.

"What's wrong?"

"Look what your boyfriend did to us."

She would have punched Ban in the face for that one, but he turned and she saw the fang marks on the back of his neck.

"Oh, honey!" Angie raised herself up on her toes to get a

better look. "We need to put something on that."

"You should see what he did to Alek's leg."

"What are you two doing here," Nik barked from behind her.

"Be nice." Grabbing an arm from both, she pulled the brothers into the house. "You guys sit down, I'll see what I can find."

"I should have killed you two last night."

Ban glanced at Alek. "Is it me, little brother. Or does big brother look well fucked this early afternoon?"

"I'd have to say he sure does, big brother. Mighty well fucked."

"If you two don't get your butts outta here—"

"What? And have your girlfriend all upset?"

"She's not my girlfriend."

"So, she's fair game then?"

Nik answered Ban by slapping him on the back of his neck, right across his still-healing wounds. Ban responded by jumping out of his chair, fangs bared and ready to fight.

"That's it! You two cut the bullshit out right now!" Angie glided back into the kitchen carrying a first-aid kit from the bathroom. But when neither brother acknowledged her, Angie growled low, "Don't make me get the balls."

Ban flinched.

"Now sit the fuck down, Ban, before I get angry." Nik smiled until she turned on him. "And weren't you doing something?"

Boy, she could be real cranky when she hadn't gotten her coffee.

⟨౮౭ఌ౮౦⟩

Angie couldn't believe how busy she'd been all afternoon. Once she wrapped up both Alek's and Ban's wounds—and Nik had thrown them out of the house—she spent the rest of the afternoon making calls. Well, after Nik bent her over the living room couch and fucked her until she saw stars.

Design house reps and some staff problems kept her going the rest of the day. Nik spent his time in his office also working. They didn't see much of each other for about five hours. But the rich sound of his voice, or that damn hillbilly accent, flowing through the hallway into the kitchen, made her wet. She had finally changed into a loose black skirt, completely forgoing the underwear. She couldn't sit around in damp underwear all day. And, for her own amusement, the black strappy Ferragamos.

Early on Miki called her to check in, but thankfully the conversation remained brief and she didn't ask any uncomfortable questions Angie wouldn't want to answer.

As she argued with Celine, her buyer and the woman pushing her to open another store in Dallas, Angie decided this would be her last call. Tired of talking and missing Nik, she wanted to shut down for the rest of the day.

"I've never liked his stuff, Celine."

"But you haven't seen any of his new stuff."

"I don't want—"

"Do you have access to a computer?"

Nik, from what she could tell, only had one computer and it resided in his office.

"Maybe."

"He's got a site you can go to."

Well, it did give her an excuse.

"Hold on."

She attached the phone to her skirt and made sure her headphone securely fit to her head without making her hair look stupid. She left the kitchen and went straight to his office. The door stood partially open, so she stuck her head in, lightly knocking.

He, too, wore a headphone and it took her a second to realize he wasn't speaking English or even hillbilly.

Nik glanced up at her knock and rewarded her with a huge grin. He motioned her in.

"I need your computer," she mouthed, then added the usual visual of her fingers typing.

He nodded and pointed, pushing his chair back a bit so she could get to the desktop.

She wasn't a gadget whore, but she knew this system would have Miki creaming in her basketball shorts.

"All right. Give me the link."

Celine walked her to the designer's site and led her around. Angie still wasn't impressed with the designer's stuff. But she was impressed to realize Nik spoke Mandarin. He spoke it well, too. She couldn't speak it herself, but she understood it and his accent was damn-near flawless.

"I'm not impressed, Celine."

"You're being difficult."

"I'm allowed to be, it's my fuckin' business."

"Okay. Calm down. I'm just saying—"

"I know what you're saying and—eep!"

"Eep what?"

"Uh..." Angie swatted at the hand sliding in between her

legs. And with no panties under her skirt... "Um..."

"Are you okay?"

Nik pushed her legs apart.

"Yes. But I've, uh, I've gotta go."

"Angie, I've been waiting to talk to you for three days about this stuff."

"I know."

"I mean you up and disappear, scaring everyone in town half to death." Nik's tongue slid up the inside of her thigh.

"Celine!" She snarled it, causing Celine to stop babbling. "I cannot discuss this now."

"Um...okay."

"I'll call you tomorrow or something."

Angie shut the phone off, snatching it and her headset off and dropping them to the floor. She gripped the edge of the desk as Nik's fingers played around her clit, his tongue teasing around her lips, but not hitting anything nearly important enough.

Then she realized something.

The man is still on the goddamn phone!

Nik stopped listening to his friend and business partner as soon as Angie bent over in front of his computer.

Wo-hoo Ling, or as the fraternity brothers liked to call him, Biscuit, kept going on and on about the last couple of million they recently made, but who cared? Really, who cared about anything when staring at the most perfect ass and legs in the world?

"You're not listening to me, are you?" Biscuit sighed out in Mandarin.

"I am too." Okay. A lie. But Nik couldn't tell very straight-laced Biscuit with his six cubs and three loyal tiger females that he currently had his hand buried inside the hottest snatch in the entire country.

"Do you even know this one's name?"

"Uh-huh." He dragged his tongue up the inside of her thigh. She always tasted so good to him, he could never seem to get enough of her. And hearing her order other people around did nothing but give him a brutal hard-on.

"I'm hanging up."

Nik pulled his face away, but dragged Angie onto his lap. He positioned her so her head rested against his shoulder, her body splayed across his. He slid his hands under her shirt, grasping her already hard nipples. "Why?"

"Because I know when I'm being ignored."

"Good point. I'll call ya tomorrow."

"I swear, you Siberians have no control—"

Nik clicked off the call. Damn South China tigers always thought they were better than the rest.

He took off the headset and set up the phone so it immediately rolled over to his voicemail. Then he went back to the beautiful woman panting on his lap.

He firmly gripped Angie's nipples again, tweaking enough to bring on a little bit of pain. She groaned in response.

"I missed you, sugar," he murmured against her ear.

"I didn't go anywhere, hillbilly."

"But you weren't right here." *Where you belong.* He squeezed her nipples again and Angie nearly writhed off his lap. He slid his hands across her skin. Nothing felt better than her flesh under his hands.

She gripped his thighs. "Stop fuckin' touching me and fuck

me already."

Clearly Angie still needed to stay in control and the touching still seemed to be her last ditch effort for that. But for some unknown reason, Nik was determined to have her trust. All of it. He just had no idea why it mattered to him.

"Not yet, sugar."

She dug her fingers deep into his thigh. "I see the 'I don't like to wait' speech hasn't quite sunk in."

He released her, pushing her off his lap. "Go sit down in that chair."

Angie glanced at the wing-backed leather chair and back at Nik. "Why?"

"Sit. Down."

Huffing in annoyance, Angie stomped to the chair and threw herself into it. She crossed her legs and her arms and glared at him. "Now what?"

"Hike your left leg over the arm of the chair."

Her face quickly slipped from annoyance to slight panic. She glanced out the big picture windows. She didn't know he had the glass specially made so he could see out but once he closed those glass doors, no one could see in. Of course, she didn't need to know that at the moment.

"Uh…"

"Hike your left leg over the arm of the chair, Angie."

Biting her lip, Angie did as he told her to.

"Good." He leaned back in his own chair, getting comfortable. "Now put your hand between your legs."

"Nik—"

"Put your hand between your legs, Angie."

If she bites that lip of hers anymore, she's gonna draw

blood.

With tantalizing slowness, Angie slid her right hand between her thighs.

"Pull the skirt up a bit. I wanna see ya."

Another desperate glance out the window, then she pulled the black skirt up so he could see her hand and dripping wet pussy. It glistened at him, making his mouth water for the taste of her.

"Damn, girl. You're mighty wet. You must like the idea of being watched."

"No, I do not," she bit out.

"Then you must like the idea of being watched by me."

Angie looked away from him and Nik fought hard not to smile.

"Get your clit good and wet, Angelina."

Her head snapped around. "What?"

"Stop making me repeat myself."

She glared at him. "And what if I don't?"

"I tie you to the bed and leave you like that all night. I, of course, will sleep in the other room so you don't seduce me into relievin' that deep ache between your legs."

"Bastard."

"Just 'cause my parents didn't marry, don't mean you can call me names."

Angie snorted out a laugh and her smile brightened his world as nothing else had before.

He lowered his voice, his rock-hard dick screaming to get out and into her. "Do it for me, Angie. Make yourself come. I wanna watch you."

Her body shuddered and she closed her eyes, sliding her

middle finger inside that tight pussy he couldn't get enough of. She dragged the finger out, and pulled it across her clit. Slowly, she circled the tiny nerve-filled muscle. Her body tensed and shook, already so close to orgasm. But she fought it. She was embarrassed. He got the feeling she'd never done this before with anyone. Once again needing to trust someone enough to allow herself to be so vulnerable. Yet she trusted him enough to let him go this far, and he knew exactly what she needed to push her over the edge.

"Angie?" After a moment, she turned those beautiful brown eyes in his direction, but didn't stop masturbating. "You thinkin' about me right now?"

She licked her lips, then slowly nodded.

"About me deep inside you? Fuckin' you?"

She nodded again.

Nik sat up, bracing his arms on his knees, his hands clasped together. "I've got you pinned to the bed. My body between your legs, my dick buried deep inside you." He paused for a moment, making sure he had her attention. "I'm holding your arms above your head. You struggle to get away, but I don't let you. I've taken control. And you can't fight it. I won't let you get away. Not 'til I'm done with you. Not 'til I've fucked you raw and made you scream my name, over and over again."

He hadn't even finished when her entire body went rigid and she groaned out an orgasm that shook her right down to the hot little stilettos she wore.

Angie couldn't believe how hard she came. But before she even had a chance to recover, Nik knelt in front of her. He lifted her other leg up over the opposite arm of the chair and buried his face between her thighs, feasting on her pussy like a starving man.

Too much. Too much Nik and his hot body and amazing tongue. But at the same time, not nearly enough Nik. She was starting to feel like there would never be enough Nik. At least, not for her.

Growling, Nik pulled away from her and lifted her out of the chair. She wrapped her arms around his shoulders, burying her head against his neck.

"You really like carrying me around."

He shoved papers, folders, everything but the computer onto the floor. "Why not? You're such a little thing."

He placed her on the desk, then dug into the back of his jeans, pulling out a condom. She stared at him. Was he even remotely serious? He didn't need to bullshit her to get between her legs. And, unlike most sane men, he didn't fear her.

He looked up at her, his hands opening the packaging. "What, sugar?"

She grinned, shaking her head. "Nothing. Just having a moment."

"Well, have it later." He whipped his cock out, sheathed it, and had it inside her in seconds. His hands firm on her thighs, yanking her to the edge of the desk.

Angie gripped Nik's arms, her fingers digging into the hard muscle as his cock dug into her.

"By the way." He smiled. "The Ferragamos..." He looked down at her shoes. "They were a nice investment."

In response, Angie wrapped her legs around his waist, making sure the heels of her shoes dug into his ass. He groaned, his hands tightening on her flesh.

"Aren't they fabulous?" she panted.

CR&CRED

So tight. So hot. He'd never felt anything like it. Like her.

After several hours of abusing the furniture on his entire first floor, they finally made it to the bed in her room. Now she straddled his waist, his dick buried deep inside her. She rode him. Hard. Apparently she used to barrel race. Explained those thighs. Horse-ridin' thighs. Thighs that could snap a man in half.

Nik buried his hands in Angie's sweat-drenched hair and pulled her down until her pebble-hard nipples burrowed into his chest. He kissed her, their lips fusing, their tongues mating. He loved how this woman kissed. Swinging from intense to sweet and eventually around to hard. Exactly like she fucked.

He pulled his lips away. "Harder."

She gripped his arms, her nails digging into the flesh. The pain biting and erotic all at once. Her pussy clenched his dick tighter as she rode him harder.

Nik never thought someone completely human could take him like this. She did, though. She took. She gave. She demanded more. And had been for hours.

Angie rested her forehead against his. "You sure I'm not hurting you?"

"Naw, sugar," he groaned, gripping her hips tighter. "I can take a lot."

"Good. Very..." she shuddered violently, "...very good."

Nik slid his hands down her hips to her ass, his fingers digging into the smooth cheeks. She gasped and smiled at the same time. He loved seeing that smile on her face. It turned his dick into steel.

"Nik..." And his name on her lips. Nothing sounded better. "I'm...I'm..."

"Do it, Angie. Come all over me."

He kissed her again, letting her soul-shaking groans pulse through him. Her pussy still spasming around him as his dick swelled further and exploded. Nik was so lost inside of her, he didn't even realize he unleashed his claws, lancing her ass cheeks until she cried out.

"What?"

"Claws! Claws! Claws in my ass!"

He retracted them. "Oh, God, sugar. Are you okay?"

Taking hold of her waist, Nik pulled her off his softening dick and placed her gently on the bed. He turned her over so that she lay on her stomach.

He winced when he saw the perfectly formed claw marks. Five in each cheek.

"How bad is it?" she demanded, trying to get a good look, but a hand against her back kept her from seeing much of anything.

"Um...not bad."

"You are *lying* to me. I can tell," she accused.

"Now, now. Don't throw around them kind of accusations." Nik jumped off the bed. "Cool your jets, sugar. I'll be right back."

Trying not to laugh, he went to the bathroom and grabbed what he needed. When he walked back out, she still lay stomach down with one leg up, the foot perfectly arched and pointing toward the ceiling. He wondered if she took dancing classes when she was a kid.

Nik crawled back on the bed. "Leave this to me."

"I did. And you impaled my ass."

They looked at each other for a moment, then burst out laughing.

Angie pointed a warning finger at him. "Don't even think about going there."

"I didn't say a word."

"You didn't have to. Your big kitty eyes give you away every time."

He kissed her shoulder, then licked off the sweat there. "Give me five minutes, and I'll make this all better."

In the end it took him twenty minutes. He couldn't help himself. The woman had such a sweet ass. He kept kissing it. Licking the wounds he inflicted.

And, some deep, dark part of him wanted to tattoo his name all over that sweet ass.

Nik cleared his throat, freaked out by his suddenly territorial thoughts over an amazing fuck.

An amazing fuck and nothing else.

"So, sugar, your tattoo. When did you get it?"

"During my out-of-control youth. For protection. Your grandmother would understand."

"You were up to all sorts of stuff back in the day, huh?" He finished taking care of her wounds, moved the first aid supplies off the bed, and settled in next to her.

"You have no idea." She threw her arm over his chest, her head against his shoulder. "But that was a long time ago, hillbilly. I'm a different person now."

He pushed her wet hair out of her face. "What made you change?"

"Fear of prison." She sounded drowsy and he knew she'd be asleep soon.

So he found the sudden roaring coming from the woods behind his house really kind of annoying.

"Go," she murmured.

"What?"

Angie kissed his shoulder. "With your brothers. That's them, isn't it?"

Not even close, but he wouldn't expect her to know that and he didn't want her to worry.

"Go," she said again.

"You sure?"

Angie let out a satisfied sigh. "Are you going to France?"

"What? No."

"Then fuckin' go." She spoke without any malice or anger. Instead, she rolled onto her back, wincing a bit as the sheets rubbed against her wounded ass. "Go. Do. Whatever tigers do at night. When you get back, I'll be here."

She didn't cling. She didn't need him to hold her through the night until she fell asleep. In fact, he got the feeling she wanted some time alone. It suddenly occurred to him this woman didn't need him. She wanted him, but she didn't need him. She didn't need him to survive. She didn't need him to make her life better.

Angelina Santiago, where have you been all my life?

Nik straddled her hips. "You're amazing."

She stretched, enjoying how he looked at her. Really enjoying how he felt on top of her. "Aren't I though?"

He kissed her and for a second she thought he wouldn't be going anywhere. Finally, he pulled away, giving her one more kiss on the neck. "One sweep around, maybe a deer, then I'll be back."

"A deer?"

"I told ya. I get hungry after that kind of fuckin'."

"Charming."

"Yeah. You are." He kissed her again. Then shifted. Right on her lap.

"Okay," she stated simply. "If that becomes a habit, you're going to start freakin' me out."

Nik licked her cheek with that huge tiger tongue, dived off the bed, and out the window.

Angie turned over, the sheet wrapped tightly around her.

Well, she'd gone and done it. Fallen for a shapeshifting hillbilly who had no desire to attach himself to one woman. And since she didn't share...

Whatever. She wouldn't worry about that now. Not with that hand slapping over her mouth. Angie barely had time to struggle before they sprayed her face with something smelling like peppermint. The last thing she saw? Eyes reflecting at her in the darkness.

Nik followed those growls. He smelled tiger, but he couldn't place it as any kin or even a neighbor. Something wasn't right, which meant Angie wasn't safe.

He hadn't gotten far from the house when he found it. A top-of-the-line portable CD player with Surround Sound and next to it a modified scent dispenser.

Staring at it for only a moment, Nik turned around and started back to the house. But he didn't get far because they came out of the trees. Quietly. Moving as if they had all the time in the world. She-wolves. Smart. Mean. And one look at them told him they were as vicious as they come.

They didn't move on him, though. They watched him as he watched them. But he couldn't ignore that scent. Not the wolves. Not even the manufactured tiger scent. Something else all together.

A gestating female. A human one.

He spun around. She stood there. A black girl. Cute. Short. She kind of looked familiar. And in front of her a good-sized black she-wolf. It took him a moment to realize scars covered one side of the wolf's face.

"Hey, sunshine." The black girl shook her head, causing her mass of shaggy curls to drop into her eyes. "All I can say is—your boys snatched the wrong girl."

She raised a rifle. Nik let loose his threatening growl, charging the wolf protecting her, preparing to drop them both on their asses. But like Angie said, her friends were fast and brutal.

An explosion in his brain flipped him back. Then nothing.

Chapter Sixteen

She forced her eyes open. Her head throbbed. Her back hurt. She felt a slight pain in her upper shoulder. She sat up, slowly, and kept her eyes turned away from the large windows that had bright morning light streaming through them.

She waited until she felt like she could look around without throwing up, then she took in the room. It was her room. In Sara's house.

"I'll kill her." She'd kill them both.

She dragged herself out of bed, stumbling as soon as her bare feet touched the carpet. Leaning against the bed posts, she took a few seconds to let the nausea pass. Who knew what wacky, untested, non-FDA-approved shit Miki Kendrick had used on her. Angie reached up and touched her head. *Thank God.* She still had her hair. She glanced down at herself. Gold sweatpants and T-shirt. Well, at least the bitches got the color coordination right.

She took several steadying breaths. Once she had herself under control, she walked out of her room.

Angie didn't have to seek her friends out. She only had to follow the yelling. Not surprisingly, they were in the kitchen where the wolves seemed to congregate.

No one noticed as she walked in, so she let the swinging door close, and leaned against the doorjamb. Then she waited.

"Tell me where he is, Sara. Now!"

Angie recognized that look on Sara's face. Her "I'm not budging" look. Zach could yell until he was blue in the face, but it wouldn't make a difference. Sara wouldn't tell Zach anything until Sara wanted to.

Conall slammed his hand on the kitchen counter. "Tell him, Miki!"

"I said I don't know."

Zach turned on her. "How could you not know?"

"*'Cause I don't know!*" Miki wasn't lying. Angie could tell. Sara kept Miki out of at least that much so this wouldn't blow up between her and Conall.

Zach ran his hands through his hair as he paced around the kitchen. "If you two think tigers are an easy take down, you're nuts. And they protect their own. Trust me when I say they're headin' this way. Now..." He looked at Miki again. "*Tell me where the fuck he is!*"

"I said I don't know. *And stop yelling at me!*"

In exasperation, Conall turned away from his mate and toward her. In surprise, "Angie?" They all turned to look at her. "How ya feelin', hon?"

"Like I've been drugged."

Conall's face turned red and he swung on Miki. "*Miki!*"

"Hey! You said I couldn't drug you. You didn't say anything about drugging anybody else. Besides, I invented a cool new aerosol. It smells and tastes like peppermint."

Zach snarled. A sound that made Angie want to back up out of the room. Even Miki didn't test him. Only one woman existed who thought it just fine and dandy to play with the man at this particular moment.

Sara stood up, her chair scraping against the floor. "Don't

think for a second I don't know the part you played in this. And don't think you can scare me. You want the motherfucker so bad, you be a fuckin' bloodhound and track his ass down."

Angie didn't believe this. What the hell was Sara thinking? How the hell could she do this to Nik? What if he were lying somewhere really hurt? Did she take him somewhere or did she kill him? Question upon question swirled through Angie's brain. Questions she didn't have answers for. And the more unanswered questions that came up, the angrier she got.

Years of anger management went out the window and she launched herself at Sara. Her hands wrapped around her throat and Sara snarled, lips drawing back over bright white fangs. Sara drew her fist back to punch Angie in the face, but before either female could do even a modicum of damage, Zach had Sara and Conall drag Angie back.

The two women glared at each other, both taking in deep gasps of air.

Zach looked at Conall. "Let's everybody calm down." He released his hold on Sara as Conall let her go. Within seconds the two women were back at each other, hands wrapped around each others' throats.

Then Miki was there. Short she may be, but the woman knew how to handle two crazy bitches in a fight. She took handfuls of hair and snatched them both down to her level.

"Listen to me, 'cause I'm only saying this once. You two bitches back the fuck off or you'll both wake up tomorrow completely hairless. You remember how that feels, don't ya, Ang?"

"Yeah, but she—"

"She started this—"

Miki yanked their hair harder. She had them both twisted in such a way that neither of them could turn to snap her little neck.

"Maybe I wasn't fuckin' clear." She twisted her fists tighter.

"Okay! Okay!"

She shoved Sara away. "Go run or do whatever dog thing you need to do, but when you get back here, you better be fuckin' rational."

Sara opened her mouth to argue.

"Hair!" Miki shouted.

Growling, Sara threw open the sliding door, shifted, shook off her clothes, and ran.

Miki released Angie. "Could you guys please excuse us?"

Stunned and a little wary, both men left. Angie rubbed her head where her best friend almost ripped her hair out.

"She—"

Miki held up her hand. "Before you even start, let me say one thing to you. When Zach first showed up to get Sara, the Alphas thought about taking her. Just taking her and turning her. If that had happened, what would you have done? Honestly."

They both knew the answer. They both knew Angie wouldn't have rested until she made sure every shapeshifting bastard in the Continental United States ended up dead for taking her best friend.

Angie took a deep breath. Then another. "Just tell me—is he alive?"

Miki nodded. "Of course he is. She wanted to make a point. Not murder anybody. At least, ya know, not anymore. So he's definitely alive. But I don't know where he is."

Angie walked out of the kitchen, leaving Miki standing there. She went back to her room and grabbed up her cell phone. They'd taken all her stuff when they snatched her back.

Angie's new clothes were dumped in a corner the way dogs will do. They even brought her baseballs and bat.

A man answered. "Yo?"

"Derek. It's me."

"Hey, beautiful. Haven't heard from you in awhile."

"Been busy. Look, I have a job for you. I need you to find something for me. Something big."

CB ℘∽℘℘

Nik slowly opened his eyes. His head throbbed. His entire body throbbed. He hurt all over.

He glanced down at himself. He was still tiger. He hadn't shifted back. And he didn't think he'd be able to. At least, not for awhile. Nor was he dead. When that crazy wolf-lover pulled the trigger, he thought for sure he was dead. But instead she tranquilized him with something. *Damn geniuses.* They should keep them in special homes where they could do the least damage.

And where the hell was Angie?

Nik pushed himself up, but his back slammed into something. He blinked, forcing his eyes to focus. He looked around. Blinked again. Then looked around again.

I can't be...they wouldn't...

"Well, well. Look who's up. How ya feelin', big fella? I bet you're hungry."

Nik turned his head toward the male voice trying to soothe him.

"Man, you're huge. It's going to cost us a fortune to feed you, huh?"

Nik closed his eyes. He couldn't look at the man anymore. Not because of the man, but because of the shirt he wore. The shirt with "Northport Zoo" etched over the front pocket in bright orange.

Those crazy bitches put me in a zoo.

C3&0&O

Angie looked at her phone, but realized she'd heard a knock at the door. Her frustration mounted as the day moved on. She couldn't find any of Nik's kin. None of his siblings answered at the numbers Nik programmed into her phone in case of emergency.

She didn't want to panic. Because with her, panic would lead to anger. And the last thing she wanted to do right now was stab her friend in the face.

"Yeah?"

Zach stuck his head in. "You okay, Ang?"

She nodded and motioned him in with a wave of her hand. "The question is, are you?"

He shrugged as he leaned against the wall. Angie could see how much Sara's anger hurt him. True, the pair seemed to argue all the time, but always with a smile or a grope. But Sara had no teasing smile now. No soft caresses on the back of his neck. Nope. Sara was really and truly pissed off.

"I'm okay," he lied.

"She'll get over this, Zach."

He winced. "You sure?"

"I know the crazy bitch. Whatever she's got going on, she's gotten it out of her system. We both have."

"And who knew Miki could be all adult?"

For the first time in hours, Angie smiled. "She has her moments. They're rare. But they happen. Especially when she realizes Sara and I won't be."

"Look, Ang, just so you know. She and Miki were really broken up when we got the call from Marrec. And Marrec was fucking devastated."

Her birth parents may have forgotten her birthday completely but that didn't mean she didn't have family. Even if she did want to kill both her "sisters" at the moment.

"Yeah, we talked. He's okay now." Angie glanced at the man who loved her friend. His shoulders slumped in defeat, his eyes staring at a rather boring carpet. Poor guy. Could he be more depressed? "And thanks, Zach."

"For what?"

"For taking your sweet-ass time coming for me. I know it cost you."

He gave a little smile, probably his first in several days. "Oh, noticed that did ya?"

"Yeah. And I really appreciate it."

"So, tell me...was my sister right? Did you fall for him?"

Angie sighed and looked out the window.

Zach opened the door, muttering under his breath, "Great. Now we're gonna have a cat in the family."

CR SO RO

Finally, after two hours, the drugs wore off and Nik was back to his old self. He could shift back to human at any time. His only problem now?

They'd put his ass on display.

I hate those women.

He didn't even know them, and he hated them.

A small establishment near the Canadian border, the Northport Zoo was a place where Angie's friends apparently had lots of clout. From what he could overhear, the zoo officials would never release him among the other tigers for several months. But, it seemed, their "benefactor" had insisted. Against the department head's recommendations, they went ahead and placed Nik in a display behind unbreakable glass.

The full tigers watched him silently. All females. Thankfully. He would be less than happy if he had to take on some territorial male.

Well, this little adventure was only going to last through today. As soon as night came, he would get his furry ass out of here. Even if he had to scare some poor security guard to death. Then he would be heading to California. He had some dog butt to kick.

Sighing, Nik looked up to find a small child staring at him. A small child busy picking his nose.

Could this get any worse?

The females stirred restlessly near him and he caught the scent they had.

Oh no. Please. Not that.

They stood in front of him, completely unaware of his presence and arguing like two ten-year-olds.

Nik didn't bother searching for a way out. There was no way out. Those two evil witches trapped him. Trapped him in hell.

Throwing up his hands in anger, Alek turned away from Ban, facing the tiger display. Alek's gold eyes stared at Nik for a moment, a frown of confusion pulling his brows down. Then he smiled. And *then* he just became plain hysterical.

Bastard! This wasn't and never would be funny!

Ban stared at Alek for several confused moments before catching sight of Nik.

As his brothers literally rolled on the ground laughing hysterically—and freaking out all the zoo visitors—Nik seethed. At this point, he needed to know only one thing, and one thing only.

When Angie sent him off the night before, did she know her friends were waiting for him?

CB&D

Angie found Sara outside petting that ugly freakin' dog.

"I can't believe Zach hasn't found a way to get rid of him."

Sara didn't look up, just kept petting the ugly beast. Long strokes from the top of his head all the way down to his tail. He let her, too, sensing her need.

"I don't understand how anyone can hate Roscoe T," she murmured.

Angie reached over and stroked Roscoe's head. "True. He's ugly, but he's loveable."

With a half-smile, "You mean, kind of like me?"

Angie rolled her eyes. "Don't even try it, Morrighan."

Finally, Sara laughed. "Oh, come on. That was a perfect pity-me moment."

"I don't pity you for one goddamn second."

"Well, I tried." Sara pulled the dog over until he was on his back. She rubbed his belly with one hand while petting his head with the other. "And before you ask, I'm not going to tell you where he is."

"I know. I wasn't going to ask. You're such a stubborn bitch, why bother?"

"Good point." Sara tickled the ugly beast under the chin. "Isn't there something else you want to talk to me about, Santiago?"

Angie took in a deep breath. "Zach told you."

"He didn't have much choice. Besides, it was the perfect opportunity. I'm not speaking to him so I was forced to listen."

"Smart man." Angie scratched her head. "So, are you okay?"

"Why wouldn't I be? I found out my mother was kind of a power-hungry scumbag like her mother, which means I will be, too. So why wouldn't I be fine?"

Angie frowned. "What are you talking about?"

Sara let out a soul-deep sigh and Roscoe licked her arm. "I thought if my mom was sane, then I'd be sane. But she was just like her. She was just like that bitch. And I'm going to be just like her, too. I'm going to destroy everything I love and care about 'cause I got the Redwolf crazy gene."

"That's a load of shit, Sara. And you know it. We all know it."

Fifty feet away, Miki suddenly stumbled out of some bushes, pulling her short skirt down. She walked toward her friends on shaky legs.

Angie raised one eyebrow. "What are you doing?"

"Nothing."

Angie leaned back, her palms flat on the grass, her long legs stretched out and crossed at the ankles. "Then why do you look guilty?"

"Fuck you, I do not."

Sara shook her head. "I smell Conall all over you."

"I really need you to stop saying stuff like that to me," Miki growled. "It's freakin' me the fuck out."

Miki sat down across from her friends, rubbing her hands across Roscoe's flank. "So what are we talking about?"

"My mother."

"Oh, you mean the Don Corleone of the Magnus Pack?"

Angie sat up straight, as Sara, her face stricken, looked at Miki in horror. The Sara Angie remembered when Sara's grandmother still breathed suddenly re-surfaced with only a few words. It really didn't take much for close friends or family to put you back in that place you hoped you'd sprung out of.

She knew she had to do something quick or she'd lose Sara to the quagmire of her obsessive mind. "No, honey. Look at me. Don't look at her." Angie snapped her fingers in Sara's face to regain her attention. "Focus on me and not the crazy bitch sitting across from us."

"Hey!"

"Quiet, Kendrick." Angie focused on Sara. "I need you to hear what I'm saying to you, Sara. Are you listening to me?" Sara nodded. "Good. Look, I've never met your mother, and she may have been a Mafia princess in training, but she had friends. People who would kill for her and die for her. Your grandmother had nobody."

Angie took Sara's hand off Roscoe and gripped it tightly. She wanted to make sure her friend heard her loud and clear. "But in the end, none of that matters. None of it. Because you're not like either of them. You're Sara. The coolest chick I've ever met in my life. You've got a seriously hot man who thinks you walk on water, a pack of people who respect and fear you, and the entire shifter universe completely convinced you and your friends are dangerous psychopaths." Sara laughed at that. "And this whole Nik thing simply solidifies that. So, if I were you, I wouldn't worry about you becoming some power-hungry bitch. Do you know why?"

Wearing that gorgeous Sara smile, "No. Tell me, O' wise one."

"'Cause, my dear, you are too fuckin' lazy. If taking over the world requires you to get your fat ass up off the couch during football season—no one has anything to worry about."

"Do you really think my ass is fat?"

"Well, honey, it ain't small."

"I think we better be careful throwing stones from that glass house, Santiago."

"I can't believe you called me a crazy bitch," Miki cut in.

Angie dropped Sara's hand and turned on Miki. "The Don Corleone of the Magnus Pack'? *What exactly is wrong with you?*"

"Don't yell at me!"

Angie turned away from Miki, her hand up and in front of Miki's face. "We're done."

Miki growled, slapping Angie's hand out of her face. But instead of ripping into her, as Angie expected, Miki focused on Sara. "Don't worry, Sara. You're sane. Weird, but sane."

Smiling, Sara asked, "How the hell do you know?"

"Hey, dude. I've done the research. I've lived every day worrying that I'd cross that line between brilliance and madness."

"Brilliance?"

"Shut up, Santiago. Anyway, I know all the signs, I've taken all the tests. You're a freak, Morrighan, but you're not an
228

insane one."

"Good to know, Kendrick."

Miki grinned like she'd deciphered the Rosetta Stone.

But Angie did feel like she'd leaped her first big hurdle. Getting Sara to deal with the truth about her mother. Not easy, but Angie had done it. Next step...the truce. But this wasn't the time or place for that conversation. No, she'd have to ease Sara into that one. But Angie was determined to do it. And she had just the idea to help her start her stubborn friend down the path.

"I was thinking, once Nik is safe back in North Carolina and desperately trying to forget me—"

Both her friends snorted at that and rolled their eyes, but she ground her teeth together and barreled on, "I thought we could go shopping."

Sara, confused by the suggestion, stared at Angie. "Why?"

"Because that's what girlfriends do."

"*Normal* girlfriends. I can shift into a completely different species. And she's..." Sara glanced at Miki, "She's crazy."

"I am not. I took the test. I thought we just had this discussion."

CB&EO

"I know, Momma. I know." Nik covered the mouthpiece of the phone and motioned to Ban. "Call me," he whispered fiercely.

Ban, laughing, leaned back. "Nik. I need you."

With a grateful nod, he returned to his mother's rant about how she wanted all "dogs" put down for their insolence.

"Momma, I gotta go. Ban needs me."

"But you're okay, right?"

"Momma, I'm fine. Really. I'll call ya later."

"All right, darlin'. I love you."

"Love you, too."

Nik clicked off his phone.

"Love you, Momma," his brothers sang to him.

Growling, Nik chucked one of the pillows at them. His brothers, after a moment of staring at him, threw pillows back. They'd been hoarding, waiting for this moment. Nik slammed pillows back at them as fast as he could. They took cover behind seats and cried "incoming".

They kept it up a good five minutes before the captain came out of the cockpit and stared at them.

"I thought we had this discussion, Mr. Vorislav."

Nik sighed. "Yes, we did."

"No playing when the plane is in the air."

"Yeah, but—" Ban began, but the captain cut him off with one look.

"No playing when the plane is in the air. Do you understand me?"

The men nodded.

"I can't hear you."

"Yes," they answered in unison.

"Good."

The captain returned to his cockpit.

"That is the last time we hire Marines for that position."

"No shit. He's downright surly that one."

Nik sat back in his seat as his brothers lambasted another

man's good sense.

Unlike the captain, though, Nik knew exactly what his brothers were doing. Trying to get his mind off Angie. At least for the moment. They'd never say it, but they both felt guilty. By taking Angie they brought the wrath of the Magnus Pack's crazy Alpha bitch down on his head.

She could have killed him. Or, at least tried. But this revenge was much more eloquent. Proof to the cats they trifled with her and her kin at their own risk. If it hadn't been his butt waking up in the zoo, he would have thought the whole thing pretty damn funny. His brothers definitely did, once they knew he was basically okay. Apparently someone called Ban and told him exactly where to find Nik.

Ban swore it wasn't Angie. He said he'd know that sexy voice anywhere. So it must have been one of her friends. They'd made their point, so the rest was gravy.

Of course, none of that mattered. Nothing mattered until he knew the truth about Angie and her involvement in all this.

And definitely not until he fucked her again.

CB&CE

"Here. Try this." Angie took the lip brush and put a dark red lip gloss on Miki's bottom lip. She leaned back. "Nope. That's not working. It's too dark."

Angie wiped the lip gloss off Miki with a tissue. She needed to do something to distract herself from the current situation. Sara still wasn't telling her where she'd put Nik, Derek still hadn't phoned her back, and Nik's family still hadn't contacted her. She could imagine how angry his mother would be. And she couldn't quite get One-Eyed Grandma out of her head either. She'd have to call one of her great aunts back in Brazil. See if she could do a protection spell for the entire Pack.

"Wow."

Angie stood and went to her makeup case. "What's wrong?"

Miki looked up from the laptop she'd been studying for the past hour. "Having a baby is frickin' expensive."

Angie glanced at her. *Talk about coming to the party late.* "Yeah. They're expensive."

Miki let out a deep sigh and went back to her computer. Before Angie could ask her what her problem was, Conall muttering "hey" to one of the other wolves outside the door spurred Miki to sudden and swift action. She jumped up and began pulling her skirt off.

"What in hell are you doing?"

"I love this skirt."

"What?"

Conall walked in and looked at Miki, one eyebrow quirking up.

"Don't you dare, Viking! I love this skirt."

He sauntered toward her. "You couldn't love it that much. Remember the rules?"

"Stay!" she yelped, holding her hand out, palm showing. And the bitch of it? Conall did stay.

Wow, Nik was right. That does work on dogs.

Conall smiled and Angie watched her best friend melt.

"Come on, Miki-baby. We're going to pick up dinner. I think you need a break from this house."

"Cool." Miki charged off the bed, throwing her entire body at Conall.

Christ, the man is a two-hundred-year-old oak. Because he

didn't move a bit when Miki slammed into him. He grabbed her around the waist, her ankles locking at the base of his spine.

"Wanna come, Angie?"

"No, thanks. But bring me back something, would ya?"

"Sure."

She followed her friends out into the hall, then returned to her own bedroom. She closed her door, and headed to the bathroom for a shower. As she washed the day off, she wondered if Nik had made it home yet. She wondered if she'd ever hear from him again. Would she hear from any of the Vorislavs? She didn't realize until now how much the whole family had come to mean to her. But especially Nik. He'd come to mean more to her than she could possibly realize...until he was gone.

Angie no longer felt any anger toward Sara and Miki. How could she? Miki had been right. If this had been either Sara or Miki they took, she wouldn't have been nearly as nice. When she told Zach she wasn't the nice one of the three, in no way had she been joking.

But she could also understand wanting nothing more to do with her or her crazy friends. Because they were part of the package. Part of her. They were as much family to her as Alek and Ban were family to Nik. Not a lot of people understood that. The Pack learned but Sara didn't give them much choice. Marrec always knew. But Nik would probably never understand.

Angie shut off the water and stepped out, quickly grabbing a towel and drying off. As she towel dried her hair, she debated whether to try Nik's sisters one more time. But she wasn't sure she could handle anymore unanswered phone calls. It was starting to hurt her feelings.

Her own cell phone went off. She wrapped the towel around

her body and rushed back into her room.

"Yeah?"

"It's Derek."

She fought her desire to cry in frustration. "Well? What did you find out?"

"Not much. Not a lot of tiger info flowing around."

"That is not what I want to hear, Derek. He's out there. You need to find him."

"And exactly what do you need a tiger for?"

"That's none of your goddamn business what I need a tiger for. I just need you to find this one."

Angie heard a noise from below her window. She walked over quickly and looked down. Half the Pack as wolves ran out the back door and disappeared into the trees. *What the hell are they hunting?* Christ, did Nik's people show up to do a little dog damage? And was there anyway in hell she could stop the bloodshed?

"All right. All right. Calm down."

"No, Derek. I won't fucking calm down. Just do what I goddamn asked you to. How hard can it be to find a seven-hundred-pound tiger?"

"All right, I'll call you tomorrow."

It felt good to finally have someone to kick around a bit. And safe, because the man wasn't in front of her to kick around in person. No jail time! "No. You'll call me back tonight. Understand?"

"Yeah. Yeah."

"Don't give me that yeah, yeah bullshit. You're being lazy." Angie turned away from the window. "He's probably right under your...eep!"

The words died in her throat as she came face to face with one pissed-off hillbilly.

Chapter Seventeen

"I'm sorry? What was that? Right under my what?"

Angie stared at Nik. His gold eyes, hot on her, swept down her body and back up again. She suddenly felt like a stripper. A really *hot* stripper who had stolen his wallet.

"I gotta go, Derek." She could barely force the words out.

"Okay," he chuckled. "I'll call you later."

"No. Don't bother."

"Yeah, but you said—" She shut the phone closed.

She still didn't know Nik well enough to read the expression on his face. He sized her up almost like an animal wondering what you were doing on their territory just before they went for your throat.

Barely stopping herself from flinching, she allowed Nik to take the phone from her hand. He carefully placed it on the dresser. Then he casually shrugged himself out of his leather bomber jacket, letting it drop to the floor. Angie debated whether she should make a break for it. She couldn't read his face. Couldn't judge his expression. She wasn't scared, but that didn't mean she wasn't wary.

Nik stepped closer to her and Angie's stomach clenched. Simply having him near her turning her insides to liquid. He still hadn't taken his eyes off her, studying her face as if he hadn't seen her in two years as opposed to a mere twenty hours.

He leaned in, rubbing his cheek against hers. She held herself perfectly still, expecting more, but he did nothing else but rub his head against hers. Like the big cat he was. She allowed herself to relax a little. Allowed herself to simply feel him against her. She instinctively rubbed him back, slow circles against his neck and chin.

She felt him against her. Knew he was safe and well. And Angie's sense of relief nearly blinded her.

Good God, I'm in love with a hillbilly!

She closed her eyes tight against the enormity of her realization, willing herself not to panic. Willing herself not to blurt out her feelings like some pathetic female.

What nut case falls for a guy after knowing him for less than a week anyway?

You know, besides my two best friends?

Nik's right hand reached up, touching her cheek, sliding down her throat, and gliding down her body. His fingers moved over the towel, brushing her breast. Angie sighed at the contact, her hands reaching up to slide around Nik's shoulders. But, with a sudden and vicious snarl, he pulled back from her. He looked feral again. Like that night he'd come charging through her window.

Uh-oh.

Nik's outward calm ended. His hand, so gentle moments before, grabbed hold of her towel and snatched it off her body. He looked down the length of her naked body and growled low. She felt that sound all the way inside her pussy, reverberating against the walls of her womb.

Grabbing her arm, he dragged her over to the bed,

snatched the top bed sheet from it. He lifted her up by the waist and threw her facedown in the middle of it.

"Hey!"

Nik ignored her, quickly ripping a strip from the bed sheet. Angie struggled to get up, but he wrapped the Egyptian cotton around her wrist and the end to the bedpost.

Oh, he has got to be kidding!

"Can't we talk about this?"

"Naw."

Another strip of sheet, her other wrist tied to the bed.

"This isn't my fault."

"Yes it is."

"How ya figure?"

"They're your friends." She felt a strip wound around her right ankle. He tied that off and moved to her other leg.

"No. They're family. And you have to make allowances for family."

"Naw." He pulled her opposite leg out tight, leaving her open and exposed. And way vulnerable.

"Come on, Nik. This is ridiculous."

"Oh, so I'm Nik now am I? I thought I was just the hillbilly." He finished securing her to the bed.

She tugged experimentally at the bonds, but they held tight. She'd kill him. If he did anything remotely funky, she'd absolutely, fucking kill him.

Of course, she couldn't deny how damn turned on she was at the moment. Her nipples hard and rubbing against the sheet-less bed. Unable to close her legs. Unable to move.

Fucking hillbilly bastard!

Nik dug through a backpack he had with him, eventually

pulling out a box of condoms. He dropped those on the side table by her head.

Apparently he was a presumptuous fucking hillbilly bastard.

"Nikolai Vorislav, I swear to God—"

"Don't make me gag ya, sugar. 'Cause you know the mood I'm in right now, I'll do it in a New York minute."

Angie hissed at him and he began to take off his clothes. First the T-shirt, then the jeans, and tennis shoes. Finally the boxers. She swallowed. Why did his cock suddenly look ten times bigger than before?

Nik moved to the bed, staring down at her.

Anything even a tiny bit funky and she would absolutely kill him. No weird S-and-M shit. No spanking. And there better be no humiliation. Or the man would never see the light of day again.

He climbed up onto the bed with her and she tensed, her entire body cringing, waiting for his next move.

When he made it she practically jumped out of her skin and fought the restraints like a madwoman.

"Forget it, sugar. My momma made sure all her boys joined the Boy Scouts. Those knots were meant to hold. So you might as well relax."

"Get off me, Nik. Right fucking now."

He laughed at her. Laughed! At her! The slimy, hillbilly son of a bitch!

He did it again. His big fingers sliding up her ankle, her calf, to the back of her knee. Then sliding back down again.

"Stop! Now!"

"The more you bitch, the longer I do this. And your skin is so soft, I can do this forever."

Damn hillbilly!

His fingers slid across her back, down her spine, across her shoulder blades. Just goddamn all over.

The bastard kept touching her. Condoms unused. No moving toward any parts that needed to be stimulated. Instead, he ran his hands over her flesh, again and again and again. Why? Because he could. Because he wanted her to know exactly how much she belonged to him.

And fuck if she didn't belong to the man. Lock, stock, and Ferragamos. And definitely her heart. Terrified as she was to admit it, she got the feeling her heart would always belong to him. Whether the bastard hillbilly was in her life or not.

Nik watched his fingers glide across her soft brown skin. She'd been trying to find him. It kept playing through his mind as he gently tortured her body.

She hadn't set him up. She didn't even know where he was. Hearing her order that poor schlub around not only made him hard, but showed him how concerned she was for him.

The ice queen, hellcat, psychopath actually cared about *him.*

Angie buried her head in the pillow, her hands clenching and unclenching into tight fists. Smiling, he slid his fingers between her legs and played around the lips of her pussy. She moaned and pushed back against his hand.

He pulled his fingers away and she half moaned, half growled in anger and lust.

"What's the matter, sugar? You okay?"

"*Motherfuckingsonofabitchcocksuckerbastardassholeprick!*"

He chuckled and her whole body tensed up.

"Now is that anyway to talk to me?"

"When my friends find out you're here—"

"Naw, they're too busy chasing tigers around their territory. They won't notice us for hours."

She glared at him over her shoulder. "Your hillbilly brothers."

"Yup." He ran his fingers across the side of her breast, just grazing the nipple. She whimpered, but he circled right back around and concentrated on her forearm for a bit. "We used to play Find The Tiger with the Pack that lived down the way a bit from my daddy. They hated us 'cause they could never find us Vorislav boys. My brothers will have them dogs out there looking for hours."

Biting back a sob of rage, she again buried her head in her pillow.

"Oh, don't worry, sugar. We have plenty of time for me to find out what every part of your body feels like. I mean, you weren't in a rush or anything tonight, were ya?"

Eighteen hours? Twenty days? Ten minutes? Angie had no idea. She lost track after the first half hour or so. He caressed her. Touched her. Ran his fingers through her hair.

Then he started licking her. He started at the instep of her left foot and kept going from there. Every once in a while his fingers or tongue would stray to somewhere vital. Her pussy. Her tits. But stray was it.

Still, without touching any outright sexual part of her, she felt close to coming. But dammit, not close enough. Not nearly close enough.

Add in that she wanted him to fuck her more than life itself and he had himself one cranky Santiago.

She cursed him. She threatened him. His family. His

livelihood. His manhood. She even threatened his brother's dog. Nik would just give that damn chuckle she'd grown to hate while his tongue or fingers kept going.

Angie hated the man. Hated him. His family. His One-Eyed Grandma. She hated his lovely mother for birthing him.

Why didn't she keep a hold of that rodeo clown? She could have controlled him. He would have been too terrified to tie her up and *not* fuck her. And why oh why didn't Miki put shifters on her goddamn List?

Three of his big fingers slid inside her painfully empty pussy. "Want me to fuck you now, sugar?"

Angie panicked. *This is one of those trick cat questions, isn't it?*

He pulled those fingers out, only to slide them back in...once. "You need to answer me."

"Yes." He'd want her to beg or something wouldn't he? Something humiliating and demeaning to women everywhere.

"Then promise me you'll never leave me again."

Promise him I won't leave...? "I was kidnapped...again."

His fingers slipped out of her. "That is really not the answer I want."

"I promise." Who could she possibly be trying to fool? She'd beg him for anything now. Do anything he wanted. Absolutely anything to have his cock shoved inside her. *Anything.*

"I don't think you really mean that." He leaned over her again, his chest pressing into her back.

"I promise, Nik. I swear. Anything. Please..."

He nipped the flesh at the back of her neck. "Please what, sugar?"

"Please, Nik. Please fuck me."

He kissed her ear. "Anything you want, sugar. Absolutely anything."

Angie's entire body slammed forward as his condom-covered cock rammed into her, her legs pulled tight because of the bonds.

Oh, thank God, Angie thought desperately as her body shook and shuddered under Nik's hard body fucking her. *Thank God shifters aren't on The List!*

Nik tunneled his fingers into Angie's silky mass of hair and snatched her head back. His mouth descended on hers as her wet, hot pussy practically seared his cock off with its heat. He reached under her with his free hand, gripping one of her luscious breasts. Lord, he loved her body. Loved how her soft skin felt under his hands. Loved that she had hips and an ass he could truly enjoy.

He roughly thrust into her, knowing she could take it. Knowing she loved it. And she did. Her delicious snatch tightening around him. She moaned, uselessly pulling against her bonds. He smiled as she drenched his cock. It happened every time she fought the restraint, which only made him crazier.

The girl worked him like no one ever had. She made him hot, made him laugh, and sometimes just pissed him the hell off. He couldn't imagine going back home without her. He had no intention of even trying.

She owned him and didn't even know it.

Against his lips, "Goddammit, Nik. God!"

He grinned and he kissed her again, never tiring of her mouth. She came like that, too, her cries sliding down his throat, filling his heart.

Nik wanted to hold on longer for her, but he couldn't. Not with her pussy strangling the hell out of his dick.

He shuddered violently, pumping hard and fast as he came and came.

Nik dropped on top of her and the two lay like that trying to catch their breaths.

Wow, she really did love the fucker. She let him tie her up and she didn't even scream. At least, not in fear or anything.

Nik pulled himself up and out of her. He quickly disposed of the condom and undid her bonds, rubbing each arm and leg to get the blood flowing. When done, he grabbed the comforter off the floor, dragging it onto the bed and over his hips and her legs.

"You okay, sugar?"

Angie nodded as Nik laid his head on her breasts and wrapped his arms around her waist. He nestled down, finally letting himself relax. She pulled her knees up a bit, allowing him to rest in the vee of her body. Whether as cat or man, he seemed to enjoy being between her legs.

She stroked his head and the two began to fall asleep, their bodies locked together.

The perfect fit.

So she found the bedroom door suddenly slamming open really fucking annoying.

Angie's head snapped up as Miki stormed in. A rifle with scope in her hands.

"Miki!"

"Hold on, Ang." Miki marched over the bed and to the window. "This is gonna be sweet." Miki pushed the glass window open, her eyes locked on something. Angie knew that look. Miki got it during hunting season.

"What the fuck are you doing?" Angie demanded.

Miki steadied the rifle in her hands, aiming it at the ground below the window. "Gettin' myself a tiger-skin rug."

Angie felt Nik's body tense and knew exactly who Miki had the nerve to aim her damn rifle at.

"*Miki Marie Kendrick!*" she bellowed.

"Don't yell at me when I'm aiming. I find it distracting."

"*Miki!*"

Sighing, Miki lowered the gun and turned around, "*What?*"

"Can you not see I'm a little busy?"

"But...tiger-skin rug," she whined.

"No."

"What? 'Cause of him?" Miki pointed at Nik, who still hadn't lifted his head off Angie's chest. He didn't seem to be a man easily shaken.

Miki was in her "zone", too. So Angie pulled out her psychotherapist voice. Soft, lilting, and intensely calm. "Well, this is a little awkward, don't you think? Remember when we talked about awkward things and how you should avoid making people feel that way?"

Miki rolled her eyes. "Yes."

"Well then..."

"Fine!"

Miki marched away from the window, back over the bed, stopping at the doorway. She turned and glared at Nik. "But you better stay on her good side." She smiled, but it was in no way a friendly one. "Otherwise, that furry ass is mine."

She turned to walk out, but Conall suddenly appeared. "What are you doing? And where did you get that rifle from?"

"Marrec sent it to me. Nice, huh?"

He pulled it out of Miki's hands. "I think we need more rules." He picked her up by the waist and walked out.

Angie let out a breath. "I am so afraid to ask what he meant by that."

She glanced down at Nik. The man hadn't moved. His head still firmly planted between her breasts.

"Comfortable, Nik?"

"Yup."

"Well, well what do we have here?"

Angie didn't even hear Sara come into the room, but she'd bet money Nik had.

"Could you leave?" she snarled.

"My house." Sara stepped closer to the bed, her arms crossed in front of her chest. She nodded at Nik. "Hillbilly."

"Canine."

Angie's head dropped back to her pillow. Could these shifters be more obnoxious?

"So? Where is it?"

"Where's what?" Nik asked.

"My apology?"

"For what? Doin' what you dogs couldn't?"

Sara growled and Angie wondered if it would be wrong to wear bright red to either of their funerals, 'cause she wasn't sure who she might kill first.

Angie looked around the room. *Where* did *she move that bat?*

She wasn't surprised when Zach walked in. *Why not?* Maybe they could get the rest of the Pack, the NFL, and the entire Vienna Boys Choir, too, to come check out Angie naked.

Zach stood next to Sara. "Vorislav."

"Sheridan."

Zach looked at his mate. "So...we're done?"

Sara started in surprise and glanced at Angie. Angie knew what Sara thought he meant. But he couldn't mean that. Not Zach. Of course, Sara would guess the worst as always and think Zach meant he was done with *her*. Not likely. Although what Sara put him through over the last few days—really, there was only so much a man could take.

And, as usual, Sara wasn't about to fight for any man. "Yeah. Fine. We're done. Whatever."

"Good."

He grabbed Sara and tossed her over his shoulder.

"Hey!"

"Quiet." He nodded to Angie. "See you in the mornin', Ang."

"Night, Zach."

"Put me down, Zacharias."

Turning on his heel, Zach walked toward the door, his hand reaching up and slapping Sara hard on the ass. "Don't you *ever* freeze me out like that again."

"Put me down!"

"I'm going to put you down. Then I'm gonna fuck ya senseless. And I'm not even going to care whether you enjoy it."

Sara grabbed his ass. "Well, I guess I'm gonna have to put up a fight then. Hope you still have some bandages in the bathroom."

Zach slammed the door shut, and Nik finally lifted his head from her chest, looking deep into her eyes as Sara yelled down the hallway, "Shopping tomorrow!"

"I told you, hillbilly," Angie sighed. "Family."

"I see it now, sugar. 'Cause only family can embarrass you that much."

Chapter Eighteen

Nik reached for her but his hand touched nothing but empty cotton sheets. "Angie?" He pushed himself up on his hands, trying to get his eyes to focus. His body so exhausted from the last two days. Fuckings. Kidnappings. More fuckings. It took a lot out of a man.

He sniffed the air, but he caught her scent everywhere, including all over him. "Angie?"

"What?" She stepped out of the closet, the door partially closed and completely blocking her from his view. She wore nothing but a pair of denim shorts, cowboy boots, and a black lace bra. She looked good enough to eat. His cock stirred and so did he.

"Come here."

"Why did you call me?"

"No reason. Just come here."

She grinned. "Were you worried about me?"

"No."

"Wondering where I disappeared to?"

"No."

"Aw, Nikolai, that's so sweet."

"Shut up." He yanked the comforter over his head. He felt her straddle his back, probably still wearing those boots.

"You are so crazy about me you don't know what to do with yourself."

She may be joking, but she had no idea how close to the truth she was. "Shut up."

She grabbed the comforter and tried to pull it off, but he held tight. "Admit it. You can't fight it." Nope. And he'd stopped trying.

"This conversation is pissin' me the hell off."

She tugged enough of the comforter away to be able to push her face in next to his. "Say it, you big kitty."

"No."

She actually *tsk, tsk*'d him. "Denial is an ugly place to live, hillbilly." She leaned in and kissed Nik on the cheek. Such an innocent, sweet touch that almost had him spontaneously coming.

How did he let this happen? How did he let this woman get into his life and under his skin? He blamed his father. Yup. Definitely his daddy's fault. Nik had defective tiger genes because of that man. Well, at least he knew his mother would make the man suffer as much as she could possibly manage.

That had to be worth something...

Angie knew she should stop teasing the man. If she kept it up, she'd probably scare him off and she wasn't even remotely done with him or his big thighs.

Smiling, she slipped out of bed, and started to walk away, but his long arm reached out and his big hand caught her around the wrist.

"Where you goin'?"

She tugged, trying to pull her arm out of his grasp. "Out with Sara and Mik, shopping."

"No. Stay." He pulled her onto the bed. Giggling, she turned her back to him, trying to get off the bed. But he wrapped his big arms around her and pulled her into his body. "Besides," he whispered in her ear, "I still didn't have my breakfast."

Angie bit her lip. *Dammit!* Much more of this and she'd forget all about promising anything to anybody. But today was more than about shopping. She needed to make sure all was right with "her girls" and to start gently easing Sara down the path to "Truce-ville". So, any fun with Nik would have to wait until her return.

Shit. Why couldn't she be selfish about her love life like other women? Friends were supposed to take a backseat. *Damn, damn, damn.*

"Later. Nik!" She caught his hand as it started to unclasp the front of her bra. "Sara's waiting for me."

"She'll wait. You'll find her sittin' by the door, just waitin'...your slippers in her mouth."

Angie, fighting a laugh, slapped his hand. "That's not funny. And get your hands out of my shorts."

"Come on, sugar. Just a little somethin'."

Knowing that if she didn't get out now, Sara and Miki wouldn't see her for another hour—or two—Angie dragged herself out of Nik's arms.

She dropped to the floor. "Bad kitty!" She picked herself up. "Honestly. A girl isn't safe with you hillbillies."

Nik snuggled stomach down into the bed, his arms wrapped around one of the pillows. His muscles bulging as he flashed her a sleepy smile. "You like us hillbillies, sugar. Admit it."

If she said yes to anything, she'd say yes to everything.

"I gotta go." She backed up to the door. She couldn't stop

looking at him. Stretched out on the bed, his naked ass calling her name. She picked up a T-shirt from off the floor, knowing she had to get the hell out of Dodge before all her best intentions went out the window.

She gritted her teeth. Honestly, the crap she did for her friends.

Slamming into the door, she grabbed the door handle, wrenched it open, and quickly left.

Angie found Miki and Sara in the kitchen. Whoever Sara had on the phone, they were doing all the talking, because Sara only grunted and nodded. Grunted and nodded.

Angie sat down next to Miki at the table.

"You ready to go shopping?"

"No. I have no money." Miki flipped the page of the catalog in front of her, barely glancing at her friend. "Nice T-shirt by the way."

Angie looked down at what she wore and rolled her eyes. "If you can't play with the big dogs, get off the porch" emblazoned across the blue tee in white letters.

"Oh, you have got to be kidding."

"In a rush this morning were we?"

"Don't start, Kendrick. And what do you mean you're not going?" If Miki didn't go, then why did Angie leave a randy hillbilly all by his lonesome upstairs?

Miki slammed the catalog down on the table. "I can't afford any of this shit."

Angie looked at the cover of the catalog. A baby furniture catalog. "And why is that?"

"Because being a professor doesn't exactly pay for the high life."

"I thought you didn't want to teach."

"I don't, but I need the money."

Sara hung up the phone and walked over to the table as Miki continued. "Conridge got me an offer from the university. If I wanted it."

Angie picked up an apple. "Who?" Miki and Sara stared at her. "What?"

"Do you not listen to me at all?"

"I listen. When I find it interesting. Why? Who the hell is he?"

"My professor. Big fight with the hyenas. *She* watched me shoot a man in the knees."

Angie shrugged. "Still nothin'."

Sara flopped into one of the chairs. "She's married to Van Holtz of the Van Holtz Restaurant chain. Filthy rich."

"Oh! *That* Conridge."

Miki rolled her eyes. "You're amazing."

"Thank you."

Sara brought her knee up, bracing it against the table, and used her other leg to rock her chair back and forth. Seemed some people never learned. Sara did that in junior high, fell back and busted her head open.

Angie shook off the image of a blood-covered Sara. "Miki, are you not staying with Conall? Did you decide to leave him?"

"I'm staying, ya know, for now." Angie barely stopped herself from laughing in the girl's face. Miki wasn't going anywhere. She loved the big bear too much. It leaked from her every pore. "But I need the job. I can't take money from a man with no money."

Sara and Angie frowned at each other.

Sara shook her head. "What the hell are you talking about?"

"I'm not living off the Pack, Sara. It's that simple."

"That's great and all, but Conall has his own money."

"I'm not going to spend the man's life savings."

"You couldn't spend Conall's life savings if you bought Scotland."

Miki, her frown so deep it changed the contours of her face, glared at Sara.

"What the hell does that mean?"

"The Víga-Feilans. They're rolling in money. In fact, his father bought this house for the Pack. As a thank you for letting them in."

Miki gripped the table with her fingers, but didn't speak.

"And Conall's money is separate from his dad's. But he'll inherit what they have, and since he's an only child, he'll quadruple what he has now. So, I really wouldn't worry about—"

Miki stood. "*Conall!*" Her screech startled Sara, who pushed a bit too hard and sure enough ended up hitting the floor.

Angie stared up at her friend. "What the fuck is wrong with you?" If this was how she was during the beginning of her pregnancy, the next nine months would be absolute hell.

Miki seethed. Her hands clenched at her side. Her teeth gritted together. "If he has all the money, he has all the power."

Sara dragged herself off the floor, one hand rubbing the back of her head. "You sure you passed those sanity tests?"

Conall strolled into the kitchen. "You bellowed?"

Miki pulled out a chair and stood on it—now they were almost at eye level. "You're rich! Filthy, stinking, disgusting rich!"

"I guess technically—" Conall stopped when Miki's fist hit his solar plexus.

"Ow!" Miki shook her hand out.

Conall didn't even flinch. "Why do you insist on doing that?"

C3❀C3

Angie held the black credit card in her hand. "I want you to realize the enormity of this situation."

"Oh, good God," Miki moaned.

"He handed you his black credit card and said 'buy what you want, Miki-baby'. First off the man *has* a black credit card. Second, he didn't flinch when he gave it to you."

Miki snatched the card back. "This is a stupid conversation. It's a fucking credit card."

The trio walked through the enormous department store. A Pack of shapeshifting females behind them. These women were clearly not in their element. The only black leather Fallons offered had Chanel stamped on it. No wonder Sara and her rough-and-tumble Pack knew nothing about this shifter-run store.

"It's not a fucking credit card. It's a commitment."

Miki shook her head. "You make me sad."

Sara sputtered out a laugh, but it died in her throat as she stopped walking. She grabbed a plaid business suit that would look perfect on her with a string of pearls.

"Explain to me again why we're here?"

"Because we're doing the girlfriend thing, and going

shopping."

"Can't we go to Old Navy?"

"No. We had the Old Navy discussion. And no GAP. And no Harley-Davidson store. So get the fuck over it people."

She smiled, making all the she-wolves take a step back. "Okay, let's go then!"

Angie started walking. "Now I was thinking we start off in the dresses, maybe hit the juniors section for Miki..."

"Hey!"

"...and then get makeovers!"

Angie ignored the whining behind her. *Like trying to put a muzzle on a dog.* She turned a corner and watched a woman walk toward her. For a moment, she thought her another she-wolf because of the big leather jacket. But even she was too grubby to be a she-wolf with her worn high-top Keds that had small holes, her jeans that had definitely seen better days, and Angie would swear the oversized Bob Marley T-shirt the woman wore might have been owned by the man himself.

"Can we go, please," the woman sniped at the gorgeous and much-taller blond women behind her. "I've never been so bored before in my entire existence."

"Could you at least *pretend* to be female," one of the women tossed at her.

Miki came up beside Angie and she grabbed onto the smaller woman by the scruff of her black T-shirt, holding her back, quickly noting the .45 she had holstered to the back of her jeans.

"What? What's wrong?" Miki looked up, locking eyes with the small blonde. "I know you. You're that bitch that was hittin' on Conall."

Startled, the woman still managed to grin. "I was not

hitting on him."

Sara walked up. "I keep smelling cat—is that you?"

"No, it's..." Angie glared at her. "That's not funny!"

"Sara Morrighan?"

Sara looked over at what Angie now knew was Victoria Löwe. Angie may be trying to take things slow but whatever powers ruled the universe clearly had other ideas.

Sara's fangs burst from her gums, her lips drawn back in a snarl.

"Sara!" Wolf eyes turned to Angie. "Be nice."

The female wolves moved up. Angie could feel their aggression swirling around them.

They started to pass the three friends, but Sara held her hand up. "Hold it." The she-wolves stopped as the lion females stood around Victoria. They were so much taller than the little lioness, she almost disappeared.

Angie, taking a deep breath, stepped forward and in between the two groups of females. "Victoria."

She nodded. "Angelina."

"I'd like you to meet Sara." Angie turned and smiled at her friend. "And Sara, this is Victoria Löwe."

The two women eyed each other cautiously as their females waited for someone to make the first move.

Angie should have seen it coming. Should have been ready for it. But, for some unknown reason, she wasn't.

"You're awfully tiny to be a lion." Miki crossed her arms in front of her chest and smiled. "Sure your mother wasn't doing a mountain lion on the side or something?"

Angie closed her eyes and growled.

CR೮Ꝺ

Nik walked down the stairs, his hands running through his wet hair. He paused at the bottom step, a smile breaking across his face.

He walked into the enormous living room and found his brothers stretched out on two of the five couches, watching TV and playing with what had to be the ugliest dog Nik had ever seen in his life.

"What are y'all doin' here?"

"We thought about leavin'..." Ban began.

"Especially after that tiny little midget girl tried to shoot us last night."

"But we're havin' so much fun here..."

"And that big blond guy said we could stay awhile," Alek finished.

Nik raised an eyebrow at his baby brother. "You're hopin' that dog's sister shows up."

"It's good for a man to have dreams."

"Pathetic." Nik yawned then nodded toward the kitchen in the back of the house. "Did ya leave any food?"

"Not really."

"And did those wolves get cranky about it?"

"You could say that." Ban made room on the couch for the dog to jump up next to him. "A few of 'em went out to get more."

"But they were not happy about it."

Nik climbed over the back of the couch and sat down next to Alek, plopping his feet up on the coffee table.

"So did you two love kittens make up?" Ban asked.

Nik stretched, feeling damn good about himself. "Somethin' like that."

"And let me guess," Alek continued, "she's *really* off limits now."

More than ever.

He'd made Angelina Santiago his. Every time he fucked her last night—and he'd fucked her all night long—he'd made her his.

But he wasn't in the mood to discuss that with his two idiot brothers. Not yet.

He held his hand out. "Remote."

Alek dropped it in his palm.

"All I gotta say is them Yankees need to hurry the hell up. I'm starvin'. Even that dog is lookin' mighty tasty."

Ban, the protector of all things except deer, elk, rabbits and cows, hugged the dog to him "That's not funny."

"Yes it is."

CB ∞ ∞

"You're shopping?" Miki demanded.

Angie shrugged. "What do you expect me to do? Just stand here? Besides, these Manolo Blahniks are adorable."

"Oh, for the love of all that's holy."

"You want a pair?"

"No!"

"No need to get tense. You're getting so moody. Must be that Pack baby."

"Stop calling her that!"

Miki sat on one of the benches.

One of the lions walked up to Angie. "What do you think?"

Angie looked at the shoe in her hand. "Bad color for you, hon. Try blue."

"Thanks."

Miki snorted in disgust. "You have got to be fuckin' kidding me."

Angie finished fixing the straps on the shoes she decided to try on. Standing up, she moved to the mirror. The salesman stood next to her. "Wow. Those look amazing on you."

She looked at herself in the mirror. "You know...you're right. These *do* look amazing on me."

Seconds after Miki made a grunt of annoyance, a sound rang out over the entire floor of shoes and accessories that stopped every wolf and lion in their tracks.

Sara's laugh.

They all turned to look at the two women huddled over in the far corner of the shoe department. Victoria had removed her denim jacket. Her sleeveless Bob Marley T-shirt showed off a Jimi Hendrix tattoo on one shoulder. Her jacket slipped to the floor. When Victoria bent to retrieve it, Angie spotted a Robert Plant tattoo on the other shoulder.

"Interesting," Miki muttered. "I bet if you looked at her high school notebooks they're covered in that stupid Van Halen logo, too."

Angie chuckled as one of the salesgirls returned with a dress for her. "How about this?"

Taking the dress by the hanger, Angie looked at it carefully. Dark red and backless, she debated whether to get it for Sara's party. She knew Nik would love her in it.

Christ, how pathetic am I?

"What do ya think, Mik?"

"What do I think? I think that lion females are really lesbians and the males are used strictly for their sperm."

Angie's head snapped up. "Miki!"

She gave that damn innocent smile. "What? It's just a theory."

The she-wolves looked down at the floor to hide their laughter while the lions glared. Well, most of them glared. One just grinned. Angie didn't have time to analyze that, instead grabbing Miki by the scruff of the neck and dragging her past the staring wolves and lions toward the dressing room.

"I swear, Kendrick. I can't take you anywhere."

"Don't blame me 'cause these bitches have no sense of humor. And you know I'm right."

Angie found the dressing room. Since it was still relatively early, there were very few customers and she had a feeling she'd have the place all to herself. *Good.* She hated fighting with a bunch of bitches over some space.

Still gripping Miki by the neck, the pair walked around the corner into the enormous room, separated into eight big dressing rooms. Busy trying to figure out which room to grab, Angie slammed right into a woman.

Dianne Leucrotta stepped back with a curse. They looked at each other and Angie almost winced at what she saw. A deep jagged gash slashed across the woman's face. From one temple, across and under her lip. And unlike Nik's wounds from the toilet and even her own, Leucrotta's still hadn't really healed. And Angie wondered if they ever would.

"Wow, I totally fucked up your face." Then Angie punched her. Leucrotta grabbed her nose and stumbled back away from them. Angie pushed Miki back and punched Leucrotta again.

"Jesus, Angie!"

"Get Sara." She grabbed the hyena by the hair and slammed her face first into one of the dressing rooms.

CB∞EO

It wasn't until someone kicked his legs that Nik woke up. Alek, snoring beside him, his head resting on his shoulder. Ban snoring on the other couch, the noise rivaled only by the dog.

He looked into the impossibly cranky face of Zach Sheridan. "Y'all get food?"

"We had a full refrigerator before you three got here."

"Where I come from, we don't let the refrigerator get empty."

"Where you come from, you marry your sister."

Before Nik could rip the man's head off—literally—Alek snapped awake. "Your sister's here?"

Snarling like a rabid dog, the wolf stomped off.

Alek winked, gave an evil chuckle, and stood up to head to the kitchen.

Nik really did have the *best* family.

CB∞EO

"You have no idea how happy I am that you're here, Ms. Leucrotta. You're exactly what I needed to make this day perfect."

As she threw Leucrotta to the floor, Sara and Victoria stormed in, Miki right behind them. They stopped and stared at the bleeding Leucrotta on the floor.

"Jesus, Angie," Sara groaned in exasperation. "I thought you worked this out in therapy—and what is that smell?"

Victoria's head tilted to the side. "Hyena."

Sara growled. "This is her?" Sara looked at Angie. "The one that came after you?"

"Yes. Notice the Louis Vuitton–damaged face."

Miki grinned. "Nice, Santiago."

Leucrotta tried to push herself up off the floor, so Angie slammed her back down with her foot. She really did like how these shoes looked on her.

"I was thinking, instead, of the two of you coming up with a truce. Maybe we could involve all three."

Angie felt the air change, the tension build, and she knew Leucrotta was shifting right under her feet.

Miki, snatching the .45 out of its holster and pulling the slide back, snarled, "You shift, bitch, and it will be the last thing you ever do."

Leucrotta let out a breath and the air surrounding them returned to normal. She'd stopped the process.

Victoria looked at Sara. "I am *really* starting to like your friends."

CR80BO

The male wolves watched as the tigers proceeded to eat and eat and eat, clearing out most of the new groceries they'd brought into the house.

Few were ever ready to see tigers feed when they were truly hungry. And the Vorislav boys were mighty hungry.

Conall watched Ban finish off a plate of fried chicken legs.

"I don't think I've ever seen anything as disturbing as what I just witnessed. And I've seen Miki dance." He looked at Zach. "If they stay for Sara's party, we're going to need another cow for the barbeque."

C8૬૦80

Sara crouched beside Leucrotta. "You're probably wondering why we haven't killed you yet."

"Although we're sorely tempted," Victoria added. She'd taken over Angie's spot after dispatching her females along with Sara's she-wolves to go deal with any lurking hyenas. Plus she seemed to really enjoy having her foot in the back of the woman's neck. Much more pressure and Angie figured she just might snap the bone.

"See, this is the deal," Sara continued. "We could kill you, but then this would keep going on. And we're tired."

"But you can't be trusted."

"Exactly, Victoria. A stereotype against hyenas, true. But we have no choice but to note past behavior. And this past behavior forced us to turn to each other to create a truce." Sara stood up and preceded to move around the room. "See, before, you guys could keep having all that fun at our expense because we were killing each other anyway."

"But we've created a truce that applies to the Cat Nation."

"And most of the Packs. Although, if I were you, I wouldn't approach the Víga-Feilans. Even though they're not our friends, they're really mean on principle."

Sara stood over Dianne Leucrotta now, staring down at her. "And do you wanna know what this truce means to you?"

"Ooh! Let me tell her," Victoria begged mockingly.

"Oh, Victoria, please be my guest."

Still not moving that well-placed foot, Victoria crouched down. She dug her hand into Leucrotta's brownish-gold locks, brutally yanking her head back. "It's simple. You fuck with us— *any of us*—and you'll have every cat, every canine within the U.S. and Canada coming after your hyena ass."

Sara crouched down again. "But the beauty part—we'll make sure to take out a few Clans on our way to you. When they find out this is all your fault, those hyenas will turn on you. There'll be no place safe for you. No place safe for your family, friends, any of 'em."

Leucrotta didn't answer, merely stared at the pair.

Sara looked at Victoria. "I don't know, Vic. I'm not sure she's hearing us clearly."

"I think you're right."

"Fine." The two women stood. "Deal with it, Mik."

Miki stepped forward and for the first time Angie heard Leucrotta's voice...as she begged for her life.

"Wait. Wait!"

"Too late." Miki aimed the gun at her face.

"No! No! No!"

Victoria ground her foot into the back of Leucrotta's neck. "I don't think I heard the right words," she bit out between gritted teeth.

"We'll stop. I swear it."

Victoria looked up at Sara. "What do you think, Sara? You believe her?"

After a pause. "No. Miki take her."

"*No! I swear! I swear!*"

The women glanced at each other. Finally, Sara looked at Angie.

"What do ya think, Santiago?"

Fighting the smile of pride she had for her friend at the moment, Angie nodded in agreement. "I say we give her a shot."

"Cool!" Miki aimed her gun again.

"I meant a chance, psychopath."

"Damn."

Victoria removed her foot from Leucrotta, but before the hyena could stand, Sara again crouched in front of her, both her hands buried in the woman's hair. She pulled her head back, their faces so close they could have been lovers.

"Listen to me carefully. If anything else happens to my friends, there is no place in this universe where you'll be able to hide..." Sara's voice dropped impossibly lower, "*...from me.*"

With that, Sara stood, dragging the woman with her. She put her on her own two feet. Pale, shaking, completely terrified, it seemed amazing Leucrotta hadn't pissed on herself.

Sara stepped back and Leucrotta moved toward the exit.

"Oh." Leucrotta's whole body clenched in fear at Sara's voice behind her. "And one more thing..."

Slowly, Leucrotta turned. "Yes?"

Sara glanced at her friend. "Angie?"

Angie stepped forward, slamming her fist into Leucrotta's face. The hyena's head smashed into the mirror behind her, destroying it as her body dropped like a ton of bricks. She probably wouldn't be moving for several long minutes, giving both Pack and Pride time to get out of the store and avoid a full-on confrontation. And Angie still owed the bitch for her ruined Louis Vuitton bag.

Sara smiled. "You always had the best right hook."

"Remember that boxer I dated? He taught me that—and not to use my teeth during blow jobs."

Miki locked her gun, shoving it back in its holster. "Well that was information I could have lasted a lifetime never knowing."

C3𝖘〇𝖘Ɔ

They all stared at the television. Twenty male shapeshifters quietly watching *The Howling*.

"If shifting was always that painful," Conall muttered more to the couch he lay sprawled across than to anyone else, "I'd never do it."

"Who put this piece of shit in anyway?" Zach demanded.

"No one. It's on cable."

Zach lifted his head off the floor. "Then why the fuck are we still watching it?"

Conall pointed across the room. "Because the remote is over there."

They all looked at the simple electronic device. At the moment, it looked miles away.

"Well who the fuck put it way the hell over there?"

Ban's hand shot up. "Sorry. That was me."

Zach laid his head back on the floor. "Damn hillbillies."

"We prefer the term redneck," Nik muttered.

They all fell into another sleepy silence, until Alek's head snapped up. "Y'all smell that?"

Conall jumped up as the banging on the door started. By the time he reached the hallway, they all stood behind him. He pulled the door open and six Pride males pushed past him. Big. Well-dressed. Boring.

"Where are they?" the lead one roared.

Zach crossed his arms in front of his chest. "Where are who?"

The lion, fangs bared, stood in front of Zach. He was taller than the wolf, but Nik was impressed the Alpha didn't back down. Instead, Zach looked kind of amused.

Ban nudged Nik. "Look, it's the pretty kitties."

One of the lions glared at Ban. "And look what we have here...alley cats. Why am I not surprised to find them hanging out with the dogs?"

Alek growled low, but Nik kept him under control with a hand on his shoulder. "Now, now, Alek. You should never attack a man brave enough to wear those shoes."

"Where are our females?" the leader demanded again. "I got a call saying they were coming here."

"Coming here?" Zach shrugged. "Sorry, don't know anything about it. But tell me, do you lose your pussies like this all the time?"

Fangs burst from gums and bodies began to shift. The lion tackled Zach the wolf. Conall, shifting quickly, went after them. Nik watched another lion go for Conall, and his Southern sense of honor wouldn't allow some lion pricks to abuse his hosts, so he shifted and threw himself at the big gold beast. But his weight shoved them all through the open door and out onto the stairs.

They fell in a mass of snarling, snapping claws and fur. He felt fangs sink into his hind leg, but it lasted only a second as Ban grabbed the lion by the scruff of the neck and tossed him away.

Nik landed on the back of another lion, pushing him off Zach. They rolled a few feet trying to get a good hold, but instead crashed into a gorgeous set of legs.

"Dude! The new shoes!"

Nik and the lion looked up to see a group of women calmly watching them. In fact, someone had pulled out a bag of chips and started sharing.

Angie reached down and brushed the top of her shoes. "Do you have any idea how hard it is to get cat hair off anything?"

She shook her head, grabbed some shopping bags and headed toward the house. "See you ladies later. I'm exhausted." She turned on those gorgeous heels. "And don't forget. All of you are coming to Sara's birthday party. Right?"

A small woman, who smelled like lion but based on her clothes and height alone simply couldn't be, nodded. "Absolutely." She looked at Sara. "Perfect time to solidify the truce, don't ya think?"

"Sure. Whatever. Wanna see the bikes?" Sara walked off toward the garage, female lions and wolves following behind her.

Miki started to follow, but Angie called her from the front door. "Get your ass up here, Kendrick."

"I wanna go—"

"No. Because apparently we have no impulse-control during this breeding process when it comes to that mouth, now do we?"

Stomping around the male lions, wolves, and tigers at her feet as if they were stuffed toys, Miki headed up the stairs. "I can't tell you how much I hate that fuckin' psychotherapist voice you put on."

"Well, when one is dealing with a nut..."

The door slammed shut behind the two human females while the shifter females disappeared among the motorcycles.

The males stared at each other, eventually withdrawing claws and fangs from vital organs. A little blood spilt but not much.

Nik wondered what they'd do next. Fighting seemed kind of wrong now that the females had a pact. But he didn't have to wonder or worry long. A small group of deer ran past heading deep into Pack territory and they all took off after them, leaving him and Conall.

Conall, not about to leave his pregnant mate alone with lions swarming over his territory, turned and trotted back to the house. Nik, however, had no such worries. Angie seemed to have quite a way with handling cats. Hell, she handled him, didn't she?

No, he had other plans for the delectable Ms. Santiago. And they definitely involved those shoes.

Nik padded around to the back of the house. She'd left the window open, so he took a step back and jumped. He cleared the windowsill easily, landing without making a sound.

He turned toward the bed and she was already there. Waiting for him. Naked. A sheet pulled up between her legs and covering her chest.

And the shoes. She still had on the shoes.

She watched him quietly, inhaling a deep breath. When she released it…it came out as a sigh.

He growled. *Teasing hellcat.*

Angie watched tiger-Nik stand at the foot of the bed, staring at her. When she'd sighed, she'd thought for sure he'd shift and tackle her by now. But he didn't, he just kept staring. Yet once again the mere thought of Nik was making her all squirmy and hot.

Then Nik did something he'd never done before around her. He closed his eyes tight, bared his fangs, and stuck his tongue out. It had to be one of the top five most ridiculous things she'd ever seen and she would have laughed, but Nik's head dipped down, flipped the sheet up and he crawled under it and onto the bed.

She felt his furry head rub against her leg, then slowly move up. Drawing his long body against hers. But as he moved up her body, he shifted and Nik's rough fur turned into hard flesh. By the time he pulled himself out from under the sheet, he was back to being human and looking as gorgeous as always.

He kissed her nose, her chin.

"What," she asked carefully, "was that look on your face just before you got under the covers?"

"I was tasting your scent. It's just a thing tigers do."

"Eeeew."

He took the sheet wrapped around her chest between his teeth and tugged it down until her breasts were bare. He nuzzled one and licked the other.

"So tell me, sugar. What have you been up to today?"

"I think I saved the world...and I bought new shoes."

"A girl who knows what's important. I do like that." He kissed the valley between her breasts, easing himself down her chest.

Angie stretched like a big lazy cat, her hands grasping the headboard. "Do you like my shoes, hillbilly? The salesman said I looked fabulous in them."

"Oh, yeah. They're nice. Now let's see if they look any better on my shoulders..."

Chapter Nineteen

"Forget it."

"Come on, Zach. For me. Please?"

"No. Way."

"Then do it for Sara. It's her birthday."

"Not if her life depended on it—and it doesn't."

Angie looked at Nik. He smirked and she knew he wouldn't be any help.

"Please. Just put it on. It will not only be a gift for her...but for you. Trust me."

"You know, compared to her..." he glanced at Miki, who immediately gave him the finger, "...I actually like you. But this...this is asking too much."

Well, cajoling wasn't working with the wolf. "Put it on, or I get the bat."

Zach looked down at her. "I'd take a bat to the head any day over this."

Angie growled. *Damn, uptight, pain-in-the-ass wolves.*

Nik had never seen a man fight so hard not to put on a cowboy hat. And Angie had tried everything short of oral sex. Of course, if she'd done that, he'd have to kill Zach and every wolf within a three-thousand-mile vicinity.

The short, Asian she-wolf who Ban seemed truly fascinated with lately pushed through the swinging doors. "She's coming."

At her wits end, Angie went for her last resort. She slammed the heel of her Prada shoe into Zach's instep.

"Ow!"

She slammed the hat on his head as Sara strolled through the door. They all turned, Angie stepping in front of a bent over Zach.

"Happy birthday!"

Sara broke out into a stunning grin. One look at it, and Nik completely forgot about the scar on her face. It meant nothing next to that dazzling smile.

Sara looked at the kitchen table covered in a full birthday breakfast, including waffles, pancakes, eggs, bacon, sausage, and anything else the catering company could think of since none of the wolves seemed comfortable with the idea of cooking.

"You guys! This is so sweet."

She turned as Zach stood up straight. The black cowboy hat still firmly on his head. His face red with embarrassment and blinding anger.

Sara's breath caught and Nik could smell her lust from ten feet away.

"Oh...my," she whispered.

"Happy birthday, girl!" Angie hugged her friend. "From me and Mik."

Sara nodded at her two friends, but didn't take her eyes off Zach. She swallowed. "Uh...thanks."

Angie smiled. "You're welcome."

Zach watched Sara walk up to him. "Look, Sara. Before you say anything—"

She cut him off by grabbing his sleeveless black T-shirt in her hands and yanking him to her. Then she slammed her lips against his.

Angie, apparently feeling pretty damn haughty, crossed her arms in front of her chest and looked at Nik.

He shook his head. Man, he loved that woman. *Crazy hellcat that she is.*

Sara peeled herself away from Zach, but kept her grip on his shirt. "You guys get started. We'll be back." She hauled him out of the kitchen.

Miki leaped off the counter, causing Conall to have one of his near–heart attacks. Nik sensed the man would have a lot of those around his slightly off-center female who had begun to grow on Nik like a fungus. She was just so dang wacky.

"Well, we won't be seeing them until the party tonight." Miki laughed.

"Yup. Which gives us time to get everything organized." Angie had taken over the party since she got back. And no one seemed to mind. She told them what to do and, dogs that they were, they went and did it.

Leaning against the counter, Nik watched Angie as she pulled out a notepad covered in all her notes for the party and her cell phone off the counter.

She had complete control at the moment. He loved when she had complete control.

"What about my breakfast, sugar?" Angie froze, the phone clutched in her hand. Her heartbeat sped up and she barely hid the panting. "I haven't eaten yet," he insisted.

She glared at him at the same time her lust punched him

in the head.

Miki stepped between them, completely oblivious. "Hello, hillbilly. Table full of food. Or make your own damn breakfast."

Conall grabbed her arm. "Come on, Miki-baby. Let's make sure the backyard is ready for tonight."

"Yeah, but—"

The big blond dragged the tiny woman out of the kitchen as the rest of the wolves grabbed food and left.

Backing Angie against the freezer door, Nik grinned. "I do like that dog."

ψ⁊ω

Angie dragged Nik's cousin Cleatus out of the DJ booth. "No offense, hon, but I think we're done with 'Sweet Home Alabama'." Four times being three times too many.

Besides, she had to do something. Miki had finally gone for her gun.

She shoved the DJ in the booth. "Get to it," she snapped in German.

As she walked away, sweet, *sweet* Tech music flowed around her. She looked at the bar where Miki decided to get in some time pouring drinks and saw her friend put the gun back in its holster. Cleatus had no idea how close he came...

Angie turned and moved back through the crowd. She couldn't believe how big this party had gotten. Pride and Pack representatives from around the country making an appearance. The word was out. The truce was on and the war was over. At least the war between the Pride and the Pack. The hyenas had become unbelievably quiet, which made everyone a little nervous. Yet Angie knew Sara and Victoria made the right decision to let Leucrotta live. If they killed her, they'd have only made her a martyr. This way she came off as she truly was—a really bitter bitch who needed to get the fuck over it.

To be honest, when the Packs and Prides began showing up, Angie worried. They didn't speak and they watched each other with open hostility. She didn't count on the Vorislavs, though. The whole bunch of them showed up except for One-Eyed Grandma. Angie had no doubt Broyna was back in her little shack probably raising the dead for her own amusement.

But young Cleatus jumped into the DJ booth, amped up "Sweet Home Alabama", and that was it. What started off as a nice little birthday party, turned into a full-blown hootenanny. Especially when some Pack from Tennessee showed up. The Smiths or something. Their name may have been plain but these people really knew how to party.

After that, Angie spent the rest of the time making sure the food was on hand, the liquor was plentiful, and that Miki didn't annoy the hell out of someone. Thankfully, Conall was ahead of her on that and tossed Miki's crazy ass behind the bar. Once back in her element, Miki was fine. But at some point she'd need a break and Angie hoped Conall was on top of that as well.

Angie cut over to the barbeque pit. "Hey, Bobby."

"Hey, darlin'. You're lookin' gorgeous this evenin' as always."

"You are such a dirty little sweet talker," she flirted. Bobby was a wolf from her home town and one of the nicest guys she never dated. She motioned to the food. "Are we doing okay?"

"I was a little worried when Sheridan ordered two more cows, but after watching those tigers eat, I see why. So far, so good, though."

"Good. Get me on the walkie-talkie if you need me." She'd

277

insisted everyone working the party have either a headset or walkie-talkie. They had no idea what a Nazi she could be when it came to running a party.

Moving away from the barbeque pit, Angie tried to find Sara. Nope. They still weren't here. Hours since the Alphas locked themselves in their bedroom. *Hours.*

She walked up to a few of the Pack standing with Alek and Ban. "Someone has to go get them."

"Are you fuckin' high?" Kelly said with that disturbingly gravel-like voice.

"Forget it," some wolf named Billy Dunwich added. "No one's goin' up there when those two are fucking."

Angie looked at Alek and Ban. She gave them her best alluring look. "Guys?"

They snorted in unison. "Not on your life, Santiago." Alek shook his head. "I'd rather start eating vegan."

"I'd set myself on fire first," Ban added.

Man, since she started fucking their brother the two of them had been less and less cooperative.

When she was about to go kick the Alpha pair's bedroom door down her damn self, Sara appeared, Zach following behind. She'd made him wear the hat, but he really looked too worn out to care. Sara, however, didn't look tired at all. Clearly her night had just begun.

Angie stalked over to her. "Where the hell have you been?"

Sara smirked. "Do you really want the full details to answer that question?"

She didn't need full details. The teeth marks all over her friend's neck told their own story.

Grabbing Sara's arm, Angie dragged her toward several Prides. "You're going to come over here and be goddamn polite, or I'll kick the living shit out of you."

"Happy birthday to me," she complained.

"You got your birthday gift from me. And you used it all fucking day."

"Dear God in heaven."

Nik and Ban turned away, but Alek stood. Transfixed. "My God, y'all. She's the worst goddamn dancer I've ever seen."

"Turn away. It'll hurt your eyes. Turn away!"

Finally, Alek did. "He must really love her."

The three men glanced back at Miki, but could no longer watch. Nik, motioning for the bartender, now understood why Conall hadn't complained when Miki started working the bar during the party rather than enjoying the event herself. Because working the bar, Miki looked graceful and cute as hell. Out on the dance floor, however, the woman was an absolute mess.

Nik leaned across the bar toward the man who'd replaced Miki. "Y'all got any grain alcohol? I need to wipe out a horrible memory."

The bartender shook his head.

"Then we'll take three shots of vodka."

"Each," Alek added.

Nik looked down to the end of the bar. The thankfully always-graceful Angie stood there comfortably chatting with two lions and Reena. He never met a woman who could effortlessly combine classy and trashy so well. Angie's jeans were Calvin Klein. Her cowboy hat and boots were made specifically for her and most likely cost her a pretty penny. But the tiny black leather halter top she wore barely covered her breasts and only stayed on because of the tiny leather ties around her neck and her waist, which Nik had quite the enjoyable time tying up for her earlier that afternoon. Add in that the thong peeking out the top of her jeans was from Frederick's of Hollywood, and Nik was a very happy man.

He smiled to himself, wondering when this stupid party would be over so he could bury himself back inside that hot little snatch that seemed made for his dick.

"You're doin' it again."

Nik looked at his brothers. "Doin' what?"

"Starin' at Angie with big, dumb dog eyes." Alek popped back his shot of vodka.

"Dammit, man," Ban continued. "You're a cat. Act like one!"

"But cats like pretty shiny things. Don't y'all think she's pretty and shiny?"

The three men looked again at Angie. At that moment, she suddenly glanced up. Her eyes widened a bit when she realized they were staring at her. After a few moments, she turned away and, with a shake of her head, went back to her conversation.

Ban sighed. "She sure is."

Nik nodded. "Yup. And if y'all get within five feet of her, I'll kill ya both where you stand." He lifted his shot of vodka. "*Na zdorovie!*"

"Cheers to you, too," his brothers responded back, laughing.

It suddenly occurred to Angie she'd lost sight of Miki. She'd been trying to keep an eye on her all damn evening but once she was no longer behind the bar, the little bitch moved like lightning.

Between the hillbillies pissing off the snobby lions, the Packs growling at each other, and Sara much more interested in Zach than upholding the truce, Angie didn't know what to do with herself.

"You can't watch her all the time, Angie."

Angie spun around at the familiar voice. "Marrec!" She threw herself into the man's arms. He hugged her so tight, she was sure he would break one of her ribs. But nothing felt better because it let her know exactly how important she was to him.

"I am so glad to see you," he barked gruffly.

"I'm fine. I promise." He finally let her go, pulling back to stare at her face.

"You sure? You sure I don't need to kill anyone?" And he would. They both knew it.

"No, sir. Everything is fine."

"Good. Where's the birthday girl? The rest of the Pack are dying to see her." Rest of the Pack her ass. *Marrec* wanted to see Sara. Angie knew exactly how much the old coot missed her friend. "She's over there...fondling Zach."

And she was, too. Sara straddled Zach's lap like a stripper giving a lap dance, her arms tight around his big neck, her voluptuous chest offered up to him under her sleeveless black Harley T-shirt.

Horny dogs.

Marrec shook his head. "Maybe I'll wait a bit before saying hi."

Angie shrugged. "That's probably a really good idea. But there's loads of food and drink, so you guys have yourself a good time. We'll talk later."

Marrec gave her a fatherly kiss on the cheek and walked off. She waved at all her friends from her Texas hometown, but she still wanted to find Miki.

Eventually, after some wandering around, she saw her. Angie was starting to realize exactly how smart a man Conall was. In order to keep the crazy bitch occupied, he'd invited Miki's geek friends from Seattle. Three guys and some girl she sort of recognized as well as a few others she didn't know. Angie'd met them before, but they hadn't been interesting enough for her to retain names. But they kept her friend busy and happy. As did Conall, apparently. Miki stood in front of him talking to her geek friends while Conall talked to some lion she didn't recognize. He had his arm around her waist, palm flat against her stomach, and his head resting comfortably on her ass. Miki's hand rested against his, their fingers intertwined.

Miki actually found someone who not only got her, but liked her anyway. Angie wanted to believe Nik was that guy for her, but she refused to hold out any false hopes for a future that didn't exist. No matter how many weird, longing looks Nik gave her across the room.

Nik wrapped his arm around his baby sister's neck and hugged her. "What are you up to?"

"Very little."

"Good. Keep it that way." The male lions seemed to have a particular interest in his sister he didn't much appreciate. He would tell her to stay near Reena, but his cousin was too busy flirting with a bunch of dogs. His whole family was going to hell in a hand basket and this time he had no one to blame but himself.

"Where's Angie?" Kisa asked.

"Being a Nazi. The girl really knows how to run a party."

"You like her, don'tcha, Nik?"

"No."

"No?"

He sighed. "I love her."

"Does she know?"

He started to respond yes, then realized he didn't really know. He hadn't actually said it to her. "I don't know."

His sister shook her head. "Typical." Kisa turned and smiled up at her brother's face. "So you are like Daddy after all?"

He snarled but his sister only rolled her eyes. "You might as well face it. I have to." She shrugged. "I like Daddy, though."

"That could explain why you're his favorite."

Kisa went up on her tiptoes and kissed her brother's cheek. "She's perfect for you, Nik. Anybody else would have killed you by now."

Angie put a cold wash cloth against the she-wolf's forehead. "Maybe you should lay off the tequila for awhile, hon."

The female nodded, moaned, then dived back into the bushes.

Angie wasn't sure, but it seemed like the wolves really weren't good at handling their liquor.

Stepping away from the bushes, Angie turned and stared in horror. Natalia, the mother of the man she loved, stood in front of the bar talking quietly to Marrec. A nice, civilized conversation. But behind her Miki had climbed up onto one of the bar stools—a ball of yarn in her hand.

"Oh, God!"

Angie made a run for it. She'd barely reached Natalia when a string of red yarn swept across the older woman's face. She batted it away with her hand, not quite sure what it was. Before Angie could reach around Natalia and wring her best friend's neck, Conall grabbed Miki, sweeping her off the seat.

Giggling, Miki loudly announced, "It was just a little

283

experiment!"

The ball of yarn hit the ground and Natalia picked it up. She looked at Angie, one eyebrow raised, looking exactly like her son.

Angie snatched it from her as Marrec stared at the ground, trying not to laugh.

"She's taking up knitting," Angie desperately lied.

Nik stood about fifty feet away, watching Ban hand over his daughter to Angie. Nik's niece, an adorable two-year-old, grabbed a handful of hair and held on to her for dear life. Angie didn't seem bothered by it at all as she talked to Ban and his niece's mother, Connie somebody or other. A vicious tigress with a killer right hook and the longest fangs Nik had ever seen on a female.

The baby looked so comfortable in Angie's arms. And Angie looked perfect holding her. Then it hit him. Like a brick to the head...

Nik didn't just love her, he wanted Angelina Santiago to have his kids...and *only* his kids. He wanted all his kids to grow up in the same family with that crazy woman as their mother. He wanted to wake up every day and find her sleeping next to him. He wanted to buy Angie more shoes and have her wear them only for him. He wanted to have sex with her all over his home in every position humanly possible. He wanted it and knew he wouldn't be happy until he got it.

Well, hell, now I'm going to have to marry the crazy, psychotic female!

He closed his eyes. Could this day possibly get any scarier?

As if in answer, a big arm wrapped around Nik's shoulder. "Hey, buddy."

Surprised, Nik looked over at Conall. "Uh...hey."

"Hey." A slap on the back from Zach. "How's it goin'?"

Eyes narrowed, Nik watched the two. "What are y'all up to?"

"Nothing. Me and Zach were just wondering when you were going to move in?"

"Move in? I'm not—"

"Of course you are. If you're staying with Angie. Ya gotta move in."

"What?"

"Didn't she tell you?" Zach asked. "They've always wanted to live together. All three of 'em. And you protected Angie—"

"And me," Conall added with a sweet smile that may fool some human female but didn't fool Nik for one goddamn second.

"So you're part of the Pack now," Zach insisted.

"Yeah. You're one of us."

"And don't worry," Zach finished, "we'll teach you how to howl."

Suddenly, Nik felt violently ill.

Angie decided to get some food and finally eat. Grabbing a plate of barbeque chicken and coleslaw she sat down on a long bench to relax and people watch. Of course, that moment alone lasted all of two seconds before she looked up to find Sara and Miki next to her.

"Okay. Fucking in our laundry room is unacceptable," Sara hotly complained.

Angie frowned, the chicken leg poised at her mouth. Nik hadn't fucked her in the laundry room...he'd fucked her in the kitchen.

"What are you talking about?"

"Two old tigers, going at it like, well, tigers."

Miki pointed. "Those two."

Angie looked over and immediately put her chicken down. Boris tried to take Natalia's hand, but she snatched it away. She stalked through the crowd toward the bar. Of course Boris didn't look hurt and definitely not discouraged. More like turned on. And Natalia may look pissed, but the flush to her cheeks also made her appear well satisfied.

Angie sighed. "Sorry 'bout that. I'll ask Nik to, uh, control his people."

"Thank you. I mean, dude..." Sara shuddered. "We clean clothes in there."

"I'll keep that in mind."

"So." Miki scratched her leg. "You marrying that tiger or what?"

Angie choked on her Long Island Iced Tea.

Miki glanced at Sara. "Told ya."

Sara shook her head. "I don't know why you guys insist on marriage."

"A societal construct forced on us from birth." Miki suddenly pointed at Angie. "And you put me in any bridesmaid dress with ruffles and it's gonna be war between you and me, sister!"

She stomped off.

Sara shrugged. "That parasite is making her so cranky."

"*Stop calling her that,*" Miki yelled back.

Sara winked at Angie and wandered off.

Angie stared after her two best friends. They both moved

with such confidence now. Sara didn't just run her Pack. She *was* her Pack. They watched her with fear, awe, and warmth. Sara would never be her mother and definitely never her grandmother. She would always just be Sara. She came up behind Zach, who was busy trying his best to hold a civil conversation with two lions and, with a wicked grin, slid her hand between his legs. The wolf stiffened, the lions instantly forgotten as he turned to face her. He grabbed her around the waist and roughly pulled her into his body. Zach looked at Sara as if she were the most beautiful woman he'd ever seen. And, Angie knew, that to Zach, Sara was.

Miki stood next to her freakishly sized giant. Conall spoke to Boris, making the old tiger laugh. Without turning away from him, Conall's hand reached down and grasped Miki's. She leaned into his side, her eyes checking out the entire crowd, most likely looking for some shit to start. She spotted it, her eyes locking on Victoria. She tried to pull away, but Conall yanked her back. Then she tried to get him to release his hold, but the man wouldn't budge. His conversation with Boris never wavered and he never lost his smile. After a few moments, Boris walked away, most likely on the hunt for Natalia. Conall leaned his—*what? Ten-foot?*—frame down, whispering in Miki's ear. She laughed, again trying to pull away, but he pulled her back, kissing her gently on the mouth. Miki returned that kiss, raising herself up on her toes.

Angie returned to her chicken, for once confident her friends were going to be okay. Still, she only managed to get one bite before Ban and Alek sat down. One on each side of her.

"So...you gonna stay with Nik?"

At Alek's question, Angie choked on that one bite of food she'd managed to get. Much more of this and she might lose a few pounds.

"That is none of your business, gentlemen."

"What if he married you?" Ban pushed.

What in the bloody hell is going on? "What?"

"Well, you human girls like that, right?"

Angie sighed. "I'm not having this discussion with you two."

"That sound like a yes to you, Alek?"

"It sure does."

"It does not!" Angie took a deep breath. "Go. Away."

"Okay." Ban sighed as the two men stood. "But remember, it takes forever for them Gucci people in Italy to get us in for our fittin' and then to make our tuxes."

"And they complain somethin' awful when we go in there last minute, so make sure you give us ample warnin'. I hate being yelled at in Italian."

Angie thought about throwing her food at their retreating backs, but she'd become completely distracted by the fact the Vorislavs actually had people inside Gucci making them clothes. Suddenly trips to Florence seemed in order.

Now smiling, Angie took another bite of her chicken leg. She'd just swallowed when Nik suddenly appeared in front of her. Taking the plate out of her hand and dropping it on the bench, he yanked her up.

"Come with me."

Without waiting for her to answer, he dragged Angie away, taking her to a wing of the house blocked off from party goers. He found a study that, without a TV, Angie knew the Pack probably never used. Like her, the wolves enjoyed their TV. Dark and completely empty of anything but furniture, the room was perfect for what Nik needed as he pulled her inside, closing and locking the door behind him.

Keeping his grip on her until he pushed her onto the

couch, he immediately started pacing in front of her.

"Is something wrong?" she finally asked.

"Look, sugar. You know how I feel about you." She did? "But I can't live here with these people. I mean—they're dogs. Literally."

"Nik, I don't—"

"Or maybe, if you're real set on it, we can build our own wing or house on the property."

"Nik—"

"But Miki's nightly yellin'—I mean, did you hear that last night?" No. She didn't hear it. But every time Conall and Miki woke up Nik, he woke her up and fucked her again. No wonder Sara kept muttering about moving the pair to their own wing. "I mean, what exactly does he do to her? And then you got Zach and Sara using everything in this house as their personal bed, and I refuse to learn how to howl for anybody—"

"Nik!"

He stopped rambling. Even stopped pacing.

Angie took a deep breath. She had no idea where this was leading, but she felt the need to be very clear. "There is no way in hell I'd live here."

"Really?"

"Really." She loved her friends, but come on...the days of slumber parties and debating who would lose their virginity first were long gone. They would always be her best friends, her sisters, but that didn't mean she needed to live with the crazy heifers. "Why did you think I did?"

"Them dogs! They said you'd wanna move in here to be close to Miki and Sara. That y'all always planned on living together."

Angie snorted out a laugh, then kept laughing.

"What? What's so damn funny?"

"I hate to tell ya this, hillbilly, but you are now officially part of the Pack."

"Everybody needs to stop sayin' that to me."

She shrugged. "Might as well face it."

"I don't wanna be one of them. You ever see them hunt? When they're done, they roll around in the muck. They act just like—"

"Dogs?"

"Exactly."

"Look, Nik. Do you wanna know why I'm sure you're part of the Pack now?"

"Yeah. Enlighten me."

"'Cause they're fuckin' with ya. And you're lettin' 'em."

"What?"

"Dude, I have no desire to move here. I love my friends. They're my sisters. And they'll always be my sisters. No matter where I live...which won't be here. Visiting, yes. Living here, no."

"Really?"

"Really."

"Thank the Lord!" Nik threw himself onto the couch beside her. "Them boys had me scared out of my ever-lovin' mind." He put his head on her shoulder and suddenly Angie didn't know quite what to do with the man. "I kept having this vision of waking up in the middle of the night hearing 'Oh, Conall. Oh, Conall'. Over and over again until the end of time."

"I'm not moving in here."

"All right then. I guess that's settled."

Angie nodded. "Good."

"Except that does beg the question of where we *are* going to live."

Angie sat forward. "What is this 'we' thing? Why do you keep saying—" She looked over to find Nik staring at her. Just staring. A cat that already had the mouse by its tail, so it was just entertaining to watch it trying to get away. "We're a 'we' now?"

"I thought I made that clear the other night when I tied you face down to the bed and fucked ya proper."

Angie looked down at her lap to stop herself from hysterically laughing. Really, how many times in a girl's life would she hear *those* words?

"Um..." she cleared her throat, "what happened to 'my kind lives alone'?"

Nik gave a deep sigh. "I've had to face the fact, sugar. I am my father's son."

Well, she already knew that. "That better not make me Natalia."

"Naw. Unlike how she treats my daddy, you're nice to me."

Very true.

"You know..." He stretched out on the couch, his head in her lap. *Acting like he owns the place.* "We could live in North Carolina. But you know, my family. Or we can move to Texas. But those wolves will have to stay off our territory. Or maybe we could move to France—no, I don't wanna deal with the French, although I do love their food. Maybe Italy?" He shook his head. "No. They can be as bad as the French. I don't want those Italian men touching you. Maybe England, except they got them funny accents. That might start irritatin' the hell outta me."

"Nik."

Gold eyes locked with hers. "What, sugar?"

She thought about making a break for it, but she'd seen

Nik move. He was way too fast for her and her baseball bat was in their bedroom.

Their bedroom. Not hers. Not his. Theirs.

Forcing herself to calm down, Angie ran her hands through his hair. Then she made the biggest leap of her life. "Maybe we could split it between Texas and North Carolina. But I'll have to be here for Mik. God knows poor Conall will need somebody to help him deal with how crazy she'll get during the pregnancy."

Nik shrugged. "That'll work."

"And we'll have to figure out what to do about holidays and stuff."

"Okay."

She cleared her throat. "And I love you, Nik." She really did. With all her heart, soul, and...

"I know, sugar. You've always loved me."

Cockymotherfuckinfriedchickeneatin' cat!

He thought for sure she'd start ripping hair out of his head. Instead she tried to push him off her lap.

"I don't know why I put up with your goddamn, motherfucking shit, hillbilly, but—"

Nik grabbed her wrists, leaned up, and kissed her, cutting off her tirade. His tongue sliding in and dragging around hers. She sighed in response, her body softening against his. His dick hardened and grew inside his black jeans. That damn sigh of hers got him every time.

He pulled back from her, releasing her wrists. Nik reached up with one hand and easily untied the leather strings holding up her top, pulling it down so he had easy access to her breasts. He sucked one into his mouth and Angie moaned, leaning back into the couch. He played with it for awhile and turned his attention to the other. Once he got both of her nipples good and hard, he looked up at her. "I love you, Angelina. I think since the moment I saw you in that airport. I love that you're ornery and rude and take absolutely no shit. I love that you make my baby sister smile and that you think my daddy's charmin'. I love how you look that split second before you come and the way you say my name when I'm inside you. I love everything about you and can't imagine a second of my life without you."

Angelina shook her head. "Thump. Thump. Thump."

He still had no idea why the woman kept saying that. And to be honest, he wasn't about to ask. She might tell him and it would probably freak him out.

Instead he tunneled his fingers through her hair, getting a firm hold and eliciting a delicious moan from those gorgeous lips. No. He'd never get enough of this woman. She was entirely too insane.

"You know, sugar, that party will be goin' on for hours and I've already locked the door." He ran his tongue along the underside of her jaw while making sure he rubbed his arms against her bare breasts. "There's all sorts of things I could do to that sweet body of yours on this big 'ol couch."

She groaned. "Then do it, hillbilly."

"Not good enough." He nipped the flesh at her collar bone, and kissed her hard. "I want you to tell me what you want, Angelina," he whispered against her lips. "I wanna hear you say it."

She brushed his hair out of his face, her hand settling on his jaw. Her eyes, filled with absolute love and trust, stared down at him. Then she smiled.

"Touch me, Nik."

Epilogue

"I blame you for this, little sister."

"I was trying to be helpful."

"Oh, you were helpful all right. I've got bare-chested, overall-wearing hillbillies on my goddamn front porch because of you." A porch Zach never even wanted. "I thought I'd only have to deal with one. But for some unknown reason his brothers keep coming."

His sister cleared her throat. "That probably has nothing to do with me."

"Oh, you are so full of shit."

She laughed. "You still sound happy, though."

"They've pulled out banjos. Exactly how happy can I be?"

"You can't bullshit me, Zacharias. I can hear it in your voice. You're happy whether you wanna be or not."

"Whatever. So when are you coming back to the den?"

"Um...ya know. Soon...I guess."

Zach watched his least favorite Pack member, the one who broke his baby sister's heart, head out on his Harley. Zach didn't like most people, but there were very few he actively hated.

"I could kill him, ya know. If you want me to."

"Don't give him the satisfaction."

"Well, you're going to have to come home sometime. You're going to be an aunt in a few more months."

"How are you doing with that anyway?"

"He would be better off breeding with the right hand of Satan."

"Damn, Zach," Nessa chuckled. "Tell me how you really feel."

"You'll see...when you come home."

"If you're ordering me home—"

"I wouldn't do that. I know you need time. Take it. But at some point, you're going to have to face him." Zach pushed himself off the bike he leaned against, heading toward the house. "And when you do, I'll be here for you."

"Thanks, big brother. That means a lot to me."

"Good. And you'll get rid of the hillbillies, right?"

"You may be on your own with that one."

"Selfish bitch."

"Back atcha, mighty bro."

Zach walked up the stairs of the newly installed porch. He looked at Aleksei Vorislav. "You wanna talk to my sister?"

The man's face lit up as he held his hand out. "Yeah!"

"Oh." Zach flipped his phone closed. "She just hung up."

Alek's eyes narrowed and Zach glared back. He didn't like the two of them being friends when his sister was in college, and he definitely didn't like the fact that the man now wouldn't leave.

Alek reached into the front of his overalls and pulled out his cell. He punched one number and waited, staring up at Zach. "Hey, Nessa darlin'! How y'all doin'?"

Zach growled low, debating whether Angie could ever forgive him for killing her brother-in-law—probably not. He looked at Ban. "Seen Sara?"

"Not since they came back from huntin' a little while ago."

"Thanks." Zach walked into his house, stopping briefly to look into the living room. Miki, at least six months pregnant now, lay comfortably between Conall's legs, the big man's body cushioning her from the hard arm of the couch. His long arms looped around her, his big hands resting on her stomach.

"We are not naming any child of mine Eunice!"

"I think it's a lovely name." Miki smiled. "There's something so 1946 about it."

"Why don't we tack a big sign on her ass that says 'my parents hated me so please feel free to mock'."

"No need to get tense. I have a list of other names."

"Such as?"

"Cerulean Blue."

Zach shook his head. He knew the vicious psychopath was just fucking with the man. Last he heard from Sara, they—yes, *they*—had all decided to name the future Viga-Feilan, Kendrick. Ricki for short. Which Zach knew Conall would be more than happy with. Of course, the evil wench seemed to be having way too much fun torturing his friend to bother telling him that yet.

As Conall let go with a volley of curses, while at the same time tickling Miki's neck so she hysterically began to laugh, Zach headed back toward the kitchen. He found it empty, so he went out to the back porch.

The porch now surrounding his house was at the insistence of his mate. She'd asked him about it once. He said no. Yet the construction guys showed up the very next day.

Zach stood at his backdoor, staring at what now lay across

said porch. *This keeps getting worse.*

He stared down at the seven-hundred-pound tiger sprawled across the wood. Big tiger head resting on enormous paws. Of course Zach had a tiger on his back porch. Why wouldn't he? *This is what you get when you mate with a nut.*

Sprawled face-down on top of the tiger's back, a beautiful sleeping woman wearing ridiculously expensive four-inch-heeled shoes, denim cut-off short-shorts, and a subtle platinum band on the third finger of her left hand...and not much else.

Gold eyes looked up at him.

He glanced around. "Sara," he whispered so as not to wake Angie.

The hillbilly motioned toward the kennels with that enormous fucking tiger-head.

He should have known. While the workmen built the porch, they also put together a wickedly nice kennel. Why? Because Sara felt Roscoe needed a girlfriend and she didn't want to keep them all in the house.

That stupid dog now had six girlfriends.

Zach came around the corner to find his mate stretched belly-down across the grass. Normally he'd get a hard-on as soon as he saw her, but he became distracted. Distracted by the orange-and-black-striped fur ball in her hands. Since all shifters were born as human and didn't shift until much older, what she held in her hands could only be one thing...

"Woman, is that a tiger cub?"

Sara cringed, then looked at him over her shoulder. "Oh, you're home early."

"No I'm not. Answer me."

"Ban needs her to stay here for a little while. Just 'til he's ready to move her into a rescue. He found her at a local circus and said they'd been mean to her and her mother. But the rescue could only handle the mother right now because she's really sick. I offered to help by keeping the cub away from her until she's better."

"It's a tiger cub, Sara. A *real* tiger cub. Not a kitten."

"I know."

Zach stared at her. For a woman who really didn't want children...

"Ban said no more than six months."

"*Six months?*"

"Don't yell."

She held the cub up, so tiny at this point it comfortably fit in her two hands. In three months or so, however, it would be the size of Roscoe. In six months it would be able to bite off Roscoe's head.

"Look at her, Zach. Look at those blue eyes. Eventually they'll turn gold, but right now they're blue. How cool is that? And she's so sweet. She just needs a little love."

"And about five hundred pounds of meat a day."

"Oh, that won't be for another year or two."

Zach sighed and rubbed the palms of his hands against his eyes.

When did his life get so out of control? He had hillbillies on his front porch. His best friend was madly in love with a psychopath. There was a half-naked beautiful woman asleep on top of one of the mightiest predators known to man. And, of course, there were tigers. He had big, hillbilly *tigers* in his home while his mate rubbed a full-blood tiger cub against his cheek and made cooing sounds.

He pulled his hands away from his face and looked down into those beautiful brown eyes. She smiled, causing the scar on one side of her face to crinkle up a bit. God help him, he never saw anything sexier.

Shit. Dick went hard.

"Six months and then it goes. Even if that means a tiger-headed blanket on our bed."

Sara crouched down to let the tiger cub go off and play with Roscoe and his harem of well-trained bitches. Then she began pulling his black T-shirt out of his black jeans.

"What the hell are you doing?"

"Getting you naked so I can fuck you until you pass out."

"Oh. Okay."

She ran her hands under his T-shirt and Zach closed his eyes, loving the feel of her against him. She pushed his T-shirt up, her tongue licking the still-sore bite she'd given him that morning. She sighed with pure pleasure as her hands slid around his waist and she laid her head against his chest. "I love you, Zach."

He wrapped his arms around her. "I love you, too, baby." Then he slapped his hand over the old wound on her thigh.

"*Zach!*" Laughing, she tried to pull away from him. "Lemme go!"

"Not on your life, Morrighan." He fell back on the ground, bringing her with him. He rolled on top of her, pinning Sara's body under his. "I'm never letting you go, you crazy bitch."

She tried to wiggle away from his hands, but he yanked her back, somehow managing to pull off her sweatpants in the process and rubbing his hand over the old wound on her thigh. He pinned her arms over her head as her body arched under his, her breath coming out in short hard pants. "You evil bastard!"

He nuzzled and nudged her shirt and bra up over her

breasts, licking the already hard nipples, his grip tightening on her thigh. "That's right, baby. *Your* evil bastard."

And he'd make sure she never forgot it. Because there was no where else he'd rather be. No one else he'd rather be with or in. Sara Morrighan was it.

For life.

About the Author

To learn more about Shelly Laurenston, please visit www.shellylaurenston.com. Send an email to Shelly at shelly_laurenston@earthlink.net or join her Yahoo! group to join in the fun with other readers as well as Shelly. http://groups.yahoo.com/group/shellylaurenston

Seth Kolski, a werewolf, hides his heritage and passes for normal. Until he meets Jamie.

The Strength of the Pack
© *2007 Jorrie Spencer*

Since his sister disappeared two years ago, Seth's solitude has intensified. Despite his deep need to be part of a pack, he sets himself apart, wary of humans who fear the wolf in him.

When Seth hooks up with his teenaged crush, loneliness and physical desire overcome his distrust. Jamie welcomes his attentions, albeit a little shyly, and Seth rationalizes they can have one night together before they part.

For Seth can never be part of a regular family. No normal woman is going to accept his freakish nature, nor his past violence. Especially a single mother determined to protect her family. However, Seth and Jamie's bond runs deeper than he knows. He cannot return to the shadows. Yet exposure may bring danger to them all.

Available now in ebook and print from Samhain Publishing.

A bizarre connection between a werewolf and a woman reveals the truth behind a pack's discarded magic lore.

Half Moon Rising
© *2007 Margo Lukas*

Private Investigator CJ Duncan can track a scent better than a bloodhound. Lately, unsettling visions of a wolf prevent her from doing her job. She sets out for Seattle to find her unknown birth father, but her quest leads her instead to a mysterious man who claims to be a werewolf.

Werewolf Trey Nolan has a secret weakness—one which leaves him powerless to protect his pack from a danger threatening to destroy their last shred of humanity. When he discovers a way to reclaim his full powers, he must act—even if it means betraying the woman he loves.

Caught up in Trey's struggle to save his pack, CJ discovers that her special powers come at a much greater cost than she ever imagined.

Available now in ebook and print from Samhain Publishing.

GREAT CHEAP FUN

Discover eBooks!

THE FASTEST WAY TO GET THE HOTTEST NAMES

Get your favorite authors on your favorite reader, long before they're out in print! Ebooks from Samhain go wherever you go, and work with whatever you carry—Palm, PDF, Mobi, and more.

Samhain Publishing Ltd

WWW.SAMHAINPUBLISHING.COM